Liar's Poker

Also by Frank McConnell

Murder Among Friends
Blood Lake
The Frog King

Liar's Poker

Frank McConnell

Walker and Company
New York

First published in the United States of America in 1993
by Walker Publishing Company, Inc.

Published simultaneously in Canada by Thomas Allen & Son
Canada, Limited, Markham, Ontario

Library of Congress Cataloging-in-Publication Data
McConnell, Frank D., 1942–
Liar's poker / Frank McConnell.
p. cm.
ISBN 0-8027-3229-1
I. Title.
PS3563.C3437L5   1993
813'.54—dc20   92-43525
CIP

Printed in the United States of America
2 4 6 8 10 9 7 5 3 1

This one's for best friends:
Celeste, my wife
and
Bruce, our uncle

Liar's Poker

$\triangledown$

1

I DON'T KNOW IF Alka-Seltzer is soluble in Scotch, but I'll tell you about the morning when I damn near made the experiment.

It was a Sunday in September, and Sunday, dig, is even under normal conditions *always* the weirdest day of the week, am I right? I mean, I *know* the days of the week are arbitrary and culturally conditioned and all that, because I watch PBS, too, but Sunday feels different. Like light is moving slower than it's supposed to move, and you're a little bit sad about . . . well, about everything, because among other things you know you've got to haul your sorry butt to work again tomorrow and the day is, like, slipping away from you, but the light is moving so slowly and you're so wuzzled in general that you can't even work up much of an attitude about being down. I mean, God maybe rested on the Sabbath, but you and I, we just get bummed.

So go ahead and tell me that's not what Sunday feels like, and I mean your ordinary, nothing-to-write-home-about Sunday. Now add a hangover—the kind where you're sure a bird flew in and made a nest in your mouth while you were asleep and your eyeballs will not stop dancing. And add that you're in a motel room, with all the sad starched unfamiliarity that goes with a motel room being a motel room—you know, no friendly smells or old-pal mess in the corner to jerk you back into security.

And, oh yeah. Add that you've spent the night balling like a gerbil on speed. But, except for you, the room is empty now.

And that's when I thought about trying a couple of Alka-Seltzers in the four fingers of Old Smuggler that were calling to me from the desk across the room. As I remember, I decided against it not because I was being smart but just because across the room seemed like an *awful* long way to go. Lucky: otherwise I might not be telling you this . . . or telling anybody anything.

So while I lay there waiting for my eyes to stop dancing—actually, hoping that they'd stop—I tried to get it together, as the kids say, that is, remind myself what I was doing there and how I'd screwed things up bad enough that I had to remind myself why I was there. Seriously, this was not one of your real fun hangovers.

Okay. I'd gotten laid, and that's, by me, always good news, since, I'll tell you the truth, I don't get laid all that often. She'd called herself Lisa, and she was about twenty, twenty-two, with long blond hair and skin that reminded you—okay, reminded me—of fresh peaches in white wine, and *she'd* come on to *me*, which since I'm pushing fifty is prima facie as my lawyer buddies say a major turn-on, and once we'd gotten to my room she'd satisfied every hope I'd had for the evening while I was getting stoned and seduced by her, like when you finally get to Disneyland and it *is* Disneyland—you know that feeling? So that was all on the plus side.

The radio was telling me that Jesus could deliver me from my affliction. That's how, ace detective that I am, I knew it was a Sunday morning, when the Top Forty stations all play a few hours of sermonettes and songs about rivers and lambs, to purge, I guess, the devil's music they play the rest of the week—sort of like why lawyers go to church.

Anyhow, Lisa was gone. That didn't surprise me, since the whole thing had been so . . . apocalyptic? Out of this world? *Weird* will do nicely. I'd have been a lot more surprised if she'd been lying beside me, smiling and asking for a cup of coffee and the Sunday paper. You know, you don't go to bed with Be-Bop-a-Lula and expect to wake up with June Cleaver. Or *I* don't.

And—aah, good, my eyeballs were approaching equilibrium—the clock on the TV/radio told me it was 10:08. Good. On a twelve-hour digital clock, 10:08 is the largest number of those little light-bars you can have lit up at one time (twenty-one, if you're interested), and maybe Lisa's age, by the way. If I could remember that, it meant I could still count and think. Maybe in a little while I could also make it to the john and the shower if I walked. Real. Slow.

One thing about Harry Garnish, he's always on top of things, especially when they fall on him. I'd been rogered from roundhouse to runcible, I wasn't going to die (yet), and my mind was still the same hair-trigger steel trap it had been for as long as I could remember.

I scratched my ass, arose (one hell of a fancy word for the way I got out of bed), and weaved toward the can, sighing at the Old Smuggler as I passed it.

I was on a case—this came back in force about the same time the cold water from the shower slapped me in the face— and also on expense account, and I was in the Morris Inn, just off the campus of the University of Notre Dame in South Bend, Indiana, ninety miles and a few planets away from Chicago, which is where I work and the only place in the world I feel—what?—oriented.

Now let's see: Had I managed to screw up the investigation, as well as my own self-respect? (I'll get to that part in a while.) Not really, the cold water kept reassuring me. I was checking on a professor's wife who was being maybe unfaithful or maybe just round-the-bend nuts. I'd come here to meet a probably certifiable nutcase priest who might drop a hint about whether and how the prof's wife was bent. I'd talked with him ages ago, when I was sober, and found out nothing except that he *was* certifiable. But I hadn't done anything, as far as I could see, to blow the investigation out of the water, or at least past "accounts payable."

Until, of course, Lisa.

Well, yeah, I thought, getting dressed and throwing yesterday's socks and jocks into my overnight bag, but Lisa had been *apart*. Crazy and troubling, but apart from why I was really in South Bend in the first place, and I'd probably never see her again, and that was—I was pouring the rest of the Old Smuggler down the sink—just swell by me.

The radio had stopped telling me about Jesus and was letting Madonna ask me to justify her love when I switched it off. God, is there anything gloomier than an empty, slept-in motel room in a small town on a late Sunday morning?

I checked out, went into the restaurant, and ordered steak and three eggs over easy. Not that my head wasn't splitting or that I was at all hungry, but any expert juicer will tell you that sometimes it's all a matter of eat or die. The fat taffeta-encased lady at the next table with her husband, an obvious after-Mass type, cocked her brow at my hands shaking while I downed my second large tomato juice. Fuck her, too. I was a working man.

I walked to my asthmatic old Duster in the parking lot—with the right kind of hangover, morning sunshine feels like a personal affront—ground it into gear, and cruised onto Highway 90 West, back toward Chicago, home, and what was for me the real world.

And that's when what I'd been repressing jumped up and did a tap dance on the dashboard in front of me. That's when I really *thought* about my night with Lisa, with no case, no digital clock, shower, steak and eggs, or fat ladies to put between me and it, just the emptiness of the ribbon-straight highway and the clear sky.

I was a recently married man, you see.

$\triangledown$

2

W ELL, NOT REALLY MARRIED, but not really *not* married either.

Married enough, anyhow, to feel GUILTY—for Catholic boys that word, more than any other, *always* appears in capitals—that's GUILTY, as I said, for my weekend "affair." (Christ, don't you hate Donahue and Oprah and those guys for forcing bullshit words like that into our lives?) GUILTY, by the way, is a word I only allowed myself to use about myself as I entered the outskirts of Gary, Indiana—a way and a half from South Bend.

Janie Regalbuto was a hooker. Not a very successful hooker, not even a very enthusiastic hooker, and there are some. But Janie's way was to make it only with johns she thought she sort of liked. Now, this is not sound business practice. Nevertheless, she seemed to do all right; maybe because she was so damned nice that it almost worked for her like a kind of shield. Even the girls from the big stables and the pimps running the big stables let her freelance without major hassle—not at all a usual thing in The Life.

Anyway, a little while ago, after I got back from some craziness in California that left me feeling crummier about things than normal, Janie and I—we'd been pals for years— started getting together pretty often for what she called nonprofessional dates. And sonofabitch if the dates didn't, as time went by, get more frequent. It felt like Janie was trying—I'm not very good at saying this—trying to do something for me, I mean do something without a payback.

Naturally, I was worried. I was even thinking about calling the whole arrangement off, and then one night I did something really stupid.

We were having a couple of drinks in the Bambi Bar, a great dingy rat's-ass bar in Skokie, just across McCormick Street from Evanston. The plan (it was summer) was to get pleasantly buzzed, schlep up to Highland Park for the Ravinia Festival, sit on the grass with some beer and fried chicken, listen to the Harry Connick big band—the guy is a one-man, living history of jazz, "The Only Music That Matters"—and then schlep back to my apartment in Skokie for a little intense nonprofessionalism. Not a bad plan.

So Janie's nursing a weak bourbon, since she's supposed to drive (in the Bambi Bar, unless you specify your brand, you don't have to ask for it weak), and I'm powering Beck's number two and explaining how Connick virtually rediscovered the piano tradition after twenty years of electronic, jazz/ rock horsehockey, when this very large guy walks up to our table.

"Janie," he says. He's maybe six foot two, maybe a few years younger than me, with a torso like a Masters of the Universe doll and to show it off he's wearing a blue—what do they call them, tank tops? We used to call them undershirts.

"Oh, hi, Curt," Janie says in her gollywhiz fashion with a big smile. "Curt McCoy, you know Harry Garnish?" Janie in a summer dress looks a lot like Annette Funicello. Janie out of a summer dress looks a lot like a Modigliani nude, enough anyway, that is, to bay at the moon.

Curt McCoy doesn't smile back and doesn't look at me. He reaches down—you can see his goddamn muscles ripple—takes the drink out of Janie's hand, drains it, and says, "Wanda told me you were here." Wanda was Janie's roommate and co-worker. "You forget our date tonight?"

"Oh, golly, Curt," she says, still smiling. "You know, I *did*. Look, honey, I'm really sorry, but I'm really tied up tonight. Can we, like, make it next week? I'll . . . you know"—she glanced at me—"make a special arrangement." Meaning, of course, a discount. I told you Janie's nice.

Curt puts down the glass and starts stroking her hair. It's one of the most threatening things I've seen.

"Naah, I don't think so, kid," he says, just stroking and stroking. "I took a lot of trouble to get free tonight, and I'm feeling ready, you know? So why don't you just tell your chubby friend here to buzz off, I mean, unless you want to spend the evening chatting with the vice cops."

Okay, I do have a beer gut. And I *hate* fighting, on the moral grounds that you can get hurt. Nevertheless, I'm figuring I can catch this yutz across the bridge of his nose with my Beck's bottle, grind his nuts, and step on his face, if I do it fast, before I get his attention. Go ahead, tell me I'm a helluva man.

But that's not the stupid thing I did.

Before I can move, Janie takes the hand stroking her hair, kisses—I swear to God, kisses it—and smiles up at him even sweeter than before.

"Curt," she says, her voice all low and husky. "You know what a coprophage is?" Now she's rubbing his wrist, too.

"Uh, no," he says, his face and voice getting softer.

"I read it in the dictionary," she coos (no, trust me, she *reads* the dictionary). "It means shiteater. And, honey, that's just what you are. Now, you want to call vice, you go ahead. You want their number? You think I haven't done half the dudes on the squad, darling? You think they ain't gonna let me off with a pinch on the ass and come down on you and your goddamn appliance store like a fuckin' wall, especially after I tell 'em some of your ideas about fun and games?"

"Hey, Janie," he says, drawing back his hand.

"Hey, Curt," she says, picking up her empty glass, licking her finger, and running it around the rim. "I think you oughta go. And don't call me again, okay, hon? Or Wanda. Or any of the girls, if you think I know them. It's a seller's market, baby. But, hey, you can't go home to wifey for a while, right?" And, you've got to believe me on this one, she pulls

out the waist of his jogger's pants and drops the whiskey
glass in the crotch. "If you're lonely, why don't you fuck
that?"

Do steroids collapse under stress? I don't know, but it was
a smaller guy, somehow, who left the bar.

So what do you do? I light a cigarette, signal for a third
beer, cough a lot. Then she takes my hand, and says,
"Thanks, Harry."

"Wha."

"You were going to fight the big asshole, weren't you? I
saw you fingering that bottle. That's sweet, Mister Garnish."
Annette beaming at Frankie Avalon in the last reel.

"Yeah. Well, hey, Regalbuto," I say. "You know, he was a
. . . uh . . . well, you know, a customer, like. Client. What I
mean—"

"He was a john," she says, the smile getting just a little
smaller.

"Yeah. That. So, you know, you lost some money on this
deal. I mean, if you want to tell me what the . . . uh . . . the
rate is these days, I mean for a professional date, I'd be glad
to, well, hell, make it up to you, okay? What? A hundred? A
century and a half?"

And that—*that*—is the stupid thing I did.

The big confrontation with Curt the Aerobics Monster
has taken place with no disturbance to the rest of the Bambi
Bar, see? Not so the aftermath.

"You son of a bitch!" yells Janie, standing up and turning
heads and yelling it so that it can't be written as a single
word. "You—you *oinker!*" (I was later to find out that, in
Janie's lexicon, that word was about five points above the
worst thing you would call your worst enemy.)

"Wha," I repeat.

"You think I want *money?*" she says. "You think this is
about *money?* Hey, Harry"—she grabs the cigarette out of
my hand and throws it at my face, and I barely dodge it—
"*fuck you.*"

There are, oh shit, tears forming in her big, sad brown

eyes as she says this and stalks out of the Bambi Bar to the parking lot.

Now you can write the rest of the scene yourself, no? I follow her to the parking lot (it was my car, for Chrissake), explain and apologize my ass off, we both smile and blink back tears a lot—imagine Henry Mancini or, if you're all the way beyond hope, Barry Manilow doing the score—and hug and kiss and never do see Connick that night.

And a week later she moves into my apartment.

And that's what I meant by recently married man.

And by this time I'm more than halfway up Lake Shore Drive, the big, loud Sears building on my left and the big, big lake on my right. The city always welcomes you back, no matter how screwed up you are, like a best-buddy Irishman at a bar who wants to stand drinks for the house and especially for you. No kidding. I've always figured that if you could convince more people to cruise LSD and really *dig* LSD when they were down, you could probably put half—okay, three-quarters—of the shrinks in town out of work.

But, like Gershwin said, not for me. Not today.

I felt like I could use a drink before I got back to my—our apartment and tried to act like it had been just a boring two days on the road. Jesus, Janie was a professional, wouldn't she have some kind of radar for that kind of thing? The Bambi Bar was only a few blocks from my place, and on a Sunday afternoon there'd always be a few guys I knew drinking there and shooting a little pool on the scarred, pre-Kennedy table. It even had real pockets, not bullshit plastic return ramps.

But I didn't feel like going to the Bambi Bar.

Off Dempster, the main drag in Skokie, there's a place called Clyde's Cavern. Clyde Crews, who used to do a little informal dues collecting for the local Teamsters (that's what they call a strenuous occupation) retired a few years ago and decided to spend his time going slowly broke running a cocktail lounge in the middle of a block containing, besides the Cavern, a Radio Shack, a mom-and-pop grocery, and a Christian Science Reading Room. (We couldn't figure if he got zoned for a bar in that area because he had friends in City Hall or guys in City Hall who hated his ass.)

Anyway, that's where I went. The place, naturally, was empty except for Clyde, staring in mourning at the cash register and the TV, showing a colorized version of *The Thing*. They'd just discovered that the wreck under the ice was a flying saucer.

Clyde served me a brandy and Heineken without comment (thanks, God). I watched TV, rehearsing in my mind how I'd do a bright "Hi, honey!" when I got back, and kept thinking, screw all professors, professors' wives, loopy radical priests, and especially their teenybopper disciples. And ordered seconds.

▽

3

YOU'RE WONDERING HOW THINGS got this messy. Truth to tell, so was I as I stared down son of boilermaker.

Well, see, I've got this funny job. I'm a private detective and I work for a sixty-plus-*plus* ex-nun—and I'm not too damn sure about the "ex" part—who can raise my blood pressure a respectable number of points just by walking into my office on a bad morning and asking me, with real concern in her voice, if I'm feeling all right. That's Bridget O'Toole, Sister Juanita that was, now honcho—honchess?—of O'Toole Agency, which is named not for her but for her father, old Martin O'Toole, who got me into the business and always told me that when he stepped down I'd have the agency to run all by myself, but who didn't know that he was going to have a stroke about the same time Reagan got elected president—no connection, *maybe*—and leave the whole *mishegas* in the reluctant but firm hands of his daughter, who intended, making me grind my teeth, to "manage things" just until Daddy was well enough to return and put his affairs in order, me in charge of the agency, and Bridget back in the nunnery.

Hell of a sentence, right? Hell of a situation.

And five days before I sat in Clyde's Cavern sucking up brandy and beer and feeling like a bottom-feeder in a fish tank, I'd been sitting in my small but cozy office at O'Toole Agency, sucking up warm Snap-E-Tom Bloody Mary mix and thinking that business wasn't so bad. I had two infidelities, one check-jumper, and three chemical dependency inquiries, for some pretty respectable business, to deal with. Life was good.

And then the phone rang. It was Bridget, asking me to step into her office. Her larger office.

Bridget has gotten tougher over her years of "managing things" for Papa; I'll give her that. Where she used to dress in big, K mart tie-dye tents—the thrill, I guess, of being out of the habit—that made her look like Mama Cass on the slum, she dresses these days in dark skirts and jackets that make her look like Mama Cass impersonating Marlon Brando as the Godfather.

You get the concept: She's large.

And large also was the other person in her office. Large, with elegantly wavy gray hair that you figured he had to brush fifty times in the morning, a charcoal corduroy suit, button-collar white shirt and—no shit—dark green ascot. He was sitting on the visitor's sofa with one leg over the other knee, smiling all faintly and nonchalant like he was just about to be asked a question by, maybe, William Buckley. All in all, quite a show.

"Professor Browder, my associate, Harry Garnish," she said. He extended a hand, not getting up. He had one of those firm handshakes, and the look in his eyes to go with it, that says Very glad to meet you, and don't let your obvious inferiority bother you for one little minute.

"Mr. Garnish," he said.

As I sat down, Bridget handed me a calling card that said, in raised script:

BARRY BROWDER III
PROFESSOR OF LITERATURE
NORTHROP COLLEGE
WILMETTE, ILLINOIS

and his office and home phone numbers. I tried to catch Bridget's eye, but she was very carefully examining the teddy bears around the rim of her coffee mug.

"Professor Browder," she began, "has come to us—"

"Please," he interrupted, "just *Mister* Browder. I think 'Professor Browder' sounds a trifle stuffy, don't you?" And smiled. I thought saying *that* sounded pretty stuffy, but hell, I was just the hired help—Harry to you.

"Very well, sir," Bridget said. "Mister Browder has come to us, Harry, on a delicate matter on which he thinks we can be of help. But I wanted you in on the consultation before we guarantee him we could be of real assistance."

See what I mean? *That* is Bridget O'Toole right down to the ground. Christ, in this business nobody ever comes to us on an *un*delicate matter—you ever see a box in the Yellow Pages for *public* investigations?—and you don't do a lot of *Geschaeft* telling people that, well, we might be able to help you out, but there are other ways of solving your delicate matter, too, you know. That maybe keeps the clients coming back if you're a shrink or a priest; they expect you to marf around and get all concerned. But with P.I.'s and plumbers it's different. They want you to stop the toilet—whatever toilet it might be, and there's lots, believe me—from running over. Right *now*.

Besides, I already didn't like Professor Barry Browder III very much (very unprofessional, I know).

So I said, "Right. Delicate matter. Marriage, money, or morphine?"

"I *beg* your pardon," huffed Browder at the same time Bridget, shaking her head at the teddy bears, said exasperatedly, "Harry, Harry."

"No, sorry, Pro—I mean, Mr. Browder," I said. "It's just usually people park their delicate matters in one of three places. Your marriage can be fouled up some way—I see you're wearing a ring—or you can find yourself a little short or a little shorted by somebody else, or you—or hey, somebody you care about—can be having a delicate matter with dope. Or booze. Or something they like a lot and can't control—that's their morphine, you know? No offense. I just thought we could cut down to the bone, here."

He relaxed a little, even folded his hands. He was dealing

with somebody he could talk down at and that made him comfortable.

"Well," he began, checking his fingernails and performing the same coprophage smile. "I'm afraid that my . . . uh, situation doesn't quite fit any of your categories, Mr. Garnish. I am, as I told Miss O'Toole, and as you've seen, a professor of literature at Northrop College in Wilmette." (So much for the just Mister horseshit.) "I teach modern literature there, and I've published four books, two of them on the work of Norman Mailer. In fact, I've also interviewed Mailer on a number of occasions."

He looked at us both, obviously expecting one of us, or both, to go "Jesus! Mailer? *No shit!*" and fall out of our chairs. Bridget saved things or at least his ego by nodding and saying, "Oh, yes. *The Executioner's Song. Tough Guys Don't Dance.* I liked those." By me, we could have been talking about seventeenth-century motets (not fair: I *know* a little about those).

"Oh, well," Barry Browder III—who was already, in my book, BeeBeeThree—smirked. "Those are some of his more popular books, though most people don't seem to get the real point of his fiction as a whole. That's one reason I wrote *Four Postwar American Novelists*, highlighting his preeminence as a postmodernist." He looked at her expectantly.

Bridget, bless her, is honest. She just stared back, poker-faced.

After waiting a couple of beats too long for a response (yay, Bridget! I thought), Browder went on.

"Well," he said, "anyway, it's used quite often, my publisher tells me, in modern literature courses around the country. My point is that I've had . . . aah . . . a quite successful academic career, especially given the relatively small and . . . aah . . . shall we say, undistinguished milieu of Northrop College. Believe me," he said, leaning forward in his chair, "I mention this only because it's an essential context of the situation that brought me here."

To be sure, I thought. I didn't look at Bridget, but Phil,

the aging philodendron that's lived in the office since old Martin worked there, radiated agreement with me from his big dumb brown-at-the-edges leaves. Phil wanted to gum this pretentious dwortz to death.

"In fact," he continued, "I am presently negotiating with a *very* major university for what could be—well, it can only be called an extraordinary career move. This is, of course, absolutely confidential."

No kidding. He really said it like, if we called the *Tribune* with this, it would push, say, a Libyan invasion of Miami Beach back to page three. I mean, self-respect is neat and all, but you ever come across a man in awe of himself?

"Everything said here is in confidence, sir," said Bridget, and I think she was a little irked, too. "And congratulations on your success. But I don't quite understand—"

"Why I've come to you?" He smiled. "Well, Miss O'Toole, Mr. . . . aah . . . Garnish, it *is* my wife, Nancy, but not in the way Mr. Garnish implied. Nancy, you see, is Catholic. I have to say, rather obsessively Catholic." The smile got a little more self-satisfied, if that's possible.

"I see," said Bridget. "And what exactly is your definition of *obsessive* Catholicism?"

"Oh." He waved a hand. "No offense. I know you used to be a Sister, Miss O'Toole. In fact, that is the main reason I thought of coming to you with this. I was sure you would understand . . . aah . . . Catholic matters."

(That was heartening. We don't turn much of a profit, as I said, but we *had* gotten involved in some beefs that had gotten the agency newspaper coverage. Maybe a nun-detective, I figured, could bring in business—you know, like the dancing goldfish, the dog-face boy, or some dumb TV series.)

"Nancy," he continued, "has always had something of a mystical bent. I mean, of course I respect *all* religious belief, and I've always been able to, well, you might say *kid* her out of any really blatant or embarrassing spiritualism." His eyes turned inward for a moment. What scenes was he remembering? I wondered.

Sister Bridget just stared.

"Except for the last few months," said Barry Browder III, segueing back into the present. "She's been increasingly involved with a group of—well, they call themselves Sethians."

"*What*ians?" I asked.

"Sethians," he repeated, a little annoyed. "I've looked up the name. It was some sort of obscure, early Christian Gnostic cult. Anyway, *these* Sethians are, as far as Nancy will explain it to me, a group of charismatics—you understand, preaching in tongues, ecstatic prophecies, all of that really tawdry stuff—and I fear that Nancy is becoming more and more involved in their little subculture. She's gone to quite a few of their weekend retreats—their big center is in South Bend, near Notre Dame—and even has given them some hefty donations."

"What's hefty?" I asked.

"Nancy has her own checking account," he said, "out of her monthly allowance and from the money she earns teaching at Northrop. But I did take the liberty of intercepting her bank statement last month; I was already concerned about this, you see. And last month alone she wrote a check for six hundred dollars to Father Steven Lee, who is the director of this Sethian Center."

"Hefty enough," I said.

"Mr. Browder," said Bridget, "I must ask you, do you believe your wife to be either unfaithful or unbalanced?"

Coming from Bridget, it caught him really off-balance. "Miss O'Toole." He flushed. "I thought I had explained—"

"You've explained," she cut in, "that your wife spends some of her time with a group of religious people about whom I know nothing except that they are religious, and that she has given them money, which, since you tell me she has her own account, I assume is her money to give. Now, are you asking us—and we are neither the FBI nor trained psychologists, remember—to ascertain the legality of this group or the sanity of your spouse? In either case, I'm afraid you're barking up the wrong tree."

And she allowed herself a little smile of her own, for Bridget, see, saying "barking up the wrong tree" is funky.

"What she means, Mr. Browder"—I had that sick feeling that we were about to let a fee slide down the sink—"what she means is that it's not real clear what you want us to . . . aah . . . do."

"Oh, well," he said, and settled back, mollified; he was boss again. "What I want you to *do* is very simple. Just see what you can find out about these Sethians, and especially about Father Steven Lee. I don't say, mind you, that they're a fraud or that they're involved in anything illegal, but I would like to know what they're doing with monthly contributions of six hundred dollars and possibly more. Some of these charismatic people are, you know . . . well, activist. And since my wife is involved with them . . ."

"Check," I said. "A Wasserman for the gig."

"Sir?" he said.

"You want a kind of security check on these guys so that nothing about them could queer this big career move you've got cooking, right?"

"Exactly," he said. "Just some discreet examination, so that if anything untoward *is* in the offing, I can confront Nancy with it and . . . well, make the way clear for us. Will you do it?"

"We will, Mr. Browder," said Bridget, "although I have to tell you that I think you're paying a good deal of money for reassurances I'm certain your wife might give you for free. Nevertheless I don't see why we can't look into this. Here's our fee schedule and our standard contract"—pushing them across the desk—"and if you find them acceptable, we will begin working on this after you leave the office."

They were acceptable, Browder signed, plunked down a retainer, shook hands all around, and left. Bridget looked at his signature on the forms and on his check and I lit a cigarette—it's good for the plants in her office—and communed with Phil. Finally she looked up and said, "Well, Harry, what do you think?"

"I think he's a prick," I said. "And I know you don't like what you call 'language,' and I'm damn sorry, but prick is the only word that covers it. But it's a job, and it doesn't even look like much work. We get these guys' brochures, run a quick check on their organization—they've gotta file for tax status and such, right?— find out they're clean, and tell ol' Barry all is groovy, and collect the rest of our tab. No worries."

She sighed. Bridget sighs at me a lot, and it's almost always bad news.

"Mr. Browder has already left us the Sethians' brochures, along with Father Lee's telephone number. That's the first thing he showed me, and that's when I called you in. And I'm afraid I agree with your opinion of our new client, Harry, but he *is* our client now, and that means we have to do what he asks of us as well as we can. I want you to arrange to attend a meeting of the Sethians in South Bend."

Ever try to take a cigarette out of your mouth but the filter gets stuck to your lip and your fingers slide down the paper till they hit the burning end?

"*Jee*zus!" I shouted, trying to blow on my fingers, lick them, and find the damn cigarette on the carpet at the same time. "Bridget, that's silly! I *hate* religious weirdos, you know that. We can do this whole thing on the computer, for crying out loud. And hell, I don't even—"

"Harry," she said. "*You* wanted to get the business, didn't you?"

She's like that. Of course she'd called me in when Browder showed her the Sethian stuff. Because she would have had qualms about getting mixed up bird-dogging a religious group, and knowing that, by me, a client is a client, she figured we would take the job and she would keep her principles, on account of *mine* come at a lower rate.

The cigarette had landed in Phil's planter. I retrieved it, nodded, and went back to my office to grumble.

4

So THAT WHOLE NONSENSE played on Wednesday, which is why on Saturday, in white shirt, black tie, and my one gray-checked polyester suit—I was trying to look like a religious nut—I was driving east on I 90, toward my first Sethian "Sharing" (*faugh*, I hate the word—I did some time in California, remember).

But Sharing is what they called it, and Sharing is what I'd volunteered for.

The Sethians' real inner-circle weekly number was on Sundays. I guessed it was just your regular Sunday Mass, with maybe some special effects—laser show, *Voyager* photos of Neptune, who knew?—thrown in. Anyway, it wasn't open to the likes of me, as I'd been told over the phone by their secretary, receptionist, whatever, a lady who called herself Dolores and had one of those phone voices that wants to tell you, soon as she gets your first name, that you're one of her favorite people in the world. "You see, Harry"—she smiled apologetically with her voice; we'd known one another about a minute and a half—"it is a Mass, but it's also . . . well, Father Steve likes to refer to it as a Witness Moment, and we like to reserve it for people who have really, you know, understood and accepted what we're all about. Of course"—conspiratorial chuckle here—"since it *is* Mass, we don't really turn anyone *away*, but—"

"Hey, no, that's fine, Dolores," I said, flip-topping a can of Heineken. "I just wanted to find out what you guys are

all about. I've read your flyers, and a couple of friends of mine
have spoken about you, but—"

"Well, you know, there *is* a way for you to do that," she
interrupted. "We have, every Saturday afternoon, a special service for people who are not yet full members of our group. We
call it a Sharing. Of course, Father Steve would like to talk to
you before an official invitation, but that's, you know . . ."

"A mere formality?" I supplied, my heart sinking. Christ,
for a minute there it looked like I could just tell Bridget that
these guys were so tight you couldn't infiltrate them without
a lot of James Bond jive (and we don't do that stuff) and go
happily back to running a credit check on the bastards.

Exactly! Dolores said, and told me just how to get to the
Sethian Center from Chicago, set up an appointment for
eleven A.M. that Saturday with Father Steve, and wished me,
sincerely, the best of everything.

Not that she had to tell me how to get from Chicago to
Notre Dame, I thought as I watched that giant smudge pot,
Gary, Indiana, glide by on my right. I'd made the trip before,
and often, and maybe one more time than was really good
for me.

My old man was a Czech immigrant ("Garnish" is an
Anglo form of a name it's just too damn much trouble to
remember how to spell) from, if you give a leaping fart, Plzen
or Pilsen to you, a town maybe forty miles southwest of
Prague (Praha to my old man) where it just so happens the
greatest beer in the world, Pilsner Urquell, has been made
since around the time Martin Luther learned to ride a bike.
And he was a plumber, and according to him the best damn
plumber in Chicago, and he thought that's what I ought to
be, too.

And I figured, who in his right mind would spend a life
making a living messing around in other people's shit? (I
know, I know, you see the irony coming already.) So, with
some saved-up money from summer jobs, and a heavy "loan"
from Pop (I never repaid it, and he never asked), I enrolled
as a freshman at the University of Notre Dame, every Cath-

olic immigrant's kid's dream of the greatest university in the world. Bought myself a goddamn blue and gold ND windbreaker, and everything. I wuz gonna be a engineer, like the joke used to go. Funny, huh?

A year later I was doing other things.

So maybe that's another reason I was pissed at having to go to the Sharing. Like I told you—if you live in Chicago and you want a quick feel-good fix, cruise Lake Shore Drive. If you're me—not that I have a lot of choice—and you want some scenery that looks, somehow, as bad as you feel about yourself, just keep straight on LSD till you're driving by the Notre Dame campus.

Now you can't really see the famous Golden Dome atop the Administration Building—you know, the symbol of the university and its proud tradition and blah blah—from the parking lot of the Morris Inn. But if you know the campus at all, you can *feel* it; it's there, at the center of the main quad, shining in the sun (hell, if you buy into the school myth, the thing even shines when it rains), smack dab at the end of the road that leads straight from the inn to the university grounds.

I'd already promised myself, when I was getting the car topped off and oil checked that morning, that I would *not* visit the campus.

I checked in at the desk—the fall term had begun two weeks before, and the place was almost empty, no fond parents staying there to see off their shiny-faced and bushytailed progeny on the seas of higher learning—dropped my overnight bag in my room, and since it was ten-thirty walked the four blocks to the Sethian Meeting Hall, Witness Center, whatever the hell they called it. Memory came flooding back—isn't that what they always say memory does, I mean, in novels? I was almost sure that, about one more block from the old frame house that was Sethian HQ, there used to be, all those years ago, a place called Kubiak's, the best bar in South Bend to get served if you were underage. And there was that funny, shadowy, and still bright light in the air, glancing off the piles of gold fallen leaves covering the street and raked into mounds in a few of the front yards I passed. Nobody was burning leaves, I figured because the smoke ate up the ozone layer and would give us all skin cancer or something, but, swear to God, *I* could smell them burning.

I rang the bell—actually, buzzed the buzzer, the place was that old-fashioned—and the front door was opened by a little old lady with bright eyes like a bird's eyes and that kind of wispy, thinning blue hair you see sometimes on old ladies that looks like it's halfway decided to migrate to her upper lip, because some of it was staking a claim there already. All in black with, just like a movie, a cameo brooch at the neck.

"Uh—are you Dolores?" I asked.

"Sorry?" she chirped (no kidding, chirped, tilting her head like a sparrow checking out a cat). "Dolores? No, no, Dolores doesn't come in weekends. I'm Clara. Are you Mr. Garnet, Father Steve's eleven o'clock?"

When I said I was, she told me to come in, come in, they were so glad I'd made the trip—goddamn if *I* was glad I'd made the trip—and glided ahead of me into a front office that must've been the sun parlor when the place was a *real* house, offered me a cup of coffee, which I turned down, and then perched behind a big oak desk, maybe forgetting I was there, while I sat on a red plastic couch with a stack of *People* and *Commonweal* magazines on the end table. Except for the *Commonweal*s, with cover stories like "The Church at a Crossroads," it could have been a dentist's office.

After about ten minutes, when I was trying to figure out how to ask Clara if it was okay to smoke (there was something on the coffee table that could have been an ashtray, but then again it could have been a pre-Columbian ceremonial chicken-blood catcher, for all I knew), she looked up, her little eyes even brighter and a smile on her face that blanked over her little blue mustache.

"Father Steve!" She beamed as the door behind me swung open. "Here's Mr. Garmush, your eleven o'clock."

The first thing I noticed, which I guess is what guys of my

generation always notice, is that Father Steve didn't have a Roman collar on. He was wearing blue jogging pants—is there such a thing?—and a black sweatshirt with one of those things, you know, a cross with a circle at the top, stitched in white across his chest. Ankh—he was wearing an ankh.

And he was a wiry guy, about my height, but wiry, with long red hair and a red beard and a Crest grin that made it impossible to guess his age. The kind of guy who wanted you to like him instantly, and you'd have to fight real hard not to.

"*Garnish*, Clara," he said, holding out his hand. "Harry Garnish. Would you like to come into my office, Mr. Garnish? Or can I call you Harry?"

Yes, and yes. The office was, I guessed, the ex–living room of whoever had lived there. Spacious enough to relax in, with no desk, just a few sofas and chairs around a big wooden cube with some papers stacked on it along with—there *is* a God—a real ashtray and a CD player in the corner uttering, right now, Paul Simon's *Graceland*. Indirect lighting. The kind of room that says, Hey, want to smoke some dope?

"So, Harry," Steven Lee said as he settled onto a sofa, picking up a manila folder from the top of the pile. "You're interested in joining us?" If the room hadn't been so under-lit, I'd swear his eyes were twinkling.

"Well, *you* know, Father—" I began.

"Steve." He smiled. "Just Steve. Okay?"

"Yeah. Steve," I said. "Well, you know. I've heard about you and the Sethians, and I was thinking—"

"What's your parish, Harry?" he said.

"Say what?"

"Your parish," he said, and his eyes *were* twinkling. "You told, aah"—looking into the manila folder—"you told Dolores when you called that you're a Catholic. So what parish do you go to in Chicago?"

"Skokie," I said. And I was, dammit, trying to think. "I live in Skokie. Avers Street. Saint Joan of Arc," I finished, with the kind of rush you get when you finish doing d-i-s-i-n-g-e-n-u-o-u-s in the eighth grade spelling bee.

"Oh, yeah, Saint Joan's," he said, fishing a pack of Dunhills out of somewhere in his black ankh sweatshirt and offering me one. Dunhill red label: best smoke in the world. I took one.

"Father Healey still the pastor there?" he asked, lighting up himself and blowing smoke in the general direction of Paul Simon's voice.

Well, Mrs. Garnish—not that I ever met the lady, she seems to have croaked before I hit what we call, I hope with a smile, the age of reason—the Mrs. Garnish in my mind, anyhow, raised no fools.

"Healey?" I said, remembering how good a Dunhill tasted. "I think you must be thinking of another parish."

He picked up a remote-control candy bar from the table between us, aimed it, and Paul died in midsentence.

"Harry," he said. "Nice try, but I go to the movies, too. Ned Healey really is pastor at Saint Joan's. We were in seminary together. And you're a private investigator. Would you like me to tell you your license number?"

Now old Martin O'Toole told me once: "Harry, my boy, if you're going to make your livin' by lyin'—which is what we do—you should study the ways of that odd creature the 'possum, and his three means of defense. When cornered, Brother 'Possum first bares his tiny teeth, tryin' to look ferocious. When that don't work, and it usually don't, he then just goes limp, tryin' to look as helpless and uninterestin' as possible. You see?"

"And what if that doesn't work?" I'd asked.

"Why, then, lad"—Martin had smiled, tipping his whiskey at me—"he just shits all over himself, don't you know?"

So, watching Steven Lee's smile and figuring I was into defense condition two, 'possumwise, I said, "No, thanks. I've got it memorized."

"Okay. So why *are* you here?" he said. "Oh, look, I know

you're not about to tell me who your client is. But you've got to admit, I have the right to know whether your, let's call it visit, could cause any harm to anyone in our little group . . . or to the group itself."

"Why ask?" I said. "I mean, you know I'm a P.I., and you know I wasn't going to tell you that. Why the—why should you believe me if I say, hey, all is cool, I'm just here checking on the plumbing arrangements for the water commission? Why not just tell me to . . . uh . . ."

"Fuck off?" he said, and burst into a genuine laugh at my expression while he tossed the pack of Dunhills onto the table between us. "Because, man, I don't work that way. *We* don't work that way. I don't know what you've been told about the Sethian Movement." A bit of a frown here. "We're pretty new, and some people, even in the church are a little scared of us. But we've got nothing to hide, I promise you."

"That why you got my P.I. number?" I said, taking another Dunhill.

The easy smile turned back on. "Harry, Harry," he said. "We may be a bunch of holy Joes and Joans but we're not suckers. You know: Live in faith, but count the cards. And I *will* tell you a secret about us. It's for free, and it's not much of a secret, and you may think I'm one silly bastard for saying it. It's this: We're just trying to glorify the Lord here."

His eyes weren't twinkling when he said that. They were misting. And whatever I may have thought he was, "silly" didn't make the list.

"So," he said, lighting up again. "You going to answer my question?"

And, honest to God, I don't know if I was carrying out Martin O'Toole's 'possum strategy or if I was really trying to be straight with the guy, who, I figured, if he really believed what he said, was in deep yogurt enough already. "Hell, Father," I said. "Tell you the truth, I'm not too sure just what I'm supposed to find out here. Sorry if that sounds like a fink-out. Maybe I'll just pack up and head home, okay?"

He snapped Paul Simon back on and leaned back on the sofa.

"Good answer, Chauncey." He grinned. "You do what you want, Harry, but as far as I'm concerned, I'd like you to come to our meeting today."

"Uh . . ."

"No, seriously, man," he said. "Come on, you know what I know now, and *I* . . . well, if I can show you I'm willing to trust you, that might be a good thing, yeah? For both of us. We start around five-thirty, six. Deal?"

I couldn't help grinning as I stood and shook his hand. "Father Steve," I said, "if you're not a helluva con, you are one very strange cat."

"Hey," he said, pointing to the ankh. "Mysterious priest, you know?"

He walked me to the lobby, where the little sparrow-lady was typing away at, I'd say, four or five words a minute. She gave him the same smile—*wonderment* is the word that came to mind—as the last time he'd entered the room.

"Clara," he said, "Mr. Garnish will be joining us for the Sharing tonight, okay?"

"Oh, good, Father!" she chirped again. "Mr. Garnish, if you'll just fill out this card, for our records."

Right. After he said my name, she got it right.

Father Steve suggested I might want to look at the ND campus, and gave me an odd stare when I told him I'd seen it. Something in my voice, maybe.

So I walked that extra block and, damn if Kubiak's wasn't still there, and just opening up.

So I went in and ordered a Löwenbräu Dark at the bar. And it was the first beer I remember not enjoying. There wasn't sawdust on the floor anymore. The jukebox—CD of course—was playing Guns N' Roses, I don't know, "I Want to Smash Your Face," or some damn thing, not Brubeck/Desmond, "Take Five." The few kids in the bar, all in black with neon trim, made me, in my polyester, feel like a Jehovah's

Witness on the skids. And besides, this was Kubiak's, but it was a *legal* beer.

So, since I was an old man, I figured I'd do what old men do. I went back to my room and took a nap.

Which, depending on your point of view, was either a great or a very bad idea, considering how the rest of my day turned out. Lisa, I mean.

$\triangledown$

5

OKAY, OKAY, I *KNOW* what you want to hear about. I'll get to it, yeah? But first I have to tell you about the Sharing. The one at the Sethian Center, that is.

Clara led me into the same room where I'd talked with Father Steve that morning. Steve was there, dressed the same, along with twelve, thirteen other people ranged around the sofas and chairs. There were some couples about my age (I couldn't get my age off my mind that whole goddamn day), some students, I guess, including one kid in a Roman collar I figured for a seminarian, and—bingo—this girl with long, like sixties long, blond hair and a smile like a sphinx, in a halter top and factory prefrayed jeans that had started a palace revolt in the Garnish hormones or whatever the hell they are by the time I was halfway into the room.

"Ah, Harry." Steve smiled. "Good. Now we can begin. Could we all stand and join hands, folks?"

And ah, shit! I thought. I hate joining hands and praying. No kidding, I *hate* it. It's one of the lots of reasons I stopped going to Mass a long time ago. I mean, you want to "community"—they love that word—with a bunch of yaboes who spend the other six days per week mainly pulling the crap that makes my livelihood? Forget it: Frank Capra gives me heartburn and Anne Frank was *wrong*.

So I joined hands, Clara on my left and the seminarian—they always look like they've just stepped out of a shower—on my right and, at least by my reckoning, a righteous 180 degrees straight across from the stone honey-hair fox.

I was expecting something nice and familiar like the "Our Father," and I was out of luck.

"Holy One!" he began, his eyes closed and the feather of a smile on his face, like he knew who he was talking to. "We stand in your presence and we stand as your presence. We call you to ourselves and we call you from within ourselves. Let the strangers among us find what they seek"—did he wink at me here? dunno—"and let us all find ourselves again in welcoming the strangers. And bless us, as we bless you. Amen."

"And now," he said as we all sat back down and he dug out another pack of Dunhills, "who's got a beef with the Lord?"

It was pretty good, I had to admit. Relaxed, comfortably groovy, and with just enough of a hint of big mystical vibes hovering on the fringes of the ultraviolet or was it the infrared? Anyway, I saw this "channeler" on the tube once—you know, one of those straw-haired, California-type, aerobics-class, drop-dead *zaftig* ladies who claimed to be possessed by a million-year-old poet and shitkicker from ancient Babylon or something. And before she went into her trance and spoke for the shitkicker—sounding like Arnold Schwarzenegger in drag—she was in just the same groove Father Steve was laying down. Yeah, sure, God and I are like that, but hey, we're all cats together here, right? In Steve's case, the Dunhills were a stroke of genius.

Of course, nobody in the room could play quite up to Steve's level. The beefs with the Lord turned out to be mainly the kind of stuff you hear in any twelve-step program or for that matter any bar, if it's late enough at night. One couple, about my age, was worried because they were losing touch with their son, now a college kid. (Damn! Most people my age had college kids.) One guy, who from his hands was a working man, was scared as all hell he was going to get laid off. One of the students, a guy, was having trouble with the sauce and another, a girl, was having trouble with eating too much (she was, natch, thin enough to make you wince in sympathy); they were both in other programs, too, but had to tell how much the Sethians meant to them.

Same old shit. But, you know, it's *always* the same old shit, and that doesn't stop it hurting. What I'd told Barry Browder was true, but only part of the truth. There are three, maybe on the outside five, basic ways to park your life in downtown hell. I'm afraid of people. I think about food or sex or booze or whatever all the time. Nobody could love me. I don't love you and I *want* to. And they're all statistics, Jack: unless you happen to be one of them. I mean, my hiccups may make you laugh like a loon; you want me, though, to laugh at yours? When they won't stop?

Not everybody spoke. Not me, not some others, and especially not frayed-jeans goldenhair across from me, who just smiled to herself during the whole show and whom I was beginning to figure for maybe Father Steve's personal revolution against clerical celibacy.

Whatever Steve was doing with his wick, though, he was doing a good job with the hurt people. He listened, he soothed, he didn't give easy bullcrap answers to the fact that these folks were in pain, and I was starting to like the guy a lot more than I wanted to. He let them talk until they were ready to stop talking. Ever try to do that?

Especially when the seminarian to my right started in.

The kid was scared. Not scared like the guy afraid of getting laid off, but scared the way you can only be when you're eighteen, twenty, twenty-one, and your body and your mind are pulling you in two different directions, and it's not just that you're not sure which one to listen to, it's that you're not sure which one *is* which one.

"I don't know," the poor kid said, looking at his hands, which were grabbing one another for comfort. "I pray. I really pray. And I know that, you know, love is all you need, like the Rolling Stones said."

"Uh," I began, but Steve shot me a glance—shot is the word—that told me to nix on the music history. God*damn* this kid was young.

"But sometimes," he went on, "sometimes it's like I just want it all to *stop*, you know? I mean, I want to stop loving Him, and I want, I really want Him to stop loving me. It's like . . . it's like I'm being swallowed, like . . . uh, an oyster. Whole. It's—"

And he didn't break down crying and he didn't moan. Just sat there, holding hands with himself and staring nowhere.

"It's like you're in a well-lighted room and you wish it would get dark?" said Steve.

The kid just nodded. His eyes were shiny.

And then Steve did something about as weird and about as right as Janie had done a few months earlier when she'd kissed jogging suit's hand in the Bambi Bar before dropping her whiskey glass down his crotch. He got up, crossed the room, and kissed the crown of the kid's head.

"It's okay, little brother," he said. "There'll be darkness. But don't worry, the light will be waiting for you when you want it again."

Everybody was quict after that, and Steve said a few things that I've forgotten—no big, praise Jesus out-chorus or request for contributions, which I'd figured would be the set closer, just a little bless us all and we should come back anytime we felt like it. And we all joined—I minded less, now—hands again, and that was it.

"Find out what you wanted?" Steve smiled at me, shaking hands as we filed out.

"Yeah." I smiled back. "You *are* one very strange cat."

"Told ya," he said, and we laughed.

It was seven-thirty, quarter to eight, and already dark and moonless. A dark and stormy night, easy on the stormy, right? And cold, the early autumn cold where the air opens your throat up like vodka from the freezer, without the aftertaste. I bundled my overcoat around my neck, lit a cigarette, which never tastes as good as when you're out in the cold, and started walking back to the inn.

In about a block I noticed a slight figure ahead of me, walking in the same direction—slight, in a parka with the

hood up, but with a butt swaying in blue jeans, by the street-
lamps, that I recognized without even thinking about it.

In another block I came abreast of her—helluva word—
and was walking on when she said, behind me now, "Hi.
Weren't you at the meeting?"

"Yeah," I said. "Harry Garnish."

"Oh, yeah," she said. "You were the last to arrive. Lisa
Bowen," holding out her hand. We walked on together.

"Staying at the inn?" she said.

"Um," I said.

"Me, too. I came in from Chicago. Wow, it's cold for September, isn't it?"

"Um," I said again. Man, when I'm making the moves,
I'm one silver-tongued sonofabitch.

"Well," she said after a while, "when I get to the inn, I'm
going to have a nice big brandy toddy."

It's the same feeling you get, you're playing blackjack,
you're dealt a nine in the hole, next card up is a seven, you
know it's crazy to call for a hit on sixteen, but, God, man,
the odds are just the odds, aren't they?

"Sounds good," I said. "Mind a little company?"

Okay! Twenty-one!

Lisa, she told me over her toddy in the Morris Inn (just
brandy for me), was a junior (how do *you* spell relief) at the
University of Chicago, majoring in religious studies, up here
to sit in with the Sethians for a term paper she was doing
on radical religious groups.

"First time?" I said.

"And last." She smiled. "These guys don't seem to have a
lot of stuff going on that would interest my prof. Hey, you
mind if I have another one of these?"

Not. At. All.

"And how about you, Harry?" She smiled, cozying back
in her chair like an ad for something, who the hells knows
what it is, but you gotta run right out and get one. "You a
religious guy?" A really amused glance, and I wished my
polyester suit was in hell.

"Naah," I said. "I'm just—well, I have this friend, he's sort of in with these guys, so I thought I'd just scope them out, you know?"

"Friend?"

"Yeah. Nobody you'd know. Older guy."

"Well, you know," she said, "I know some older guys. I like older guys." And, next hand, I thought, and this time I'm dealt a queen face down.

Go for it.

"Yeah?" I said. "Well, look, *this* older guy is going to head up to his room and deal with a little Scotch. So, Lisa—" and you got it, I paused.

"Is it older Scotch?" she asked, putting down her second, untasted toddy.

What the hell. I know, we're all used to instant replay on the tube, you know, you can watch Michael Jordan walk on air for that perfect, Balanchine slam-dunk again and again, if you've got a VCR. But (if I have to tell you this, you got *problems*) some things you can't replay, except somewhere way past where words work. Just figure; it was weird. In the best sense of weird. First time all day I hadn't thought about my age.

Which brings (and brought) me back to Clyde's Cavern next day, staring at the last inch of my second beer and thinking about my age, and a lot of other stuff, all over again. Clyde ambled down the bar.

"*Uno más*, Harry?" he said.

"Thanks, man, no," I said.

"Hey, Harry? You don't look so good, you don't mind me saying."

Old Clyde. "No biggie, lover." I force-grinned at him. "It's just Sunday, don'cha know?"

"Yeah," he said as I walked toward the afternoon outside. "Crummy fuckin' day."

So now where? Where else, except home, was there?

$\triangledown$

6

JANIE WAS THERE, SITTING on the sofa next to Bandit, the cat wreckage who adopted me when he discovered I was partial to fish sticks and always warmed up more of the suckers than I could eat. Bandit was watching TV: the "WGN Movie for a Sunday Afternoon" was *42nd Street*, and he freaks on musicals. Janie was stroking him behind the ears and reading this hefty book Bridget had lent her, last time Bridget came over for dinner (we were doing stuff like that now, too): *The Second Sex*.

And, by God, she did it. As I walked in the door, she looked up, smiled, and said, "Hi, honey!"

Christ. Remember that "Outer Limits" where Robert Culp lets these guys turn him into a space monster so that everybody on Earth will unite against what they think is a threat from Mars or something? And how, right after they give him the there's-no-turning-back-after-this injection, his cute wife tells him she's pregnant and their life is going to be so great? And Culp, already monsterfying inside, has to act as if all is cool? "The Architects of Fear"—that was the episode.

I didn't manage things as well as Culp. Sue me. Since she'd moved in, Janie had tidied the bejeezus out of the apartment, given Bandit flea baths and a scented collar (he was too stupid to notice anything), left The Life, and been . . . well, fucking wonderful, and yes, if you want to reverse the adjectives, be my guest.

So scratch "Outer Limits." I felt more like Freddy Krueger wandering onto the set of "The Cosby Show."

So, naturally I dealt with the situation like any normal man. I picked a fight with Janie.

You don't want the details, do you? I mean, hell, they're always the same, anyway; the specific words are just chips in the game. You know: You're late. Well, where's dinner, for Chrissake? You been drinking? What the fuck's it to you? Yeah, you have. Hey, you getting moral with me? And so on and so forth, and razza razza, with the damn cat looking from one to the other like, hey, does this mean no tuna fish tomorrow morning?

So I slept on the couch that night, secure in the knowledge that nobody was going to make me feel like shit just because I'd treated them like shit. H. Garnish was no asshole, am I right?

Bandit did get his tuna in the morning. And there was coffee and eggs and herring waiting for me when I got out of the shower, which I love and which today I ate in kick-your-self-in-the-ass silence while Janie talked to Bandit. When I was leaving for the office she asked me what I wanted for dinner.

"Hey," I said, "want to go out tonight? The Corinthian Columns, maybe?"

"Okay, if you want," she said. " 'Bye," and gave me one of those kisses that feel a lot like CAR-RT-SORT letters. All very "Ozzie and Harriet," without the laugh-track.

Christ, I thought as I drove to O'Toole Agency, does she *know?*

I realized, walking into the office, that I'd been so bummed that morning I hadn't even read "Garfield," "Shoe," and my horoscope for the day in the *Tribune:* bad karma. And I haven't looked back to check it, but I'm sure my starchart for that Monday, translated, must read something like SHIT: INCOMING.

Brenda, our 90-proof receptionist, was already in place for the day—her portable radio playing New Age music, a stack of important-looking manila folders, which may or may not have contained anything, at her left hand, and a mega coffee mug, which at eight-thirty A.M., odds were, probably *did* contain coffee, at her right.

"Morning, Harry." She beamed at me. "Hey, boss lady says to check in with her, soon's you can." Brenda is closer to my age than Bridget's. But she's been at O'Toole since old Martin's days, and remembers Bridget as the cute nun daughter—Shirley Temple played by Sidney Greenstreet—and so she adores Bridget running the show, thinks it's precocious and, that word again, *cute*. Go figure. I told her I'd see Bridget right away.

"Hey, Harry," she said as I was leaving. "You don't look so good, kiddo. Everything okay?"

Right. That was Clyde Crews, Janie, and now Brenda, the three people I'd seen since Lisa, all telling me I was radiating weirdness. Check that. There'd been the lady in the Morris Inn watching my hands shake. Four. Ever see that old Peter Lorre movie, *M*?

"I'm swell, Bren." I weakly grinned. "Late night, you know?"

"Aww, Harry, you dawg," she said. If only everybody else was that easy.

Bridget was ensconced—that's the word for when you put a candle in a candleholder, and believe me, with Bridget in her office, it works—Bridget was ensconced among her plants. I gave my usual silent nod to old Phil, lit up, and took my seat.

"Harry." She leaned forward, her eyebrows making a V over her nose. "Is everything all right, dear?"

Five.

I explained to her—I was getting good at this—that life had never been more splendiferous, Garnish-wise. I also explained to her that I had visited the Sethians, that they seemed to have one hell of a good intelligence-gathering network, since I'd been made before I walked in the door, but that, as far as I could tell, they were a bunch of harmless, if maybe paranoid compulsive cuddlers. The non-Sethian cuddling, I figured, was nobody's problem but mine.

"So," I concluded, "I think we can just bill Professor Barry Browder Three for time and charges and call it a wrap."

"They had checked on you before you arrived?" Bridget said, communing with the bears on her mug.

"Well, yeah," I said, lighting another cigarette. "Father Steve was very up-front about it. They're being, I don't know, hassled by the church or something, so they—"

"Father Steve?" she said.

"Wha," I said.

"You call him 'Father Steve,' " she said. That's a very friendly locution for someone who tells you he's done a background check on you. Do you trust this man, Harry?"

"Well," I said, and thought, wait a minute. Had I been bolloxed by this guy? Like one of those movies about religious cults and shit, where the guy finds himself being smarmed and hugged out of his gourd by the brainwashing, brainwashed crazies? And if that was so, what if Lisa . . .

What if Lisa was part of the scam?

No. Couldn't be. I'd been with the Sethians for less than twelve hours, for Chrissake. Unless you counted Lisa, and then—but no.

"Bridget," I said, lighting a third cigarette. "I'm giving you my impressions, right? What else can I give you?"

"All right." She sighed her that's-not-the-right-answer-but-let-it-pass sigh. "But I don't feel that we can really let Mr. Browder's inquiry end just on that inconclusive note. Harry, I want you to go to Northrop College—"

"Say *what?*"

"And ask around about Mrs. Browder," she went on, as unperturbed as if I'd farted in the middle of her fifth grade math class. "She's a writing counselor there, and you might be able to talk to a few students, a few faculty, who know her. Just, you know, find out what their impressions of her are. Since you're so good at impressions."

It was the irony—Bridget almost never does irony—in that last line that snapped me out of my general funk.

"Hey, Bridge," I said. And she *hates* to be called "Bridge."

"Hey, Bridge," I said. "Brother Browder, far as I know, didn't hire us to check up on ol'—what's her face?—ol' Nancy. We were hired to do the Sethian folks, yeah? Now what's this crap, you want me to ask around the college—you know I hate college—about little wifey? You think the good professor's going to pay us for that? What's our scenario here, you don't mind me asking?"

"Harry," she began in that patient lecture tone that always tells me I'll be screwed by the time she finishes her first sentence. "If Nancy Browder is involved with the Sethians, and if the Sethians claim to be carrying on the work of the church, then *I* want to know that they're honest. And I think Professor Browder can afford a little extra time and expense to secure us in this knowledge."

Oh, boy. That meant I was caught between two religious fanatics, one of them my boss, a client I thought was a self-important dork whose case I didn't even want, and my own, my very own, first infidelity, since, you see, I'd never thought about being faithful before. Like I told you, SHIT: INCOMING.

So I drove up to Northrop College.

$\triangledown$

7

R*EALLY* UP. I*F* BY "up" you mean north. (I could never, in geography, figure how some rivers, like the pain-in-the-ass Nile, could flow from the bottom of the map to the top, but that's another story.) To get to Northrop College, you hit Sheridan Road and keep the lake on your right. Sheridan is the northern spur of Lake Shore Drive and it thrusts as far toward the North Pole as it can, petering out like an out-of-breath, out-of-water salmon near the Wisconsin border. But "up" another way, too. From Evanston, you hit the Gold Coast suburbs of Wilmette, Winnetka, Glencoe, and Highland Park, and with each progressive suburb you tack another thirty or fifty thousand on the price of a lot, till in Glencoe you're seeing drop-dead houses on the road that are the carriage houses for the mansions they shield. "Up" as in, it could turn you into a Marxist.

Northrop College is near the beginning of this whole capitalist theme park. It's in Wilmette, not far from the Baha'i House of Worship. Now the Baha'i Temple, which is what Chicagoans call it, invariably freaks out the out-of-towners. Set in the middle of upscale American suburbia, it's this massive, alabaster-laced dome that's got nothing to do with the Frank Lloyd Wright wannabe houses surrounding it. It's supposed to look like a mosque, they tell me. *I* think it looks like a rocket ship from one of those science fiction magazine covers that I loved in the fifties, and that's why I love the temple. I don't know much about the religion, except that it's about you should try hard to love everybody and try *real* hard not to fuck anybody over, and since Dizzy Gillespie was a member, that's good enough for me.

So if Notre Dame had its Golden Dome, Northrop College had, sort of, its alabaster one. On lend-lease, as it were.

It wasn't a campus, really—I mean, not that monastic, twilight zone, hey you're on a different planet feeling of hush that you figure goes with deep thought. It was a sprawl of low-slung cinder-block buildings right across the street from a row of laundromats, bookstores, pizza places, and record stores, with only a big redwood sign—NORTHROP COLLEGE OF LIBERAL ARTS: FOUNDED 1957—to proclaim itself. Kind of a brave little big sign, I thought.

I found the English department after asking about four students and taking three wrong turns. I was figuring—not that I gave much of a damn—on not running into Barry Browder, and my luck held, though I did pass his office door and, by God, there on a little fake-brass plate was "Barry Browder III"—"III": what a dwortz.

The English department receptionist was this beautiful young, I guessed Eurasian, woman in denim overalls and a white turtleneck. (Student intern? Rrrowrr: shut the fuck *up*, Garnish.) I told her, old master of disguise that I was, that I was thinking about taking some courses at Northrop and was wondering if I could talk to somebody in the writing program.

"Uh, do you mean *creative* writing?" she asked with a smile. "Shonnie," the nameplate on her desk read. "That would be Professor Middlebrook, but he isn't on campus today."

"Well," I said, wondering, creative writing? What the hell was the opposite of that? "Well, I guess I mean, well . . . writing. You know, essays, letters. Writing. I'm sounding dumb here, right?"

"You're not sounding dumb," she said, and said it so nice that I hated to be lying about the whole thing. "Why don't you try CASE?"

"CASE?"

She chuckled. "Center for Academic Skills Enrichment.

CIA, HUD, you know. Organizations love initials, don't they?"

"Yeah, acronyms," I said, and that earned me a couple of raised eyebrows. "That sounds good. That where Mrs. Browder works?"

"Nancy?" she said, and her eyes smiled along with her lips. "You know her?"

"Not really. Pal of mine said she was really good, though."

"Oh, she's swell!" Shonnie said. Kids were saying "swell" again? Christ, maybe I was coming back into fashion, like slow dancing. "You'll love her. Here, let me draw you a little map how to get there." And she did.

"Hey, thanks." I grinned at her. "You've been nice to an old man."

She looked me in—dig, *in*—my eyes and she said, "You don't sound dumb, and you're not an old man." The contact lasted maybe a millisecond, but who gives a shit for clock-time? Feeling sad and exhilarated all at once, I left.

I found my way to the little CASE Quonset hut (Shonnie gave great headings) and, on a dare with myself, walked in. Nancy Browder wasn't supposed to see me, of course, but I was still in a raw mood about Janie and, well, you know, ol' Shonnie hadn't especially cleared up the mental sky, so I was figuring, bag the investigation.

"Sorry, no smoking." The skinny little guy in a white beard behind the reception desk smiled.

"Right," I said and tossed my cigarette out the door. "Just thought I'd take a look at your literature. Okay?"

"On the shelf there," he said, pointing to the opposite wall and staring at my cig smoldering outside the door like I'd just taken a dump in his prize dahlias. A polluter and a litterbug. Well, screw, Jack.

I was pretending to read the descriptions of the CASE Writing Program—Jesus, the people who wrote this crap were going to teach other people how to write?—when a slight woman in a blue dress buttoned at the collar came out from one of the cubicles in the back. About my age or a little younger with a worry cleft between her eyebrows and short brunette hair. You know—the kind of face, you figure the worst thing she ever did, she let her fella go all the way the week before they got married.

She was Nancy Browder, just like but maybe a little thinner than the photo her husband had left in Bridget's office.

The guy with her looked about six and a half feet—square. Blond hair down to his shoulders, a long pendant earring, and arms sticking out of his black T-shirt like legs, big as anything I'd seen since Ted Kluzuski used to play ball.

"Going to lunch, Nancy?" said the whitebeard, non-smoker prick.

"Going home, Gary," she said. "My next appointment's not till three. See you in a few hours. And I'll see you, Billy," turning to the jolly pink giant, "this time next week."

He grinned, shook her hand, and left as she walked back to her cubicle. I put the folders back in the rack, lit a cigarette as I sauntered toward the door—Gary could suck eggs in Cleveland—and followed the big guy as he crossed the street dividing the campus from the rest of the world.

And that was the first and last time I saw Nancy Browder.

8

JOLLY PINK HEADED FOR a place called Woodstock Pizza—
"Michelob on Tap!" Long tables with benches, kids all over,
a big TV on the wall playing a rerun of "Gilligan's Island,"
and, just like at Kubiak's, some metal band on the jukebox.
This time it sounded like they were singing, "I Worship
Your Pain," who knew? And this was where students gathered to talk?

The big kid was sitting with a bunch of pals and sucking
on a jumbo Coke by the time I came in. I hadn't noticed it
before, but across his black T-shirt were iron-on letters spelling out THOR.

The place was crowded enough that I had an excuse to sit
near Thor and his gang with my sausage submarine and beer.
I chewed and sipped till their conversation lulled—time it
yourself sometime: After twenty minutes max, in any group
everybody will fall silent for a minute or so, just like rounds
in a prizefight.

"Excuse me," I said into the silence. "All of you folks go
to Northrop College?"

Friendly nods all round. Old farts are fun to talk to, in
small doses.

"Well," I said, "I don't want to interrupt you kids, but I'm
just in town for a few days, and I thought I'd look up an old
army buddy who teaches here. I'm just not sure he'd want
to see me. Anybody here know a Professor Browder?"

That got a general laugh, a kind of uncomfortable laugh,
and Thor turned it into a crack-up when he said, "Barry

Browder. Mister World Lit? He was in the army? Whose?"
Not a fan. Good.

"Ours," I laughed along, "but not so you'd notice. He still
hard to get along with?"

"Well," they all sort of hummed in unison.

"Hey," I said, "don't worry. 'Old army buddy' at my age
doesn't mean I love the guy. Just might feel like checking in
on him, auld lang syne, that stuff, dig?"

Thor nodded sagely. Young guys always understand the
odd ways of old farts. "I had two classes with him. What was
he like in the army?"

"Well," I improvised, "the kind of guy, always looked like
he smelled something bad in the corner of the room and had
'B.B. III' stamped on all his personal stuff."

"Oh, wow!" He laughed. "I have to tell you, Mr. . . . ."

"Garnish. Harry's better."

"Okay. Your pal hasn't changed much. He's really smart,
I guess, but boy, does he come on cold." The chorus nodded
sagely.

"But you took two classes with him?" I asked.

"Had to. You can't do an English major here without doing
Professor Browder."

"Hey," I said, "you guys know if he ever got married?"

"Oh, Mrs. Browder's great," said a girl who'd been hanging on Thor's arm (that arm was big enough, you probably
could hang on it).

"Yeah? She's a teacher, too?"

"Well, sort of." The girl went on. "She's what we call a
Writing Counselor." I liked that "we"—explain it real slow
for the poor dumb old fuck. "Helps students plan their papers, organize their time, you know. And she's so friendly.
Not—"

She'd been about to say, of course, "Not like her prick of
a husband," but she remembered that we were old army
buddies, and she was a polite kid.

"Good," I said. "Any kids?"

"Well," began the girl, smiling into her Coke, the kind of

smile that tells you, hey, if I felt like it, I could give you some really good shit. "They've got a daughter—"

"Hey, Heather, I've got to split," said Thor, rising. "Nice talking to you, sir. Hope you enjoy your reunion." And left.

Sir.

I chatted with the rest of the kids through another sandwich and another beer, and went away with not a hell of a lot more than I'd learned in the first ten minutes. Barry Browder was generally regarded as a supersmart pain in the ass, which didn't exactly make me gape in astonishment, and everybody—even the ones who'd never been to see her—thought that Nancy Browder was basically Sally Field in *The Mother Teresa Story*, and what that all told me was that I might as well not have bothered to make the drive in the first place, and I hate driving, anyway. Heather never got back, somehow, to the Browders' kid, just that she was named Andrea, and was a student at Northrop, and at least in this crowd wasn't about to be voted Queen of the May.

I left Woodstock's, after expressing geriatric gratitude to everybody, with a headache ("Gilligan's Island" and heavy metal is too fuckin' much for only one pair of ears), heartburn (two sausage submarines is too fuckin' much for anybody), and heartache—not a word I use a hell of a lot, but I'd just spent the day talking to a bunch of kids and finding out *bupkis* and for what? and now I got to drive back to the office, report that I'd wasted my time on something I didn't even care about, and then drive home to a woman I'd screwed over and she knew something was wrong and I didn't even have the balls to tell her I'd been a bastard.

Some kind of life. And I could have been a plumber.

All of which I'm thinking to myself as I walk to my car. And trying to phrase how I'm going to tell Bridget this is it, there's nothing to find out about Nancy Browder or the goddamned Sethians except that they're just as fouled up as everybody else and they haven't made a law against that yet, and let's pick up our check and close the case, and underneath all that wondering how I was going to act like Robert

Young when I got home to Janie, when what I still felt like was the Smog Monster—remember that movie?

And all this is what I'm thinking as I unlock my car, noticing that it's just past four and that the sunlight is already getting reddish as it reflects off the Baha'i Temple's alabaster dome, and I find myself picked up—that's picked up, the way you pick up a liter-mug of beer—and set down on the trunk of my Duster as I hear a voice say, "All right, Mr. Garnish, I think we should talk."

Thor.

$\triangledown$

9

H<small>E DIDN'T LOOK ANGRY</small>, really, I mean, for a guy who had just picked you up and put you back down like a chess piece. I tried a smile (always smile around big guys—got me through fifth grade recess, and I've never forgotten it).

"Not a bad idea," I said. "You go first."

"Fair enough," he said, and he wasn't smiling. "I don't think you were in the army with Professor Browder."

"Really," I said, always there, just like Robin Williams, with the topper.

"Look," he said, "you come around asking about Professor Browder and then about Nancy—about Mrs. Browder like you're just off the bus. But ten minutes before you came into Woodstock's you were in the CASE office when she and I finished our counseling session. You followed me, didn't you?"

Right. Once again into 'possum defense condition two. What with Steven Lee, Janie, and now this guy, as an expert undercover sleuth I was building myself one hell of a track record these days.

"Bingo," I said, 'possuming my ass off. "Guess I'm getting old. I didn't think you'd noticed me. Okay, Thor—is that really what they call you?"

He wasn't biting.

"Okay," I went on. "I'm a private investigator. Want to see my license? No? And what I'm doing is, I'm running a security check—you know about security checks and such? —on Professor Browder. Nothing sinister. He's being considered, see, for this big damn appointment. I don't know, something to do with some kind of national council on college teaching, and I'm supposed to be finding out how students feel about him and such."

"Bullshit," said Thor.

"Hey." I spread my hands. "You want another story? I'll make one up, okay? And how you gonna know the straight one? I told you I'm a P.I. and that means, like, lawyer or used-car salesman and that means, like, liar. And I haven't mentioned that if I felt like it I could haul your sweet ass into court for assault, have I? You mind I get off my trunk? It's an old car."

For a manhandler he was a nice guy. He tried hard not to grin as he gestured me off the car.

"Yeah, I'm really sorry about that, Mr. Garnish," he said. "It's just that—"

"That you're a big guy and when you get excited you forget sometimes how fuckin' big you are. That it?"

And the grin came through.

"Well, hell, man, you're a polite mugger anyhow. They really call you Thor?"

"Well," he said, "my name's Billy. Billy Donner. And—"

"And 'Donner' is German for 'thunder,' and everybody knows the comic book, and you're stuck with it. Don't worry, man, it's better than being a Harry all your life. Now, look. You're a smart kid. You made me in the CASE building, you followed me to my car, and congratulations, man, I didn't notice you. So, I gotta ask you, why? You worried about Professor Browder's reputation, or what?"

He sputtered. No kidding, really sputtered, and I don't know if I'd ever seen anybody sputter before.

"Prof—Professor Browder?" he sputtered. "Aww, *Jeez*us. You think I—listen, I hope he gets this big appointment or whatever, and I don't want to bad-mouth him, everybody says he's a great teacher and all. But it's like I said back there, he's really a major turn-off."

"His wife, then," I said.

He creased his brow. It was half an acknowledgment, half a wince.

"Yeah," he said. "Mr. Garnish—"

"Harry."

"Okay. A lot of the kids around here really love that lady. I mean it. She works with us, she cares about us, and, hell, she gives a shit. You know? And then . . ." He paused. "Look, man, can I talk to you, like, off the record?"

"Thor," I said, "if you think about it, you don't have much choice but to finish what you were going to say, do you?"

He grinned again. "Yeah," he said. "Okay, it's that people sort of worry about her, you know?"

"Worry?"

"Worry. She's, you know, so damn nice, and she just looks—I don't know—*sad.* I mean, I've—and a few other kids have, too—I've gone to see her in her office, and I swear she looked like she'd been crying, something, before I came in. You just, a lady like that, you just feel protective about her, you know?"

We stared at one another. Was the kid having a thing with Nancy Browder? Nancy Browder of the brown short hair and the praise-Jesus Sethians and the nothing-to-write-home-about body? I'd seen a hell of a lot stranger pairings—or was it couplings?—in my years in the business. Or was the bullshit about how much the students cared about her not, after all, bullshit?

Damned if I knew. And, come to think of it, if Thor and Mrs. Barry Browder III were banging their heads off, damned if it was my business. I had been hired to check up on her religious connections, and information I wasn't being paid to retrieve was information I didn't have to deliver.

I know, I know, you got it; I didn't like my client much in the first place, and even if he had messed with me, in a kind of polite way of messing, I was starting to like the kid. Bag it. I didn't really trust him, but I decided to believe him.

"I'll buy it," I said, and his brow uncreased just a little. "And, if you want to believe me, I've got no intention of making Mrs. Browder any more unhappy. But I gotta tell you, my friend"—I rubbed my elbow where he had grabbed me— "you gotta work on your ways of showing compassion."

His brow recreased. "Oh, God," he said, "did I really hurt you? Look, Mr. Garnish, there's a campus infirmary—"

"Don't sweat it, man, I'm just real good at doing guilt," I said. "But I'll tell you what. I don't feel like going home right now." And it hit me that Janie was still in the back of my mind, and that I wasn't just thinking about maybe getting a little more out of Thor, but was telling him the righteous truth. "If you want to buy an old man a cup of coffee somewhere, I'd like to ask you a few more things—nothing that's going to get your friend in any kind of trouble, Scout's honor."

He wasn't sure he trusted me; that was on his face like a road sign. But he was also a nice kid, and sorry he'd treated me like a mail sack. So we strolled back to Woodstock's.

Where, after two cups of coffee, I'd learned that Nancy Browder really was a kind of one-woman UNICEF for the kids of Northrop College. It was a rich kids' school, Thor told me, except for a few scholarship cases like himself, and like most rich kids' schools, hired its faculty on the basis of how "distinguished" they were (whatever that meant) and not on the basis they gave a damn about teaching or talking to the students. Enter Nancy, who, Thor said, used to invite kids over to her house regularly to just talk about their problems and their questions. Until she had to stop because, Thor and the grapevine (there's always a grapevine, which is how I make my living) said, her husband decided it was just too goddamn intrusive upon his research and writing time at home, and then she just began holding the meetings with the kids in odd rooms around the campus when enough of them felt like getting together.

I asked him if she ever talked to the kids about religious stuff.

"Not really," he said, looking at his clasped fingers. "But it's funny you say that. I mean, I wasn't raised much of anything, you know? But Nancy—Mrs. Browder—sometimes she says things, you get the idea, she really *believes* in something, and it kind of makes you wish you could, too. Is that silly?"

I didn't think it was silly. Secondhand I was getting to like the lady as much as I was getting to like her student. Or her whatever.

And I learned that Billy Donner, less than half my age, was from southern Indiana—New Albany, just across the Ohio from Louisville, and that he was at Northrop because he'd been the ace kid in his high school and against his daddy's wishes (yeah, he said "daddy") had applied for admission as a scholarship kid, and gotten it.

"So what's your father do, Bill?" I asked.

"He's an electrician," he said. And he said it proudly.

And I learned that Billy played electric bass with a local heavy metal band. This I learned when I said something obscene about the third metal song to come on the jukebox. I won't repeat it here.

"No, man," he smiled. "You've just gotta open your mind. Don't fight the music. Hey, what do you like? Simon and Garfunkel?"

"Bullshit," I said. "You ever hear of bebop?"

"Oh, wow, Bird and Diz and Max Roach," he grinned. (This I guess is when I knew I'd been right to like the guy.) "Well, just let this take you the way bop does. Honest to God, it's the same energy—you just gotta *hear* it."

His group was called Redrum, he told me. "That's 'Murder' spelled backward, like in *The Shining*, you know?" He talked about it with the fire in the eyes of all lost lovers.

"So, you finish up here, you figure on becoming a rock star?" I asked. "You've got the looks."

He shook his head, smiling. "Naah, that's just, what, my passion. I finish up here, I'd like to be—well, I'd like to be a teacher. Like . . ."

And he didn't finish the sentence, but I knew, and he knew I knew, he'd been going to say Mrs. Browder. So I finished my coffee and we shook hands and I reassured him that he'd told me nothing, absolutely nothing that could come to harm for Nancy (Christ! Now I was thinking of her by her first name), and I walked back to my car while he went I don't know where.

A nice kid. A *good* kid. I couldn't really care much if he was poking his writing counselor.

And, as with Nancy Browder, that was the first and last time I saw Billy Donner, whom his friends, because they loved to kid him and because he took kidding well, called Thor.

$\triangledown$

10

AND THAT (at least I thought at the time) was that.

I reported to Bridget the next morning that nothing I'd found out cast any suspicion on Nancy Browder, except that she seemed nicer and a hell of a lot better liked than her spouse (so I'm not an objective reporter—who is?) and, with one of her industrial-strength sighs, she agreed that we might as well tell Brother Barry we were dead-ended and hand him the tab.

"You know, Harry," she said as I was leaving her office. "After all this time working together, I'm not . . ."

"Not what?" I said into her pause.

"Well, frankly, I'm not sure we have, let's say, the same perception of what the job we're doing really is."

Funny, in the years we'd been together, I realized, and the years I'd been bitching (that's the word) about her, this was the closest she'd come to a quarrel. I fished out a cigarette, my favorite defense mechanism. And glanced at Phil, who was no help as usual.

"You're saying you don't really trust me, aren't you, Bridget?" I felt odd bringing the words out.

She picked up her coffee mug and stared at the teddy bears.

"I'm saying," she said, "that I sometimes wonder—no, I often wonder—if one of us, and it could well be me, isn't working on some basic misunderstanding of . . . of things." Now she looked me in the eye. "Do you know how warmly F-Father always spoke of you? 'My best lad,' he used to say.

'He's going to be a'—now, what was it? Oh, yes. 'He's going to be a crackerjack!' "

She smiled, a little mistily, and dammit, so did I. We were both remembering, in different ways, that funny and canny old man who'd always had something to say and who now, sixty miles north of us, was lying in bed with a tube in his arm, for a long time speechless.

"Bridget," I said, looking at the burning end of my cigarette. "Are you saying you think I ought to resign?"

She looked genuinely surprised. "No, Harry!" she said. "No! That's not what I meant at all. I meant—well, I'm sorry, perhaps I should think more about this myself. I do admire you, Harry . . ."

(Goddamn if I could figure why.)

"And I'm sure everything will be all right. Say hello to Janie for me."

And if she'd been looking for the right button to push to make my day complete, she couldn't have found a better one. "Hello" was damn near *all* Janie and I were saying to one another these days. And for a lot of days after.

I don't know. It was like Barry Browder, that blowfish, walked into the office with his bullshit little problem and all of a sudden, as dumb as when you choke on a fishbone and everyone else at the table goes bugfuck slamming you on the back, I was under some kind of siege. I mean, a detective is a guy you hire to find out stuff, tell you what he found out, and then he goes back over the rainbow, right? He's not a faith healer or a Steven Lee, gets all tangled up in the pain and dreck he deals with. He's more like a plumber. And this dumb case, that as far as I could see wasn't even hardly a case at all, had somehow monkey-wrenched my ass, and just when, factor it all in, I was beginning to think said ass was in not too bad shape.

Okay, okay, you're right. I'm avoiding talking about the thing with Janie.

What? You never went through a desert place with a lover? Or a "significant other," as they call it these days? (A wuss-out phrase, I figure, invented by the same folks who decided we should call it "bathroom tissue" instead of "toilet paper.") If not, then we don't have a lot to talk about.

Anyhow, in the next few weeks, while telling myself that the Browder case was over, and would eventually disappear altogether like a bad hangover, I managed to invent more ways to make Janie feel shitty than there are chess openings. Nothing big, mind you—no Stanley Kowalski smack 'em alongside the head, throw the dinner dishes on the floor, end-of-act-three stuff. Just the little things, the ones that linger like paper cuts. You know . . .

Over dinner: "Come on, do you *have* to feed the fuckin' cat from your plate? He didn't used to be so spoiled."

On Sunday afternoon: "Christ, do we have to go to a movie? I work all week, you know?"

At random: "Well, *you* sure the fuck are quiet. What the hell's the matter?"

And (this was a *good* one) in bed: "And who taught you *that?*"

The last one I got to use less and less as the days went by.

When I was loaded enough, and that was happening more these days, sitting on the sofa staring at the late weather report while Janie and Bandit silently got ready for bed, I could almost work it out. Get loaded enough, you can always work it out—almost.

I was treating her like shit and I knew I was doing it because I'd cheated on her. Cheated? How the hell do you cheat on a hooker? Easy. Because she's not a hooker, she's an ex-hooker, and she's a really good person, and she put your ass back together when you were strapped six ways from Tuesday. And she really likes you.

So what? you say to yourself (and if you've never carried on a dialogue like this with yourself, then you don't know from loaded)—wha'd you do was so wrong? One night, man! One night with a fox you'll never see again, and what the hell, who's to know, and wouldn't any guy? Why so bent about this?

And that's the "almost" part. I could never get quite loaded enough to get round that last question. Why not just tell Janie I'd fucked up, apologize my ass off, and go from there?

Ever play liar's poker? You've got a dollar bill, the other guy's got a dollar bill, and you both describe killer five-card hands you've got, using the serial numbers on your bill as cards. And the point of the game is you can—no, you're *supposed* to—lie about what you've got in your hand, but if your bluff is called and you *are* lying, you lose the dollar.

The trick of winning, see, is to make the truth in your hand sound like a lie, and vice versa.

It's a stupid game. We all play it all the time. September slid into October and things were getting chillier.

Same-o same-o at work. Barry Browder had taken our report and paid his bill with a predictable grump and I was happily back to running down bad checks and spying on pharmacists' assistants who liked to sample the goodies. Well, not happily, exactly. Bridget and I didn't seem to have a lot to talk about these days, and in a weird way I was starting to miss being driven up the wall by her conversation. Janie finally persuaded me to ask her over to dinner one night. She made lasagna, she and Bridget talked a lot, and I mainly stared at my empty plate and my never-empty-for-long glass. On a scale of great evenings, it was maybe a little above cleaning out the grease trap in the sink. The last thing I remember clearly—that's, I mean, before the usual fuddled images of somehow getting your clothes off without falling on your ass and falling asleep to the absolute, stony silence of the person in bed next to you—was when Bridget and Janie were having coffee. I (try to contain your surprise) was having a little coffee and a lot of brandy.

They were talking about movies, about, believe it or not, *Gone With the Wind*, and talking with that forced animation people put on when they're trying, painfully, to ignore the fact that there's a drunk sitting at the same table. The kind of forced painful animation you always notice and resent, especially if you are the drunk sitting at the table. I could see that Janie was close to crying, and so I was sure Bridget could see it, too. And so I poured myself some more brandy in what was left of my coffee, just so nobody would think I was out of control or anything.

"Did you ever read about the search for someone to play Scarlett?" Bridget was saying, maybe just a decibel or two louder than she need have talked. "It was a national event! People all over the country were sending their nominations in to MGM."

"I didn't know that," said Janie, smiling and shaking her head. "Did you know that, Harry?"

I stared into my cup.

"Yes," said Bridget, after a little-too-long pause. "And Vivien Leigh was the last person to test for the part. In fact, when she got it, she was hardly known in America at all."

"Gee," said Janie, and I knew what they were doing. They were trying to keep this dumb-shit conversation about nothing going just as long as it took until I admitted that I was bored out of my skull. In other words, a fucking conspiracy.

So I fixed that.

"Did you know about that, Harry?" said Janie again, smiling hopefully into my silence.

I poured a little more of the good old into my cup and lit a cigarette. Time to devastate these plotters, I figured, with my witty and very carefully pronounced speech.

"Well, Janie," I said, "you see, much as it may surprise you, I'm not quite as old as Bridget, here. I mean, you may have gotten that idea, us being in the same business and all. But, no. I ain't that old. So, you see—"

Janie had started to say something. Well, not actually say something, but she made one of those little gestures, you know, a jerk of the head, a twist of the shoulders, whatever, that tell you somebody's about to speak. But I was unstoppable.

"No, no, no," I went on. "You asked me a question, I'm answering your question. Now what was your question? Oh,

yeah. Did I know about the famous search for Scarlett
O'Hara for *Gone With the Fucking Wind*? Matter of fact, my
dear, I don't give a damn. I mean, I hate the fuckin' movie,
I hate the fuckin' story, and who gives a flying fuck about
who got to play Scarlett? All actresses are whores, right? And
Scarlett was a whore, right? So what's the big goddamn
deal—sorry, Bridget, I know you don't like profanity—but
what's the goddamn deal about which whore gets to play the
whore? Whores are like . . . unh . . . interchangeable, right?
Like, hey! Like pieces of an Erector set. Har! Get it? Erector
sets."

They didn't look like they got the joke. Bridget was staring
at me like her face was carved out of granite. Janie was staring at me, and now her eyes *were* damned near running over,
with a question just behind her face that she was afraid to
ask and that I was suddenly afraid she would ask.

"Well," I said, saving the moment with my usual grace
and stubbing out my cigarette, "that's what *I* think. I gotta
go to the john."

I got up and walked into the bathroom, ramming my right
shoulder against the doorjamb, and closed and locked the
door. I don't know how long I was in there. I didn't even *go*,
you know? Just stared at myself in the mirror for a while,
had a glass of water, and then another.

When I came out Bridget was gone. Janie was doing the
dishes, and when I offered to help her she did one of those
things (you know, those wordless little shoulder hunches
and turnaways?) that told me my presence was considerably
less than required. So I went into the living room, had myself
another brandy and a cigarette, and tried to play with Bandit,
but the little bastard skittered away when I reached for him.
Fuck him, too.

I got up late the next morning. Janie had already gone out,
but there was a fresh pot of coffee on the stove.

Came Halloween.

Halloween's always been one of my favorite days. I mean,
it's not even a holiday—ever see a sign, "Closed for

Halloween"? But that's what I like. It isn't a holiday but it feels like one, anyhow. Thanksgiving—who would consecrate a day to consumption for the sake of consumption, a day built for next-morning hangover and early Christmas shopping? The Fourth of July? Forget it—hang a yellow ribbon from your nose, burn the burgers, get a beer-in-the-sun headache, and make believe you're a patriot because this year you remembered to vote. Christmas and Easter—well, hell, the nuns and the brothers nailed it that they were about some very serious stuff going down in what Bridget likes to call "mythic time." And all the churches on those days get overflow crowds and fat collection boxes, swell, but aren't they really about, you find yourself jacking yourself up to be extraspecial happy on those days because the calendar tells you, you'd better be? Or you're weird? I've got this shrink friend, Marge, who tells me her business always goes over the top on those days, too.

"Cognitive dissonance," she said over a couple of Johnnie Walker Blacks in the Red Boar on Halstead (this was before Janie).

"Hey?" I said.

"Cognitive dissonance," she said. "Two contradictory messages sent on the same channel. You know, like, 'I love you so much I'd do anything for you and I'll see you Wednesday if it doesn't rain.' We do it all the time to one another, don't we, Harry?" And she smiled at me over the rim of her glass. It was a difficult friendship.

"But," she went on, "with holidays it's a matter of mixed signals for the whole culture. See—hey, let's have another couple of shooters—see, the word 'holiday' comes from the word 'holy day.' Get it?"

I signaled for two more Johnnies.

"Okay," Marge sighed. "I'll give you the user-friendly version. Here you have a holiday, a holy day, supposed to be a special, shared, not just everyday time, right? But what makes it special? You don't have to go to work that day and you better shop early for all the stuff you'll want because the stores'll be closed. See? Not a holy day, not Shabbas, just another day off that reminds you, like every day off, that your real life is when you go back to work. Tells you it's special and tells you it's really not. Cognitive dissonance."

Marge is a very bright person, but I think what she was talking about was the same thing as what I told you about liar's poker: Your straight flush is a winner just because the other guy isn't sure whether you've got it or not.

Anyway, that's why I like Halloween. It's not a holiday, but, even in the workday world, if you open yourself up to it, it feels more like a holiday than lots of the official ones.

It's for kids, right? They all get to dress up as ghouls or demons or famous politicians and go around the neighborhood demanding candy just because . . . well, just because. But it's *not* for kids. Because if you buy the candy to give the kids, that is, if you're not a total asshole, then you're making believe, too. You're pretending that the ghosts and goblins are at your door and that you can placate them with a gift so they'll be friendly ghosts and goblins, and on that workday night you're letting the darkness, the three-in-the-morning terror we all spend our days ignoring, have its way for once in the year, because it's all in fun. Officially, it's All Souls' Day on the church calendar, the day before All Saints' Day, and I've always thought it was very neat that, when we decide on a celebration, we pick the feast of all the souls, including the damned, instead of the feast of all the saints. Hell. The saints don't need it.

Anyway, came Halloween.

Janie hadn't said a word—not a word—about my performance the night Bridget came over. Bridget, at work, hadn't had to say a word. That woman can do a full paragraph with a cock of the eyebrows and a shrug. But, you know, things had been percolating down to the point where I didn't feel like such a bastard all twenty-four hours a day. We could talk, even share a careful joke once in a while about something stupid Bandit had done, the phone bill, whatever. And Janie had bought these big bags of miniature Baby Ruths,

Snickers, and such, for the kids in the neighborhood. Everything felt like that moment when you're having a muscle spasm, and you think it's just about to relax instead of getting worse.

So, Halloween night, I came back home with a pumpkin, a couple of videos—*Seven Footprints to Satan* and *Blood Feast*, that's all they had left at the store—and a jug of cider. A whim, you know?

And when I walked into the apartment there was Janie in the kitchen, popping up a second batch of popcorn—goddammit, Be-Bop-a-Lula as June Cleaver—and there was a fresh bottle of rum and a tray of cold cuts and cheese on the coffee table. I looked at her and she looked at me and the stuff I was trying not to drop and we both laughed. A nice laugh. A real nice laugh.

"Well, hell, baby," she said. "Happy Halloween." And let the popcorn pop away and walked up and gave me a hug.

So we spiked the cider and put on *Blood Feast* and noshed to our hearts' content. Hell, she'd even gotten me prosciutto, and that stuff is expensive. And at about six or so the first of the neighborhood demons showed up, and we oohed and aahed over the really keen Freddy Krueger mask he was wearing, gave him a Baby Ruth, and went back to the sofa.

Which was, maybe, the nicest evening I had all during this crummy business I'm telling you about. Bandit loves prosciutto, too, and I was even feeling good enough to give the little bastard a strand or two. The kids kept coming—one of them was wearing a Nancy Reagan mask, and I gave that one a whole handful of Baby Ruths—and we got mildly, comfortably buzzed on the rum and cider. *Blood Feast* is a classic bad movie (we'd both seen it before) and *Seven Footprints* is bad beyond belief, but, like every horror movie I've ever seen, not bad enough that you can't see that there's something, well, hell, important going on under all the ditsy dialogue and phony gore, something sort of serious, sort of like the whole silly and serious business of Halloween itself.

Anyway, we watched the movies and took turns going to

the door and mixing the cider and lying on the sofa, turning
to one another once in a while and smiling or sighing, and
it was so fucking nice.

I think nice is underrated, don't you? Every—what?—
forty minutes and usually when Janie was smiling at me, I'd
remember Lisa and the wild stuff in the Morris Inn, but I'd
grab another handful of popcorn or another swig of cider,
sigh, and smile back: dig, angina you can live with.

And about nine we remembered we had to carve the
pumpkin. A little drunk and laughing, we did, even though
I'd forgotten to get a candle to put inside, digging great gobs
of pumpkin meat out of the thing and laughing about how
orange and messy our hands were getting.

I dug a Magic Marker out of the kitchen drawer and traced
the face I was going to carve: real scary, with jagged teeth
and fierce eyes, well, as fierce as a pumpkin's eyes can be,
anyhow.

But, "Naah," Janie said, shaking her head. "Give him a
happy face."

"Wha," I said. "He's a fuckin' Halloween pumpkin!"

"So?" she said. "He can't be a happy Halloween pumpkin?
Geez, Harry, even a goblin's got to lighten up sometime.
Here, gimme the goddamn Magic Marker." And she took it
from my hand, and, no kidding, it was the first time we'd,
well, touched since she'd hugged me when I came home.

She drew a happy, actually a loony, face on the opposite
side of the damn thing from mine and we carved out both.

By ten-thirty the kids coming to the door had dwindled to
a few stragglers whose moms, I guess, didn't really care how
late they stayed out or whether they wound up with razor
blades in their apples, the cider and rum was mostly gone,
and WGN was running *Dracula*. Bandit was blitzed out between us, nose buried in his paws.

"Hey," I said, about the time that Renfield first enters
Dracula's castle, "how about I roast the pumpkin seeds—a
little salt and oregano, like you like it?"

She looked at me and her brown eyes seemed like they'd grown larger. "I think I'll just go to bed, honey," she said.

And you've had conversations like that, don't tell me you haven't. I stared back, and shrugged off a hundred pounds of grief. Just like that.

"Janie . . ." I began.

"Harry," she said. And she took my hand. So corny and so right. "It's a good night. Let's go to bed, okay?"

Ever break a leg? You know, when they take the cast off and it hurts like ten kinds of sonofabitch every time you put your weight on the sucker, so you figure to yourself, okay, this is the way it's going to be from now on and I might as well get used to thinking of staircases as obstacle courses. And then one day you notice that, dammit, you're actually walking and it doesn't *hurt*. And you're pretty sure that it won't start hurting again. The feeling is almost like your body or something or someone is forgiving you.

That's the kind of love we made: careful, almost shy except we knew one another so well "shy" was a funny concept, and maybe even a little sad. It was a goddammit-I-miss-you love, and if you've ever been there you know what I'm talking about. The doorbell rang, I think, three or four times, the last of the trick-or-treaters, but neither of us heard it until the next morning, in memory.

And next morning was Sunday. We woke up smiling at one another (it had been a by-God while since we'd done that), made sleepy love one more time, and stumbled together into the kitchen to make coffee.

Janie had bought kippers the day before and hadn't told me. When she brought them out of the fridge, with a flourish, kippers and eggs being my all-time favorite breakfast, I didn't know whether to laugh or take her back to bed. Bandit solved the problem by going for the kippers like Rommel pushing into Egypt, so we decided to fry them right away. I went to fetch the paper, thinking, damn! maybe you do get to go back to Oz.

And there it was, page one of the *Tribune:*

NORTHROP STUDENT, PROF'S WIFE DEAD:
DRUGS SUSPECTED

With photos of Thor and Nancy.

I must have made some sort of noise (I really don't remember) because Janie came in from the kitchen saying, "Harry? What's the matter?"

And I must have looked at her a certain way. I must have looked at her the way I'd been looking at her ever since . . . well, ever since Lisa, that way you look at a lover that only a lover would notice, that way that says you've got something to hide or something you won't share or just something that keeps you apart. Because with the headline had come back, for no reason I could understand, my own sense that I was somehow involved—no, that's not the word—somehow tainted with whatever was going on in the messy life of the Browders. Okay, okay, had come back the memory of Lisa.

Janie got the look, especially, I guess, after all the ghosts we both thought we'd laid last night. And she said nothing, just clamped down an answering look on her own face and went back into the kitchen to finish doing the kippers and eggs.

So Halloween hadn't worked, I thought. We hadn't placated the goblins. Janie's happy face on the pumpkin had been the wrong one, and Oz, as far as I could tell, was still shut down for repairs. Maybe indefinitely.

11

THE *TRIB,* FOR ONCE, got its headline wrong (yeah, that's a joke). Billy Donner was dead, all right. But Nancy, the article went on to say, was in coma—maybe not reversible.

They'd been found in a Wilmette motel (the Getaway Lodge, it was called) by the maid on Saturday afternoon. Nancy Browder had checked in, under her own name, Friday night into a single. Next day, around four P.M., the maid, a little worried about the "Do Not Disturb" sign that had been on the door all day, used her pass key to peek into the room. She found a blond giant, on his way to turning blue, lying in bed naked beside a little brunette woman, also naked, whose breathing sounded, the maid was quoted as saying, "like one of those leaf-blower machines." When the cops and the paramedics were summoned, they found the classic gimmick—bent spoon, matchbook, Baggie with a little brown shit still in the bottom and, natch, the needle—on the night table. Clear case of overdose. The *Trib* of course didn't say that, but what the hell, it didn't have to. Mrs. Browder was in intensive care at Saint Philomela Hospital in Evanston. Her husband, Professor Barry Browder (they left out the III), was not available for comment.

So, I figured, standing in the living room while Janie stared at me and Bandit tried to express his anxiety about the herring overcooking on the stove, I'd been right. They were poking. Well, screw, you know? Not my problem that I didn't guess they'd been using, too. Shake it off, enjoy your Sunday and your kipper and eggs and maybe, if you get lucky, a little more of last night's solace.

Right. And elephants fart diamonds. I didn't know what exactly it was that was making my stomach hurt and sending that tingly, Christ-am-I-having-a-stroke set of invisible fingers up the back of my skull. The feeling that I'd missed something. That I should have said something. That I could have done something. No, that's the kind of bullshit you get in the detective shows on the tube, where David Janssen or Tom Selleck comes to this big goddamn revelation (usually just before the last commercial break) and sees how he's gotten it all wrong, but now he's hip to the real situation, and so after they sell you a little salad dressing, whatever, he tear-asses off to fix it all up.

Not my scene. If somebody ever did show me a clear-cut diagram of the way things were put together, I'd probably run screaming from it because, from what I've learned about people's lives, there ain't no shape, just a hell of a lot of needs and griefs that get more tangled up with one another every day. Every damn day.

So what there was, was just this feeling that something stupid and silly and beyond-words sad had happened, and that somehow, and I was damned if I did know how, I was involved in the stupidity and the silliness and the sadness. Like the hung-over queasies, yes? You can't localize them but you can't deny them, either.

Breakfast was, call it quiet, and that's all I'm going to tell you (Bandit wound up with most of my herring, I wasn't hungry), and the rest of the day was a very careful attempt by both of us not to open any wounds, and Jesus, can that be hard work. The Return of the Browder Curse, I kept thinking—make a hell of a thirties Universal horror film. By ten o'clock I was even too tired to get drunk. I just sat with a bowl of Rice Chex and stared at a rerun of "I Love Lucy," which I always hated, and then at a rerun of "Father Knows Best," which I always really hated, till I was sure Janie was asleep. And then climbed into one weird dream.

I was a student at Notre Dame, in Keenan Hall, my old freshman dorm. And Janie was my roommate, though nobody was supposed to know it (I kept wondering how we kept it from Father Burtchaell, the hall rector). Anyhow, I was taking this course from Barry Browder, and it was the end of the term and the final exam was the next day, and I hadn't read any of the damn books assigned for the class. So I opened them—I don't know, Shakespeare, Homer, Norman Mailer—and, by God, they were all in code, like the notation of games you get in the chess and bridge columns in the newspaper, and I was scared. So I tell Janie—she's lying back in bed, naked, and somehow we've just been balling while I was reading, too—and she says, "So why don't you just fuck the prof's wife, honey?" And smiles.

Which seems like a great idea. Next thing I know, I'm in bed with Nancy Browder (same dorm room, who cares where Janie went, I tell myself in the dream, this is a dream), and it's aces until the door opens and in comes Barry Browder, or maybe it's my old man, or maybe it's Martin O'Toole, and—this is, at least by me, weird—as we keep on balling, Barry/Daddy/Martin says, "Well, Garnish, you obviously pass the course. But if you ever tell me that you did this, I'll have to kill me." That's right: I'll have to kill me. And I look down at Nancy, but she's not Nancy, she's Lisa, and she's smiling dreamily; she's bringing this hypodermic toward my arm, and I know what's in it and I don't really care.

And I woke up with Janie clutching my arm, saying, "Harry. Harry. What is it?"

I'd been moaning stuff in my sleep, she told me, that sounded like "Fuck the wife—don't tell" and shit. I looked her in her worried and pretty—okay, okay, dammit—her good face and told her it had been a nightmare about the movie I'd been watching on the tube. She asked if I wanted to make love. I told her maybe in a while, I should get some sleep first, and rolled over. That was four-thirty A.M.

I didn't go back to sleep.

Bridget had heard the news, too. And more.

"Harry," she greeted me as I walked into the office. "We have to talk."

And "Harry," she said as I settled into her office and lit a cigarette, "Barry Browder is going to be here at ten o'clock."

There was only one sane question to ask, and I asked it. "For Christ's sake, why?"

"Because," she said, "he's convinced that his wife could not have been having an affair with that poor young man. Because the police, he says, refuse to listen to his claim that this tragedy is anything other than an accidental double suicide . . . or perhaps not accidental. And because"—here she gave me what the Irish call a "straight look"—"he is not at all satisfied that we have disclosed all the results of our investigation to him. I was on the phone with him for over an hour last night, and I'm exhausted."

"Well," I said, watching my smoke curl around Phil (he *likes* secondhand smoke), "what do you want to do?"

"What I want to *do*—" she began, her voice rising, and then she caught herself. "What I want to do," she repeated, calmer, "is see him, with you, at ten and respectfully tell him that, saddened as we are for his trouble, we can't really pursue a case that the police have already decided upon, and that we don't have any more information than what we gave him at the end of our work for him. Does that satisfy you, Harry?" And, again, the straight look.

"Well, hey," I said, still watching the smoke curl, "I don't see much else we can do, right?" I didn't like her look, and I didn't like thinking about that nice kid, Billy Donner, turning blue with a lot of shit crashing through his veins. But most especially, I didn't like the prospect of screwing with this scene anymore at all. Maybe if we just put it behind us (tough luck, it happens) things could get back to what used to pass for normal. (If *we* put it behind us? Who the fuck you kidding, Garnish?)

Thing is, I'm not really excellent at thinking things through.

Came ten o'clock and I shook hands with Barry Browder

and I tried to hide the cringe. Whoever the guy had been who'd come into the office six weeks earlier with his en-graved card and his ascot, the guy I'd taken an instant dislike to, wasn't there anymore, if he had been in the first place. You hear about people looking "shrunken" after something really bad happens to them. Browder didn't look shrunken—he looked like he was about to have a blow-out through the top of his skull. His eyes kept wavering, like there was some-thing just out of the corner of his vision he was trying to catch. His handshake tried too hard to be firm. His brushed white hair was kind of brave and more sad than it was brave: you know, trying to say "It's all right, I'm still me, even after they took me apart."

"If you ever tell me, I'll kill me"; that silly line from my dream kept running and rerunning in my head.

"Mr. Browder," said Bridget after the preliminaries were over and done with, and her lower lip was trembling, not so you'd notice but after these years I can, "believe me, we can't begin to tell you how terrible, terrible we feel for your . . . for your distress"—(good ol' Bridget, she swerved away from saying "loss" just in time)—"but there's really nothing we can do, except of course share your grief."

"No!" he said, and it wasn't a commanding no, it was the quaver of an old man. "I can't accept that. I can't—I won't—believe that Nancy could do this thing. Look, the police have already made up their minds. You're my last chance. You must have found out something about these people, these . . . Sethians."

"Wait a minute," I said, though I'd promised myself not to say anything. "You think the Sethians had something to do with this?"

"Who else?" he said, waving his shaky hands before him like an octogenarian trying to shuffle a deck. "Look, these people had their hooks in Nancy. That's why I came here in the first place. And when you said you'd come up with noth-ing on them, I did a little checking on my own. Read their pamphlets. Wrote to their headquarters—did you know their headquarters are in Spain?—asking for a full, a full disclosure of their ultimate intentions. Yes, and I only got a form letter response. But, you see, they knew who I was now; they knew I was on to them. And then—and then this."

He stopped shuffling his invisible deck and was silent, breathing real shallow. Remember Bogart as Queeg breaking down on the stand in *The Caine Mutiny?* That was the feeling. God *damn,* the guy's wife had been turned into a cabbage and he was hating himself for having her investigated and he was looking, scared shit, for somebody to put the weight on. Carrying that kind of load, I figured he was staying pretty sane.

"Mr. Browder," said Bridget, "please, sir. You're going through a terrible time. Can't you, for your own good, try just to be as quiet as you can and not lacerate yourself with impossible demands for vengeance? You have a daughter, don't you?"

That seemed to calm him down, or at least bring him back into earth orbit. "Andrea, yes," he said.

"She needs you now, Mr. Browder," said Bridget. "Help her pain, and it will help your own. All of this"—shaping the whole business about the Sethian conspiracy into a ball with her hands and throwing it away—"can be sorted out after you've healed. Go home and heal with your daughter, Mr. Browder."

He stood up, maybe a little straighter than when he'd come in, or maybe it was just my imagination. "You're right, I suppose," he sighed. "Andrea's at the hospital now. I'll just . . . umm . . . I'll just take her home."

And turned to leave while I reached for a cigarette and then, don't ask me why, stopped.

"Ms. O'Toole? Mr. Garnish?" he said, turning. "There's a . . . well, there's a memorial service for the boy, and for . . . well, you know . . . at Northrop on Wednesday. I've decided that I really should be there. Just to show that I don't for a minute believe . . . well, just that I should be there. Do you understand?"

I didn't but Bridget said she did.

"And," he went on, "I'd appreciate it if you two, if you think it's . . ."

"Of course, sir," said Bridget. "Thank you."

He smiled for the first time. "Thank you," he said. "Nine o'clock, in the main auditorium." And left.

Now you don't want to hear about the three weeks of grousing I got into the next forty-five minutes, asking Bridget how the hell she could commit us to for Christ's sake that, or about how crummily the next two days went while I tried to get the whole thing out of my head and out of my life and in the process behaved to everybody who came in my path like a rabid Chihuahua. I've already told you what a charming fellow I can be when I really put my mind to it, haven't I?

Nope. What you want to hear about is Wednesday. It was one of those odd November days, as far as I can tell you only get them in my city, when the air is as cold and clear as a new carving knife but the sun hasn't gotten the message yet that it's coming on winter, so it feels as warm as a day in July, and your body, not knowing how to react to this cocktail, feels just . . . well, lighter. The kind of day mortality feels like last night's bad dream. I can't explain it better: Spend a November in Chicago.

So I drove Bridget to Northrop College and we filed into the main auditorium, along with maybe two, three hundred kids and faculty. Some kids got up on the podium and talked about Billy (or Thor, as a couple of them called him) and, yeah, a couple of them broke down. And Dr. Pearce, the college president, got up and said some solemn and good things that I don't remember.

I mean, what's to say about the dead? Ever write love letters? Letter after letter, you're trying to find a new way to say something that there's no new way to say. Iloveyouiwantyouineedyou. How many changes can you play on those chords? But you keep writing the damn letters, just because not to write them is even worse than falling on your ass trying to say something new when you do write them. Same with death: Ilovedyouimissyouihurt.

So Dr. Pearce was really kind and as impotent as anybody else trying to talk about the Big Crap-out. And then he introduced Barry Browder.

Browder came to the stand with a couple of sheets of paper in his hand. "Today," he began reading from them, "we're gathered to mourn . . ." and his voice trailed off on "mourn." He stared at the paper for a couple of hours (probably no more than thirty seconds in real time) and then raised his head, looked around the auditorium, and said, "God bless you all for coming," and walked off the stage. To dead silence.

And that was it. Almost. As the assembly broke up, a lot of people lined up to shake Browder's hand. Bridget insisted we get in line, though I was ready for home and Löwenbräu. So, when we finally got up to his section of what was by now a disorganized crowd, he took Bridget's hand warmly and thanked her and me for coming and then, gesturing to the girl who was standing a few feet behind him, talking to a couple of students, said, "And this is my daughter, Andrea. Andrea, I'd like you to meet Ms. O'Toole and Mr. Garnish."

She smiled sweetly and said hello. But we'd already met. It was Lisa.

$\triangledown$

12

In sophomore year in high school, in reading period, Brother Benedict caught me with four or five tear sheets from *Playboy* folded carefully into the copy of *My Antonía* I was supposed to be reading (that, by the way, is the only reason I still remember the name of the damn book). Now Benedict was a tall, skinny guy—looked like Daffy Duck drawn by El Greco, as I remember—and the most intimately mean guy I've ever known. He took the book out of my hands (damn! I hadn't heard him behind me), looked at the tear sheets, looked at me, snapped the book shut, rapped me over the top of the head with it, and continued on patrol.

Dig. The tear sheets and Miss October were still in the book, and Benedict hadn't said anything. So I was free, if I wanted, to go back to exploring the contours of the (remember, I was a sophomore) undiscovered country. With everybody else in class watching me and wondering why the hell I'd been swacked. Never felt so naked in my life.

Until I shook Andrea/Lisa's hand and told her I was glad to meet her.

Know that thing with the eyes? I mean, when you look at somebody you share a secret or maybe just a wish or, hell, maybe just an aversion with, and you know, way past anything you could say, that you're both having this, like, speed-of-light conversation. Without words.

That's what Andrea/Lisa (okay, Andrea) and I did in the time it took to shake hands. I remembered everything, she remembered everything, and I didn't know what this was all about, and she did, and she also sure as hell wasn't going to tell me what it was all about, and I was, as you might want to put it, whipped. And, just like with Benedict in reading period, she and I were the only people in the room who knew how naked I was.

Don't ask me what we talked about, I was too busy conversing with Andrea at 186,000 miles per second to pay much attention. Anyway, Browder thanked us for coming and Bridget marf-marfed lots of sympathetic boiler-plate, or I guess you'd call it marshmallow-plate, and I drove her back to the office.

"You're very quiet, Harry," she said as I pulled into the parking lot in front of the minimall where our offices are. "Is something troubling you?" It was the first time in a few weeks she'd spoken to me with that old concern in her voice, and I realized, kicking myself while I realized it, how much I'd missed that.

"No sweat, Bridge," I said. "I guess funerals or memorial services, whatever, and I don't get on too well together. Look, I'm just going to drop you here, okay? There's a few things on the Zueck business I have to check out, and I might as well get them done today."

The Zueck business stood to make us a few bucks, actually. This guy, Zueck, was accused by his former boss of stealing some computer software from the video-game company the boss ran, and of planning to use them to set up his own video-game outfit. The thing was, though, that these were not your regular arcade kiddie video games, like "Intergalactic Space Fuckers" or whatever. We're talking, here, double-X-rated videos that you can't buy over the counter—S & M, you name it, with real impressive graphics (I'd seen them), which was why the former boss couldn't exactly call in the Fair Trade Commission or the copyright fellows, and which left us to do a little, well, a lot of discreet asking around and try to scare the hell out of Brother Zueck, to the tune of a lot more bread than we normally got for a gig. It was the kind of work I enjoy, even if I do know about as much about software as I do about needlepoint, actually less. Civilization had sure as hell come a long way since Brother Benedict caught me with Miss October inside Willa Cather.

Bridget sighed and nodded. She didn't like taking the Zueck case, but I'd talked her into it. "Be careful, Harry," was all she said.

Of course I wasn't going to do a thing about the Zueck business. I wasn't sure what I was going to do, but it was going to have something to do with going back to Northrop College and trying to figure out why Barry Browder's daughter had screwed my brains out (thinking about my life for the past month or so, that was a real apt way of putting it) and how the hell she factored into the whole equation—if there was an equation.

I hate working for no bread, and I'm always telling you that I basically want to be left the fuck alone. But that's just it. This wasn't about "investigating" (hate that word), this was about finding out where I was and who I was. Okay, this may sound silly, but goddammit, I felt like I'd been raped. But why?

First stop, though, was the Corinthian Columns, not far off Sheridan on the way back north. Never try to look for your soul on an empty stomach, and why anybody in Chicago ever eats at home is beyond me, since you can't drive a block without passing a place that the food will curl your toes and make you shout yaha, yaha! Fried whole squid— *kalamarakia* to you—potatoes and spinach boiled together, and a few glasses of Mavrodaphne, which makes Mogen David taste, no kidding, subtle, and reality gets to look, I don't care what your beef with life is, habitable. Matter of fact, since I really didn't want to be doing what I was going to be doing, make that a second dish of *kalamarakia* and a little more Mavrodaphne. I hadn't had much of an appetite at the apartment lately, as I'm sure you'll understand.

"Hey, Harry," said Claude as he served up my second helping of everything, "you never have a second bottle of Mavro, afternoons. You okay, buddy?"

That's Claude Polutropos—"not *Nick,*" as he'll snarl at you after a couple ouzos—who's he swears "one hundred ten percent" Greek but is, after all, named Claude and who looks more like Elmer Fudd than Omar Sharif (who's not Greek either, I know, but you get me). And hell, I thought as I poured some Mavro, this is cat number five? six? what? telling me I look like shit. One goddamn helping on the side and I was turning into a psychological Elephant Man.

"No sweat, Polly," I said, using his after-closing crap-game name. "Just the usual barbed wire, but a little more of it lately. Greeks got a saying about that?" It was an old routine but I guess I must have looked even worse than I thought.

"Yeah, a couple," he said, taking the wine bottle out of my hand and plunking the cork back in. "First, *To pathei mathon.*" Except he said it toe *paw*-they maw-*thown.*

"Wha," I said.

" 'Suffering is Wisdom,' " he said, tucking the bottle under his arm. "Aeschylus. The *Agamemnon.* And second, get the fuck out of here and do whatever you're trying so fuckin' hard to keep from doing, but don't get shitfaced on my time. This"—holding up the wine—"is on the house because, Harry, you ain't gonna have it here."

So I bargained him down to a cup of Turkish coffee (and I've never had real Turkish coffee, whatever that is, but Polly's version could raise the eyebrows of a day-old dead raccoon) and, as my lately favorite philosopher had suggested, got the fuck out of there.

So what would you do? That's not a rhetorical question. I mean, you pay a call on the daughter of the everything-but-deceased, the afternoon of her momma's memorial service yet, to ask her just what she meant by straddling you from stop sign to straightaway. You ask at the main gate of the college if they have an Office of Weird Stuff. Call her dad and say something like, "Hey, Barry, ol' bro, sorry about Nancy's little problem, but you got any idea why your daughter Lisa—oops, Andrea—should have driven ninety miles east to seduce my aging ass?" Maybe if I'd done some more of the

Mavrodaphne I'd have been dumb enough to try one of those hands. Stoked with about a thousand milligrams of Claude Polutropos's caffeine cocktail, though, I made—maybe for the first time since I'd walked into Bridget's office and met Barry Browder—a halfway nonfuckedup decision.

Professor Middlebrook, Shonnie the drop-dead receptionist had told me, was the head of the Writing Program. So, what the hell, Halloween seemed to be going on a little long this year anyway, I found the office and knocked on the door. Trick or treat.

The guy behind the desk was tall and thin, even sitting down and I mean thin, like the first muppet spindly alien to come out of the space ship at the end of *Close Encounters of the Third Kind*. And hardboiled-egg bald in a floppy I'd guess purple wool turtleneck and (you have to trust me here) those little half-moon glasses that, at least for me, immediately telegraph "prick."

Okay, I'm not predisposed to like academic types.

"Yes?" he said as he peered at me over his tiny slivers of prosthesis and, when he'd focused enough to see that I wasn't another acne-survivor freshman, "sir?" he added an eighth-note later.

"Professor Middlebrook?" I asked. "Ernest Middlebrook?" I'd checked his name card on the office door.

"The same," he said and half smiled, maybe a little puzzled about who the hell I was, but obviously pleased to hear his full name pronounced.

And, hey, thanks, old Martin O'Toole, then I knew what I was going to say. "Find where the bloke ties his goat," Martin had said, smiling like he always did at some private joke you knew he'd never let anybody else in on. "Find where your man ties his goat and then feed and feed and feed the beast. It's the only way, lad."

"Professor Middlebrook," I said, still standing at the doorway so he, dig, should have the pleasure of inviting me in. "I know you're a very busy man, sir. And I'm not really connected with the university—"

"College," he corrected. "Northrop is only a college. That's because, you see, we don't dispense the Ph.D.," except he pronounced it pee, aitch, dee, with the kind of curl of the lips you get when you accidentally bite into a whole clove of garlic in your Caesar salad.

"Yes, sir," I said, getting a stronger fix, I thought, on this guy with every twitch he twitched. "See, I'm afraid I'm not much of a college type."

"Not a problem," he said. "Please come in, sir. And do close the door. I don't think we have to worry about harassment charges, eh?"

Say what? Screw it. I came in and closed the door.

"So," he said, leaning back and fishing out of his pocket one of those long damn brown things that you can never figure, unless you see the pack they came from, if it's an expensive cigar or a silly cig, "how may I help you?"

"Thanks," I said. "My name's Harry Garnish, Professor, and I'm a private investigator." I handed him my card.

And he threw his funny brown cigarette at my face. Well, actually, in my face.

"Out!" he shouted, spindling to his feet. "You bastards really enjoy this, don't you? Out!"

"Hey, man—" I began.

"Don't man me, you toad," he said (*toad?* I thought). "I've answered everything I'm going to answer. And just because that boy is dead—my God, you couldn't even wait for him to be cold in his grave, could you?—just because the boy is dead, don't you dare think that you're going to be able to squeeze any more pain out of me."

I started to say something again—his goddamn cigarette, I noticed, had burned a hole in my one Dior tie—but he wasn't having any.

"Out! Now!" he said again. "Unless you want me to call the campus police."

So I got out.

Jesus.

I guess I'd forgotten, from my almost-one-year at Notre

Dame, what colleges were like. I mean, you work at a job like mine in a city like Chicago, you really do get to live with the assumption that the whole place is one big spiderweb or one big hall of mirrors—everything, that is, is connected to everything else and no matter where you start, you'll find your way to the place you wanted to go. Maybe all cities are like that but I only know my town, and sometimes it feels like my town is an entity, like it knows itself and if you live in it long enough it knows you.

Not a campus, though, not even a campus in a big city. It was like one of those weird little towns on "Twilight Zone": you know, where all the people share this great big secret, like they're all vampires, and you don't get to be in on the great big secret until the great big secret has swallowed you up. College campuses, secret societies, and black holes: By me, you can have them all.

So what do you do? I decided to fraternize some more with the natives.

Woodstock Pizza was still selling Michelob on tap just across the street, and I was having an adrenaline clutch from Polly's Turkish coffee and from just having had a cigarette thrown in my face, so the logic, as they say, was unassailable.

So was the luck. There weren't many folks in the place this time around and, for a welcome change, the big TV was turned off and the music playing was—hello, hello!—Steely Dan, "Doctor Wu" from the *Katy Lied* album, with the kick-ass Phil Woods alto solo in the middle of the tune. God, I figured, was maybe trying to make up for all the fucked karma he'd been putting me through lately. And there, in the corner, talking to another girl, was the kid I'd talked with—how long ago was it, now?—when I'd first come here and met Billy Thor Donner, who was dead.

He'd said her name—yeah, Heather. And as I carried my beer over to their table, another Martin O'Toolism came to mind. "Lad," he said once, "when you've got to break into a closed game, you could do worse than announce your presence with a loud fart or the equivalent thereof."

So I did. "Hey, it's Heather, isn't it?" I said, sitting a decent interval down the bench from the two of them and smiling into their annoyed alarm. "You probably don't remember me, but I was here a few weeks ago asking about Professor Browder. You were in here with a bunch of kids and with Billy Donner, remember?"

A little bit of pain crossed both their faces when I said the name, and maybe a little crossed mine as I said it, and Heather said, "Yeah, I remember you," and the other one started fiddling with her french fries like she was getting ready to split. "Didn't you say you were just passing through town?" Heather asked.

"Well," I said, keeping the smile in place, "see, I was what you might call lying."

"Let's go, Heather," said the other girl, standing up. And Heather, sucking out the last of her Coke, started to rise.

"Hey, wait," I said. "Look, I told you I was lying. How the hell more honest could I be? I'll tell you, I'm kind of lost here, and I'm—hey, this is no bullshit"—I could see that they were both about half snagged on what I was going to say next, and I thanked my stars that I'd learned life by playing poker—"I'm really pretty bent about what happened to Billy and to Mrs.— Mrs. Browder. Could I just have a minute?"

Now, look. When I semichoked on saying "Mrs. Browder," I knew that the voice-crack was going to reel them in. And I also knew that it was a genuine voice-crack. Goddammit, I was starting to care about these people, and I think I told you already that caring is not one of the things I like to do one hell of a lot. So I was either acting or I was being honest. It struck me right then that I'd been in the business long enough, damned if I could tell the difference.

Anyway, it worked. "Denise?" said Heather, settling back on the bench. And Denise sat back down, too, though looking at me like she half expected me to grow a third eye all of a sudden or sprout antennae.

"So what do you want?" said Heather.

I decided to try the truth, for a while, at least.

"Look," I said. "I'm a private eye. No, don't wince, I know you girls are smart. . . ."

"We're not girls, mister," said Denise, whose hair was in autumn-leaf ringlets and who had a face like a very hip Shirley Temple, if you can imagine that, and while she said it chomped, meaningfully, a french fry in half.

"Yeah. Sorry. Ladies."

And, swear to God, they looked at one another and both cracked up. What the hell?

"I missed something?" I said.

"Forget it," said Heather, "it's not your fault." And what I heard behind that (don't tell me I'm not sensitive) was the question, "How the fuck old are you anyway, man?"

"Well, yeah," I went on. "I know you guys are smart"—that got a passing grade—"so you know that 'private eye' means paid snoop and no romance, right? It's what I do. And when I was here last time, talking to Heather, here, I made up that stuff about being Professor Browder's old army buddy because that's what I do, too."

"No sweat," said Heather. "We didn't really much believe you, and we thought you were kind of weird anyhow."

Swell, I thought. "Swell," I said. "I knew I had you guys in the bag. So anyway, here's the straight poop. I'm running what we call a security check on Browder. See, he's up for this appointment—okay, I can't tell you exactly what, but it's big, right?"

Like I always say, the truth is a nice place to visit but, well, you know.

"Anyway," I went on, as they looked at one another, checking me out again, "what bugs me here is that I thought I'd gotten everything nailed down pretty good, and then this happens. Now I really liked Thor, you know, Billy Donner—"

"Omigod, man," interrupted Denise, not looking at me but examining a french fry in her left hand dripping gobs of ketchup from the end, "that's almost as feeble as the old army buddy story. Now you've had your minute. So what's your real problem, Mac?"

I swear to God, I didn't know anybody still called anybody "Mac." Maybe stuff always comes back into style, yeah? Like wide ties and chicken-fried steak.

"Okay," I went on, not denying or affirming my lie (isn't that what they do in Washington?), "I'm just asking around, dig, but like I say, I liked Thor—"

"We loved Thor," said Heather.

"Right. And, well, look, I just had a talk with this guy, Professor Middlebrook, and—"

"Oh, *Jee*zus," said Denise. "Did you tell him you were a detective?"

"Well . . ."

"Okay," said Heather, glancing at Denise and nodding significantly. "Look, this isn't a good place to talk." And in fact Woodstock's was filling up. "Denise?" Denise nodded. To me: "If you're really serious, you want to come to our apartment? It's walking distance."

Like Denise had said: *Jee*zus.

$\triangledown$

13

THE APARTMENT TURNED OUT to be a two-bedroom and utility kitchen affair that made me, for maybe the first time, a little proud of my own pad. A kind of nondescript lump of space (sorry, but that's all I can think to call it) played at being a living room, with a sofa, two chairs, and enough stereo shit and speaker wires trailing around the place, it looked like an MTV sound stage. The kinds of posters you'd expect: Jim Morrison on one wall, Axl Rose on another, but on the third, a really huge drawing, in colored pencil and under glass, yet, of what looked like some kind of giant exploding flower, and in the middle of the explosion, or the foreground of the explosion, this giant, sexy, nude black guy holding out his arms in either crucifixion or welcome. The guy's face was unmistakable.

"Hey," I said as I sat on the couch, "that's Jimi Hendrix, right? That's great!" And I meant it.

"Yeah," said Heather, shrugging and walking into the kitchen. "I did that. Hey, you want a diet pop? Or we have some white wine left, too."

Neither one sounded good to me, but I didn't have a chance to turn them down. "This isn't a social call," said Denise, taking the chair across from me. "Look. We loved Thor. Everybody loved Thor. And everybody loved—loves—Mrs. Browder. And this bullshit about them being together and overdosing in some goddamned motel is bullshit. Now the cops aren't going to do shit, and nobody else is going to do shit, so if you think you can do shit, then we'll talk to you. But if you're going to jerk us around with more shit about Professor Browder and high-level jobs and shit, then you can walk right back the way you came. Am I making myself clear?"

"Clear as shit," I said. She looked at me for a second and then busted out laughing.

"Okay," she said. "So I've got a vocabulary problem. Sue me."

"Kid," I said, "you sound like me."

"I'm not a kid," she said, and everything we'd won with the laugh we lost with that. And with her look.

"All right," I said, "fuck this. You want honest. Honest you got. I'm an old man, notice? I don't know how the fuck to talk to you so I don't offend your goddamn sensibilities. I don't even know what your fuckin' sensibilities are, okay? This gay guy, a couple, few months ago in California damn near had to beat the crap out of me before we realized we were friends. And we *are* friends—sonofabitch has AIDS, and I'm not too goddamn thrilled about it, okay?"

"Hey—" she began, as Heather came in from the kitchen with two cans of diet pop.

"Hey, bullshit," I went on. "I'm old. You understand old? Well, why should you? Old, kid, yeah *kid*, is you don't spend your time hoping for the perfect piece of ass and you do spend your time looking for a pair of shoes that don't hurt. That's one hell of a good drawing of Hendrix you did, there. You know what he'd look like, he was here? Like me, dammit, and just as tired. But gray. 'Cause, and maybe you don't know this, and I hope you never will, junkies get gray."

"Look—" she began again.

"How about I just leave?" I said, getting up. "You kids have this all figured out, and it's all the secret shit you know that you'll tell me if I'm just a real good old fart and let you feel superior for a half hour, right? Well, girls, it don't work that way. Let me explain this to you. See, I told you I'm a P.I., right? Ever hear of incipient consent? No? Well, in Illinois it means that you know I'm an investigator, you agree to talk to me and then you decide to clam up, I can tell a court you *were* willing to talk to me and then clammed up and a lawyer can use that to make you very seriously uncomfortable."

It was, of course, a lie: one Martin O'Toole had taught me to use if I ever thought I was dealing with the easily misled. I was half right.

"Oh, wow," said Heather, holding the cans of pop like they were defensive weapons.

"Oh, wow, is right," said Denise, curling up in her chair and obviously enjoying this. "That's totally bullshit, isn't it? God, you must get tired of lying your way to the truth like that. You do this all the time?"

What could I do but spread my hands? "Hey," I said. "You have no idea."

We stared.

"You poor bastard," she said.

It works that way sometimes, doesn't it? You scam your friends, you scam the people you give a rat's ass about, and as long as you can keep the scam on line you figure it's all going to work out in the end, anyhow, and then (and, dammit, you can never tell when *then* is going to be) you end up spreading your hand for a total stranger. Just because, like Denise said, you're tired.

"All I want is a little help," I said. "Mind if I smoke?"

"Okay," she said. "About Middlebrook. He's our campus poet. Got a couple of books of poems out, teaches this seminar in—you believe this?—The Spirit of Creation, I swear to God. Everybody wants to sign up for it. Sit around and listen to the great man stare into space and recite his own shit.

"You really admire this guy, don't you?" I said.

She smiled, a nice smile. "So you caught me," she said. "Hell, I think he's a creep. I took his damn class, and I felt cheated the whole time I was there. I mean, I want to write. And paint. And—God, there's so much I want to say, you know?"

I'd forgotten what it was like. Or maybe I'd never known

what it was like. She wasn't talking to me—an old and suspicious fart who belonged in her world like a real frog belonged on "The Muppet Show"—she was talking, with moist eyes, to whatever it is you think you can be at that age, and for some, that's damn near everything. Like I say, I'd forgotten. I hoped.

"So what did he do to you?" I asked. It was not the right thing to say.

"Well, that's none of your fucking business, is it?" she said, and we were instantly back to the bad half of this tap dance between friendship and gunfight we'd been doing all along.

"Hey—" I began.

"Hey, Dennie," said Heather at the same time. "Chill out, all right? It was just a question."

"Question, my ass," she said. "Look, man, are you working for Middlebrook? Or for the fuckin' college? You better tell me, and don't give me any more bullshit. I'll know if you're lying. Heather"—Heather was about to say something—"shut the fuck up."

At that moment I thought that Denise probably would know if I was lying. Not a bad guess, since everybody since this whole nonsense had started seemed able to tell, one way or the other, if I was.

"Game, set, and match," I said. "I'll say this once, and after I'm finished you can either give me that glass of wine you mentioned and three or four Excedrin if you've got them or you can throw me the hell out. I'm not working for anybody right now. I didn't know Nancy Browder and I only talked to Thor for maybe an hour but I liked the bastard. I don't like that he's dead. I don't like that Nancy Browder is maybe worse than. I can't tell you any more than that, and I can't even tell you why I think something stinks about what happened to Thor and Nancy. It's personal. And I'm supposed to be a private eye and to tell you the truth I don't.know.what.the.fuck.is.going.on.here. I don't even know if you kids—girls—guys—fuck it!"—and they both laughed—"can really help me. But I've got to start somewhere. That's all you get." I lit another cigarette.

They were quiet for a minute, looking at one another. And to my surprise it was Heather who spoke first.

"We only have regular aspirin," she said. "How much wine?"

"How big's your glass?" I asked and she, swear to God, winked at me and went back to the kitchen.

"You talk about personal," said Denise after a while. "I'll give you personal. I hate Middlebrook's ass because he tried to get into mine, that personal enough for you?"

"Hey, wait," I began. "I didn't want you to have to—"

"You didn't want me to have to make you embarrassed, isn't that the way the game works? Guys never want to hear about this shit. Young, old, makes no difference. So you asked, so I'm telling."

"Dennie. Maybe—" Heather began.

"No!" she said, and it sounded like the NO! you heard from Mom when she told you, at age two, to get your finger out of the light socket.

"So I signed up for the Great Man's course. I was a fuckin' poet, right? I deserved to be there, and I was going to stun the guy with how good my stuff was, right? I mean, man, I was serious. Oh, sure, Patti Smith, Jim Morrison, Bowie, all those guys, I knew them. But I also knew Hopkins, and Stevens, and Williams, and Sexton. Ah, shit—hey, give me a sip of wine?"

She was about to cry.

I held my glass out to her but Heather was there with a full one. Had she heard the request before I did?

"So, yeah," Denise went on. "I take the class and I read my shit out loud, and I'm really scared when I do this, right?" She giggled and it was not a nice giggle. "And Middlebrook, he's really kind and nice and warm about what I bring in to read. You know how that felt?" And she took a gulp of wine.

"So, yeah. He asks me to come to his office, sometime, talk about my 'works.' That's what he said, 'works.' So, I went. It was a Friday afternoon."

"Den, for Christ's sake," said Heather.

"See," said Denise, smiling in a way I didn't like a whole hell of a lot, "Heather's the only other one who knows about this. Didn't tell my mom, or Greg—Greg's my boyfriend—or . . . well . . ." She took another gulp of her wine.

Remember what I said about hanging your butt out for a total stranger? The best I could do, I figured, was shut up.

"So you can figure the rest, yeah?" she continued. "He loved my poetry and thought I showed real 'fire,' and by the time he got to 'fire' he was holding my hand, and I tried to take it back but he kept holding it. And then he was stroking my hair and telling me that I needed to 'liberate my imagination.' I mean, Jesus. He didn't know what bullshit that was? What bullshit everybody knew that was? And that's what my poetry meant to him, that it told him I was probably dumb enough to fall for that bullshit and fuck him for his fuckin' respect? You know what I told that sonofa*bitch*?"

"I can imagine," I said. I couldn't.

"You couldn't," she said. "Hey, your name is Jerry, right?"

"Harry."

"Okay, Harry. You want to fuck me, Harry? You want me to give you"—and she whispered this word in a whisper that was as scary as anything I'd ever heard—"head?"

"Look—" I began.

"Oh, shit, *Denise*," Heather said.

"For the last time shut the fuck up!" she snapped. "Heather's my best friend; she won't tell. I won't tell. I won't tell your wife, your momma, your priest, whoever. No fooling, man. How about it?" And she started massaging her right breast with her left hand.

And, goddammit, I found myself thinking: well, wait now—why *not*?

And then she broke into laughter.

"Would have, wouldn't you?" she laughed. "And how silly do you feel now, Harry? Now that you know it's not going to happen. Now that you know I can make you cheap that easy."

"Goddammit, you—" and I bit back on the next word.

"Right," she said. "And now you know how I felt when good old, sensitive old Ernest Middlebrook told me he liked my poetry and then tried to get inside my pants. Now you know what I felt like. Don't you, Harry?"

"So what happened then?" I said. I kept thinking about Janie, and I really didn't want to be thinking about Janie.

Because Janie belonged to Chicago and to the world where a guy comes into the office, asks you to check out what his wife is doing, and you do that and then you play the rest of the hand by the numbers. This was something different. And whatever it was, I didn't like it.

My face must have shown what was going on. At least Denise didn't spend any more time taking what was left of my ego apart.

"What happened then?" she said, smiling. "You're a guy, Harry. You know what happened then, don't you?"

"Unh, excuse me?" I said.

She looked at me. Hard. "You're kidding," she said.

Wha.

"Sonof*abitch*," she said for the second time in the same way. "You know, Harry, you just might be savable. What happened is I told the fucker that if he didn't back off I'd call the campus cops. What happened is that he told me that I was a hysterical woman and that I could never get away with—this I remember word for word—'trying to damage his reputation,' just because he told me my poetry wasn't good. *Wasn't good*, the fucker! What happened is that he told me that if I tried to talk about this, he'd truly fuck me up on campus and make sure I didn't graduate." She was on her third glass of wine, and she was crying for true. "So, darling," with one ghastly smile, "you wanted to know about Middlebrook?"

"I wanted to know about Thor," I said.

"Oh, yeah," Denise said, and she was a little drunk and I figured was entitled to be. "Thor. Well, don't you know, Middlebrook tried to fuck Thor, too."

14

"I FEEL LIKE SOME MUSIC," said Heather, going to the stack of CDs. "Anybody mind?" Nobody spoke.

"Thor told you this?" I said, finally.

"Oh, hell, man, Thor told everybody he knew!" She laughed. "See, he took the famous Spirit of Creation course, too. You didn't really know him. You don't know how serious he was about his music. He could recite Bob Dylan. By the hour."

Over the speakers, and way too loud—is everybody born after 1950 hearing impaired?—came Paul Simon's *Graceland*: "These are the days of lasers in the jungle."

"So," Denise went on, "naturally he wound up in the Great Schmuck's class. And guess what? His poetry had 'fire,' too. And it turns out, one late afternoon in Middlebrook's office, he needed to liberate his imagination, just like me. Ain't that amazing?"

"And Thor told his pals?" At least now I understood why there was a cigarette burn in my best tie.

"He told his pals, he told his old man, and he told the administration, man." That was Heather. "That was the big flak, all last year. Everybody was joking about 'Middlebrook-Gate.' You know, like Watergate?"

"So they covered it up?" Don't tell me the Garnish isn't swift with the ancient history.

"Covered it up?" Denise again. "Hey, man, the god of all the poets never even heard of Billy Donner. Or maybe remembered him vaguely from class. Or maybe, well, you know, did see him in his office once, but certainly never said anything like, you know, he'd like to get inside his pants. Billy must be crazy, right? You know, another drugged-out longhair metal freak." Again, that mean little giggle. And now I knew why it was a giggle and why it was so mean.

"So nothing happened," I said. It wasn't a question.

"Hey," said Denise. "Did you know Thor—Billy—was a scholarship student? We don't get many of those at dear old Northrop. We're all rich fuckers, you know? But Thor's father, he's an electrician, plumber, something, down in Indiana. Can't really afford this place, but he's got—had—this supersmart kid."

There was a lot of self-hatred in what she said, but that wasn't what had given her the giggle from hell.

"So the president of the college," Denise said, "or somebody—you think maybe they have a dean of sexual harassment?—let Thor and Thor's daddy know that if they didn't press all this, then Thor could keep his scholarship and graduate with a big goddamn degree from this wonderful place."

Except she didn't say "wonderful," she said "wun'rful." But I knew she was getting blitzed already, and, like I say, entitled to.

"So," I said, and I was trying to be really careful picking the words this time around. "So there was a big hoo-haw over all this and it all got laid to bed with no ripples, is that it?"

Denise may—just may—have caught where I was going. Her eyes anyway focused all of a sudden on me and "Yeah" was all she said.

"And when all this was going down," I went on, lighting another cigarette and staring very carefully at the carpet, "did you ever go to anybody—I don't know, a dean, a professor, somebody—and tell them that Middlebrook had pulled the same shit with you?"

"You know," Denise said, "why don't you go somewhere and fuck yourself?" And threw the rest of her wine at my face. Well, actually, in my face.

"God, Dennie!" said Heather, jumping to her feet while Denise, who was exhausted from a lot more than just throwing the wine, slumped.

"It's okay," I said. "It's okay." And that was to Denise. "I sounded like I was accusing you of something and I wasn't, but I'm a pretty clumsy bastard. Heather, you think you got maybe a towel somewhere?"

At that Heather gave an embarrassed little laugh and went into the kitchen, and even Denise, who was getting steadily drunker from the adrenaline that was now dancing around in her cerebral cortex with the chablis she'd snorkeled (it steamrollers like that, you know?) tried a little, diffident (I like that word) out-of-the-corner-of-her-eye smile.

"Hey, man," she slurred. "I'm sorry. Sore spot, right? I mean, maybe I should have—"

"No, you shouldn't," said Heather, coming back in and handing me a dish towel. "Dennie, you know how hard you've worked and how much you want to be a writer. You need Middlebrook. You couldn't have helped anything."

"Uh, wait," I said, drying myself. "You need this guy? This guy that—that—"

"That tried to climb into my big black car?" Denise laughed. "Hey, Harry, don't blush. It's a line from *Politician*. By Cream, y'know? Sure, I need'm. Big man, y'know? Letter from him means a lot. Spoze to mean a lot. And, you know"—and I've heard and read the word *ghastly* a lot of times, but I swear to God the smile she gave me then was the first time I got what it meant—"he really kind of has to write it for me, hey?"

I got it. You play, you pay, right? And I couldn't really get too damn self-righteous about Denise blackmailing Middlebrook. Served the bastard right, I figured, until I started thinking about Lisa/Andrea and me. As you always wind up saying once you start deciding who deserves what they get and who doesn't: Oops.

"Okay," I said. "One more question? What do you guys think about . . . aah . . . Andrea Browder?"

I hadn't expected them both to break out laughing.

"The Little Mermaid?" said Heather, who was first to recover from her laughing fit. "You know her?"

"Well," I said, "just from the memorial service, you know."

"Well," said Denise, mimicking me, "that's about as much as you want to know Lady Andrea, ol' buddy ol' pal." I looked to Heather, since she was at this point the one most likely to give me a sober opinion.

"The thing is," Heather said, "she's—she's a bitch. I mean, you know, her father is Mister Distinguished Bigshit Professor"—you could hear the capital letters in her voice— "and she, like, totally plays on that and treats the rest of us like we're tourists here, you know? Plus she's got this bod, and boy, does she use it. Well." And she fell silent.

I didn't have the heart, or was it the nerve? to tell her that from where I stood on my half of a century, the idea of having a bod applied to goddamn near every woman I'd seen on the Northrop campus. That had been the start of my problem, a few weeks ago, on another campus, now hadn't it?

"So that's it?" I said. "She's a bitch?" This was not information that did me a hell of a lot of good in my investigation, whatever it was, by the way, I was or thought I was investigating.

"Thass not it," said Denise. "You must be smarter than you look, Harry. Yeah. The ol' princess, see, was hitting on Thor, too, for a while back there."

Now this was interesting. "For a while?" I said, trying my damnedest to look uninterested and lighting another cigarette.

"Denny," said Heather, "I think that's enough, don't you?"

"Hell, no," she said. "I'm just getting started." And poured herself another glass of wine.

"Look." She leered at me, and past a certain level of intake the only way you can focus on somebody else is a leer, and don't tell me you don't know that. "Look. 'Bout the time, last year, Thor was blowing the whistle on Middlebrook—

isn't that what you called it, blowing the whistle? No? Oh, well. Maybe I said that. Maybe I read it somewhere."

"Andrea and Thor?" I said, trying to get her back on track.

"You got it!" she said, as if I'd just suggested the idea. "Look. 'Bout the time Thor was blowing the whistle on Middlebrook. God, that sonofabitch. Well, anyway. See, the CFM ice princess, old Andrea—"

"CFM?" I interrupted.

"Come fuck me," she said. "She decided, like, Thor was just the guy she ought to—how do they say it?—bestow her favors upon. I mean, truly. Chasin' his ass all around the campus. I don't know, maybe she figured it was kinky slumming, yeah? Rich professor's daughter and the poor boy stud from the other side of the tracks. Like a Prince video or something. I mean, man, everybody was talking, thought it was funny as hell, you know?"

"Thor thought it was funny, too?" I asked.

"Aww, *fuuuuck!*" she said, letting her head bob back against the cushion, and I was shocked, because I'd never known that you could get three syllables out of my favorite word. Heather made a movement like, she'd decided Denise was too drunk to talk to an outsider. I made a movement like, it's okay, I'm a highly trained professional and everything's just fine. My lie worked.

"Fuuuck," said Denise one more time. "Heather? Hey, listen, kid, I think I might take a nap, okay? What—your name is Harry?" she said, looking at me.

"Check and checkmate," I said, nodding to Heather to put on the coffee, turn down the bedsheets, do whatever it took to get this nice and seriously damaged person back in the pocket.

"The pocket": that's what jazz musicians call the moment when you're playing—just playing—and it's like the whole world is concentrated around *this fucking moment*, this moment right *now!* and none of the ordinary, everyday shit, none of the guilt or the debt or the pain you owed anybody else mattered worth a damn, because you're in the pocket, you're in the pocket, and besides dreams this is the best place you're ever gonna be.

That's where Denise wanted to be, and she was almost there. She was snockered enough and she was nice enough (no shit, she was just a nice person) to deserve to be in the pocket, and her friend Heather (I should have such a friend, sometime) was more than willing to help her get there. It's funny. I never did find out if Denise and Heather had ever gone to bed with one another. That's what you've been wondering, yeah? Me, too, when I was there. But at that moment when Denise was obviously so drunk that she really couldn't talk anymore, and Heather was all concern to keep Denise from falling on her ass, it hit me that it just didn't matter.

Well, that's not entirely true. Let them be lovers, I thought as I walked back to my car—it was around four and the light was already beginning to fade—or let them be friends enough, for Christ's sake, they could crawl into bed together and cuddle up like sisters, pals, spoons in a kitchen drawer, and hide out from the dark. They'd earned it. Hell, we've all earned it, and I don't know if we ever get to the point where we don't need it. Nothing complicated here, I'm not a complicated man. No big philosophy of life, not even much good advice. But, you know, if the world is an awful place that you know, sooner or later, it's going to break your heart, then, seriously, you could do lots worse than save up and savor those moments when you're half awake and half asleep and you've got your arm around your best friend and you think to yourself (it doesn't have to be in these words, but, really, it always is) I will never be safer or happier than I am right now.

Okay, I was getting sloppy and okay, I was thinking about Janie and about how long it had been since we'd been like that. Even worse—I was remembering that one time, not all that long ago, we had been like that. I was thinking, if you want it flat out, that I was one lying and bullying sonofabitch. But I was also thinking about Denise and Thor and Nancy Browder, who'd all, I couldn't put it together but I knew I was right, gotten themselves caught up in and maimed by—by what? By all the little lies and big lies and half-deceptions and half-truths, all the bullshit we cobble together every day, like Silly Putty with a bad smell, to build a dike between ourselves and the truth. Denise and Thor and Nancy hadn't wanted to help build the dike, so naturally they'd been somehow ground up and worked into the clay.

Damn right I hoped Denise and Heather were hugging one another.

Know the Beach Boys? The song, "Wouldn't It Be Nice?" Sweet, bouncy song about how much the guy loves his girl and how much he wishes they were married because then they could play together all the time, all very cotton-candy shot through a rose filter, and then, at the bridge, the guys sing, in the most plaintive of voices, about how they could be happy if they got married. It knows how bitter it is, but doesn't for a minute admit that it knows, which makes it all the more bitter. Damnedest song I know.

Which are the cheery thoughts I was having as I passed the English building on my way to my car. And there, maybe half a football field away from me, were two figures in the dusk pushing and shoving. Well, actually only one of them, the shorter and fatter was pushing and shoving. The other one, who at this distance looked like an Ichabod Crane wannabe or Ray Bolger in *The Wizard of Oz*, was just trying hard not to be pushed and shoved, and at the same time to walk, dignified, and not run away—tough job when you're being pushed and shoved.

It wasn't Ichabod Crane or the scarecrow from Oz, of course. It was Ernest Middlebrook, the old student-grabber and cigarette-thrower himself, trying I guess to get to his car. Come to think of it, between a chicken schoolteacher and a straw man sadly lacking a brain, my first impression hadn't been all that far off.

The other guy I hadn't seen before, but as I walked toward them I could hear him, half grunting and half muttering with every shove.

"You're just going to walk away from this?" he was saying. "Big deal professor, you think you can buy your way out of this, too? Answer me, damn you! I can still go to the papers, you know that, I don't give a damn how much money you got. You stand still and talk to me, damn you!" which seemed kind of illogical since, as he said it, he gave Middle-brook another healthy shoulder-lunge in the back.

"Now look," Middlebrook said, "I told you I didn't want to have to call the police, but—" And then he saw me.

"You!" he said, and I couldn't help remembering the way Jack Benny used to say, "Well!" "I knew it. You're working for him, aren't you?" He pointed at shorty. "You set this whole thing up. What are you going to do now, beat me until I tell you what I want you to hear, you Nazis?" And he started to scream for help.

Not that there was anybody else on the horizon, and not that he got very far. I don't know if I've told you this, but I'm not exactly Jean-Claude Van Damme. The last time I was mugged, coming out of a Loop bar at closing time, when the two guys (yeah, only two) knocked me down, I knew just the right Tae Kwon Do move: I held out my wallet with my left hand and told them to have a nice day. They (honest) laughed and left. (With my wallet, sure.)

But I was tired and I'd just heard some pretty unsavory stuff about the poetic Mr. Middlebrook, and also there was a hole in my tie. So as he started to raise the hue and cry, I did something I don't think I'd ever done before. I slapped him across the face.

Just slapped him. Hard enough so that his glasses were knocked askew. It made him look Jerry Lewis-goofy as he stood there, shocked, stock-still, staring at me with (and now I kicked myself, as I usually do when I act on impulse) his lower lip trembling.

"Hey, sorry, man," I said. "But you two guys were acting pretty crazy, and the last thing I need right now is a mob scene. And believe it or not, I never saw your dumpy friend here before in my life. And I came over here because, dammit,

I thought you might need some help. Hey, you all right? I
didn't belt you that hard."

Because he was still just staring at me, his body rigid
as—did you ever play that kid's game, statues? So I surprised
myself again. Don't ask me why, but I reached up and ad-
justed his damn glasses for him.

That had an effect. He focused back on the real world, and
said, "You're really not in league with this man?"

I liked that, "in league."

"I'm really not," I said, "and I bet he's going to let you get
to your car unhassled now that you've got some company,
ain't that right, stranger?"

No, this wasn't rescuing professors in distress. But I figured, sleazeball as he might be, Ernest Middlebrook, if he
felt in my debt, might be able and willing to map out a little
more of the sleaze for me—give me some hint of why Nancy
Browder and Billy Donner had wound up as they had.

But he just stared at me puzzled, not relieved. "I don't
understand," he said. "You say you're—"

"Who the hell are you, mister?" said shorty, who'd been
watching the scene confused, but with his fists clenched. I
looked at him for, really, the first time.

He reminded me of the middle-aged Jimmy Cagney: all
chest and shoulders with legs that looked too short for that
torso and cocked forward on the balls of his feet, as if waiting
for a blow and ready for a counterpunch.

"This gentleman," Middlebrook said to shorty, with an
odd and unpretty little smile, "says he is a private investigator, Mr. Donner"—and it was my turn to do, internally, a
Jack Benny *Well!*—"so I'm sure the two of you will have lots
and lots of smelly little things to talk about, even if you don't
already know one another. And now, if you gentlemen will
excuse me."

And he turned to walk away. From that afternoon in his
office and from the blow-his-brains-out look on his face
when I slapped him, I was pretty certain the guy was working
on the last few ounces of bravado he had left in his nervous

system. Still, it was a brave act. Brave enough that, given what it was probably costing him, I couldn't bring myself to see him screw that one up, too.

Mr. Donner started to move toward him and to say something, and I put my hand on his arm and said, "Wait. I knew Billy, and I need to talk to you. Okay?"

It was mentioning the boy's name, of course, that did it. "You knew Billy?" he said, staring at me, Ernest Middlebrook forgotten. "How the hell do you come into all this? All right, look, I'll talk to you," he said before I could answer. "Damn, I'll talk to anybody, if it can get me to the bottom of this mess. But I want a beer. You want a beer?"

Now I don't very often feel this way, but at this point in this particular day, I wanted a beer about as much as I wanted a cold sore. Nevertheless, sighing inside, I told him sure, guys always talk more honestly over a brewski, right?, and we trudged back to Woodstock's, which at that time of day was blessedly almost deserted. I bought him a pitcher of Miller Genuine Draft and me a large coffee (told him I was nursing a headache, and I was) and we settled into a back corner of the place to talk.

Edward Donner ("Bud," he insisted, to his friends) was only seven or eight years older than I was, and was indeed a master electrician in New Albany. He'd built his business up from scratch over a period of thirty years, and now he had a crew of six electricians working for him and he didn't even have to take out more than an eighth-page sidebar in the local Yellow Pages because if you'd lived in New Albany for any time at all and you needed some fast and good work done at a reasonable price, you knew you called Bud Donner. And his wife, Billie (that's right, Billie) had died giving birth to their only son. Billie had been taller than Bud—that had caused a lot of dumb jokes when they'd been dating all through high school, but hell, they didn't care— so it must have been her genes or whatever they were that made the boy so large.

"Yeah, he was a monster even coming out of the chute,"

laughed Bud more to himself than to me. "Eleven pounds, can you believe that? Eleven pounds!" And he shook his head, moist-eyed and smiling.

He was pretty well into his pitcher by the time he got to that point in the story, and it hadn't taken him long; my coffee was still warm. And he hadn't asked me, since the scene on the lawn, what I was doing in all this grief. So what to do? Use what Heather and Denise had told me and brace him with the fact that he'd—or Billy had—taken hush money from the college to cover up Ernest Middlebrook's problems with his wick? Or ask him why he'd been assaulting Middlebrook? Or ask him if he'd ever heard Billy say anything, hint anything, about a Mrs. Browder? He was still smiling, still shaking his head, and his eyes were getting moister.

I smiled—wow, eleven pounds!—and shook my head in sympathy, and took a sip of my coffee.

"Yeah," he said. "I don't know, the doctor told me the kid's size didn't have anything to do with what—what happened to his mother. And hell," he said, smiling at me, "nobody can help how big they're born, can they? Hey, I'm gonna get another pitcher, you mind? Be right back."

I minded a lot. Whatever I wanted to find out, and I wasn't even sure what that was, I didn't want this obviously good and obviously sorrowful man getting himself so blitzed he would run into a tree or a state trooper on his way back home. But what do you do? I'd spent a lifetime, it hit me as he stumped back up to the cashier, trying not to tell people what to do and trying to keep the hell out of their private little desert places. In that respect, I guess, I was kind of an anti-Steven Lee. But, much as I'd gotten to like Lee, that's, by now, what I was. So I just waited for him to come back.

"Where were we?" he said, pouring himself a glass that just barely managed not to foam over, and snorkeling it before the foam even had a chance to start settling.

"Well," I said, "I was going to ask you, Mr. Donner—"

"Hey," he said, a little foam mustache on his upper lip, "come on. Bud."

"Bud," I said. "I was going to ask you . . . uh . . . you know, I was at the memorial service for Billy this morning, and I don't remember seeing you there."

And this morning, I thought as I said it. Jesus Christ, this morning! It felt more like a week; scratch that, a month. It was (I checked my watch, couldn't stop myself) less than twelve hours since I'd stared into Andrea Browder's eyes and realized that she was the Lisa who'd taken me around the North *and* South poles and, in the process, left me without any compass points at all to tell me where, or for that matter who, the fuck I was. And now I was talking to the on-the-edge father of the likable kid whose death? suicide? murder? was somehow part of the reason I'd wound up having that silent and scary confrontation with my young and (it was the mood I was in) poison lover.

Bud brought me back to the question I had just asked. "Memorial service!" He scowled. "God damn their memorial service, they think that's going to fix anything. Bastards. Hey"—and he looked at me with that half-squint you always develop when you're on the verge of being snockered but aren't quite ready to admit it to anybody, especially yourself—"Hey, Harry," he said. "Look, buddy, I'm glad you were there. You knew Billy, right? You must've seen what a good boy—what a good boy he was. Everybody said that, you know? I mean, he was one in a million. Really good boy." And he reached for the pitcher.

And I got there before him, and poured as much as I could, which was most of it, into my empty large coffee cup.

"Hey!" he said, and then broke into the drunk's smile, which I knew well from both sides of the face. "Okay, I'll get another one."

"No you won't, Bud," I said. "You staying somewhere in town, or you driving back to Indiana tonight?"

He reached into his pocket and took out a motel key. "Days Inn," he said, "just down the road. But, look—

"You look," I said. "You don't know me from Adam's off ox. You don't know if I'm working for the college, trying to keep the lid on what happened with Middlebrook and your son, and the deal you cut with the college to keep it all quiet."

At that he turned maraschino red and started to get up. I stopped him by pointing my finger at him. No kidding, I was on one of those righteous trips where you know what you're saying is for the other guy's good, and you know that you and the guy you're talking to are being carried along on a moral riff that's got its own rhythm and authority that neither one of you can deny.

The big problem is (I realized as I pointed my finger at him and it, naturally, worked) that you can only slip into that groove when you're telling the other guy what's good for him. With your own bad self? Forget it. I was saving Bud Donner's ass, and he knew it and I knew it. But what he couldn't know was that I was still drowning.

"Yeah," I said, as he sat back down. "I know. And you've got to know—"

"Jesus," he said, and he hunched his shoulders, as if waiting to be struck, and the Cagney association came back to me again. "Bill never did anything bad, you know? I mean, even when he was just a kid, he'd—look. When he was, I don't know, thirteen or something, I don't know, his class had this field trip. They were going to go to New York, visit all the places, stuff. Had to sell raffle coupons, you know. And Bill—well, everybody loved Bill, so of course he sold, I guess, twice as many coupons as anybody else. Twice. And, came time for the trip, you know what he did? You know what he did?"

"No, Bud," I said, and decided it was time for a sip of the purloined beer. "What did Bill do?"

He rubbed his big hand across his stubble and stared at me like he was about to reveal the Manhattan Project.

"He didn't go," he said, his eyes shining, and obviously waiting for my question.

I complied. "Why was that, Bud?" I asked.

"Because," he said, "it turned out that the trip was planned over Billie's—you know, his mother's—birthday.

And Bill and I always—we always used to make that kind of a special day just for the two of us."

And, oh-oh, I thought. Could Bud, who seemed like such a nice, uncomplicated guy, have laid enough guilt on Billy Donner about his lost-in-childbirth mother to screw him up somehow, and not even know he was doing that?

Well, you know, maybe that's what families were all finally about. I mean, everybody has to get warped somewhere, right?

"Yeah," he went on. "You know, Bill always carried this photo of his mom in his wallet. It was even there when they ... uh ... found him like that."

And something started to take shape in my mind, and I wasn't really too sure I wanted it to. It was just—okay, I'm no shrink. But then again, if you ever turn on your TV, anything from Bryant Gumble to Oprah and Geraldo to "Divorce Court" to, for crying out loud, "Cheers," isn't everybody in one way or another speaking fluent Freudian? It's kind of like a thirteenth-century stonecutter in Paris saying, "Hey, I'm no theologian, dig?" Bullshit, you're not.

So you already see the little scenario I was composing. Here was Billy, big and sweet and maybe so absent of malice it was almost a birth defect, raised by a father who mourned, and kept on mourning, the mother Billy could only know through photos and reminiscences and through guilt at having killed her by being born.

And here was Billy, bigger and sweeter and bristling with talent, on his own for the first time at Northrop College and as far as I could tell the prince of the campus. Chicks loved him (did they still call them "chicks"?). Guys loved him. And ...

And he'd been found dead with a lady who was his writing counselor, and who was kind and compassionate, and who was old enough to be—as I said, you see it already. I kept remembering the gleam in his eye when he'd told me he wanted to be a teacher, like—and not said the name, Mrs. Browder. Or was it Nancy that he'd stopped himself from saying?

I could see that Bud was sliding into that sorrowful place—it'll happen if you start drinking and don't drink enough—where the booze has clarified your pain but hasn't built up enough pressure to stifle it. I felt for him (hell, we've all been there, no?) but I didn't want him loaded, both for his own sake and because there was something else I wanted to know, and if you believe that jive about guys are easier to question when they're fried, then you've never questioned a guy when he's fried.

"Helluva kid," I said. "Well, listen, Bud. You know I'm not working for the college, don't you?"

"Oh," he said, waving his hand in front of his face. "So how come you know my boy?"

This was going to be the hard part. "I'll tell you the God's truth, man," I said. "You know I'm a P.I. Well, I wound up here a little while ago working on a case—nothing at all to do with Thor—with Bill—but, you know, I ran into him, talked to him, liked him. He was a good boy, Bud." And since that was the first thing I'd told him that was entirely the truth, naturally it was the thing that hurt him.

"Oh, Jesus!" he said, rubbing his eyes. "Yeah, he was a good boy. . . ."

"Okay, Bud," I said, "now listen. When I heard what—what happened, I just wanted to, I don't know, you know, ask around a little, maybe figure out why—"

And that was a wrong move, too.

"Why?" he shouted, turning the few heads there were in the place. "I'll tell you why, goddammit! Because he should never have been here with these—these—look. I told him he didn't need college. Billie—you know, his mother—Billie and I, we'd planned, like, if he was a boy, you know, well, he could just go into the business. I'd have it all set up by then, best electrical service in New Albany, and he could just, well, write his own ticket. We *planned* that for him. And then, his fucking teachers—"

"Bud," I said. "Hey, man, you're shouting."

"Well," and he gave a little smile. "His fucking teachers

told him all this shit about his promise, his potential. What the fuck do they know? They make as much money as I do, you think? But, no, he's got to go to college. So I say, well, all right, Bill, you know your mom and I"—and damn right I winced—"had other ideas, but it's your life, boy. And what happens? Another goddamn teacher, this sonofabitch Middlebrook. Christ, you know they let these guys get away with shit like that? Bill told me what happened; I wanted to kill the bastard. With my boy? Fuck you! And then . . ."

I just waited. This part he had to get out by himself.

"Well, and then, you know," he said, with that repressed giggle everybody does when they're about to admit the inadmissible, "you know, Bill did want to stay in school, and the college guaranteed that he'd be—that they'd make sure he graduated, and all. And it's damn expensive, yeah? I mean, sending a kid through a place like this. So Bill and I, we had this long talk. I mean, he took some persuading, but, well, you know how kids are." And he smiled.

I didn't know how kids were, but I knew his smile was as awful as anything I'd seen for a while. Bill had taken some persuading? All I'd ever know about the kid, whom I'd liked a lot, was what I was going to hear from now on from people who'd known him. That's what it meant to be dead. And what I was hearing now was that old Dad—Billy Donner had called him "Daddy," I remembered—had talked him into taking the hush money not to blow the whistle on some jerkass professor who'd tried to get into his pants.

Christ. The kid must have felt like the dimensions of the world were shifting.

So the next question more or less asked itself.

"Yeah, man," I said. "Look, we all do what we gotta do, it's cool. But did Bill ever talk to you about any of the other teachers here? Like, I don't know, he ever say anything about, you know, Nancy Browder?"

"No!" he shouted. "That's a fucking lie, him and that woman. He never talked about her, I don't think he even knew her. See, you're just like all the fucking others. You think he was really—you think he really was running around with a woman like that? Old enough to be—you think he couldn't get any of these young pussies around here he wanted to? You think he'd go for an old snatch like that? You think—listen, he never, *never* did any fucking drugs in his life. I'm telling you. This was a goddamn set-up. This was a goddamn thing, I don't know, the fucking college tried to make my boy look bad. You think my boy—our boy—who the fuck are you, anyway? I ought to fix your fucking face, you know that? Who the fuck are *you?*"

I've seen enough guys in grief, okay, I've seen too many guys in grief, I knew just to sit there and let him chew his own guts. He didn't need my help, and anything I said would just make him chew harder. When he wound down, exhausted the way you only get after great sex or great rage, I told him, quietly, that I thought I should be getting back home and thanked him for his time. And I asked him, quietly, if he'd be okay to drive himself back to the Days Inn. He said yeah, and we walked back to our cars—they were in the same lot—together. Not talking. It was as close as we'd come to friendship. I let him alone with his failure and doubt and he let me alone, not trying to convince me I hadn't seen those things. And between us, his boy—Billie's boy—whom I knew better now than I had when he was alive, and whose own failure and doubt could not now be shared or concealed. Not anymore.

I wasn't sure if we would shake hands when we parted in the lot. But he extended his, and I took it.

"Look," he said. "You're okay. I'm . . . well, I'm . . ."

"It's okay, man," I said. "You're hurting. Fuck, you're *supposed* to. I find out anything, I'll let you know, yeah?"

And damn if he didn't give me his business card. And started to say something else and thought better of it. And walked into the dark.

$\bigtriangledown$

15

I<small>T WAS ROTTEN OUTSIDE</small> by the time I got back to my car, about seven-thirty, and this morning's sunny cold had decided, for a finale, to turn into a dark-of-the-moon, scrotum-tightening cold night with spitting ice/rain for grace notes. It felt like a different season, and though Chicago does that a lot, this time it felt like about how long my day had been. Plus, since my car heater had decided to take the rest of the day off, I got to slip and slide back down Sheridan Road as chilled inside the car as it was outside the car, which was also as chilled as I was inside.

The apartment was dark when I let myself in, except for the light in the kitchen where Bandit was munching away, with a junkie's placid face, at a very large bowl of kibble mixed with sardines. It was the kind of serving you leave for your cat when you expect him to be alone for a while, which, along with the way things had been going lately, was maybe why I wasn't too surprised at the note taped to the refrigerator door. Remember what I said about love letters all sounding the same? I expect all these kind of letters do, too. It said:

Harry. I don't know what's wrong, but this just isn't working out, is it? You're so unhappy all the time. And I feel like it's my fault. I'm sorry, ~~hon~~ Harry, but we're not doing anything good for each other. I'll call you in a couple of days, let you know where I am and everything. I'll be all right and I hope you will, too. God, I'm sorry, honey. Be good, Janie. P.S. There's some corn beef hash

*on the stove, with mushrooms the way you like it just
heat it up. I'm sorry.*

"She's sorry," I told Bandit as I got the brandy down from
the shelf with the Frosted Flakes and the cigarettes. Bandit
kept right on eating. "She's damn sorry, you know?" I continued, filling a mug with half that morning's cold coffee and
half good ol' Ernie and Julie Gallo and not bothering to stir.
"Slipped up, too. Crossed out 'honey' the first time she wrote
it, but let it stand the second time. Made hash, too. Is that
a kick, little brother, or what?" Bandit looked up for a minute
(swear to God) and went back to his dinner. Maybe he was
interested in what I was drinking so thirstily.

"Well," I said, refilling my mug, "damn if I know what
she's sorry about, dig, considering who's the asshole around
here. Hey, you want some hash with mushrooms? *Good* for
you." And I set the pan from the stove down beside his food
dish and fixed my third mug—without coffee, now.

Like, really, sometimes numb is good for you.

Not that numb ever lasts as long as it's supposed to. Six
the next morning I woke up, on the couch, in my skivvies,
with the TV playing (now you're not going to believe this,
but it's really no shit) *The Lost Weekend.* Right when Ray
Milland hallucinates that big damn bat eating the head off
the cute little mouse poking through his wall, right? And
starts screaming his ass off.

"Too fucking pat," I told Bandit, who had decided to spend
the night nesting on my belly. "Don't you think?" And he,
as usual, reserved his opinion. All cats should be politicians,
or is it the other way around?

It was going to be one of those days, I decided as I show-
ered, dressed, and wolfed cornflakes (all the hash was gone)
when the chance of hangover and the chance of bonecrush-
ing regret were in such a delicate, perfect balance that you
could actually walk between the two of them and, in a weird
way, function. Like this comic book I read once—*Hellblazer*
it was called—where this guy who was going to die saved his

life by selling his soul to two demons who hated each other's ass, dig, so they had to let him live to avoid a big war in hell. That particular morning, it made perfect sense to me. The Zen of screwing up, hey?

So, what to do with my busy day? Not go to the office, that was for sure. Track down and try to talk to Andrea Browder, that was what I had to do and I'm here to tell you, I felt just about goofy enough to do it. So around eight-thirty I called the agency to let Bridget know I'd be out most of the day working on the Zueck case. (You dirty old hacker, I thought, dialing the phone. I should buy you a beer, all the excuses you've given me.)

And that's when my luck, as it will do, ran out.

"Harry?" said Bridget, answering the phone (damn! where the hell was Brenda?).

"Bridget!" I said, while Bandit, surprised at my tone of voice, jumped off the kitchen table. "Hey, glad I caught you. Listen, I can't come in today, I've got—"

"I think you should come in today, Harry," she said. And I'm not sure I can tell you how the word *should* sounded when she said it. Just add up all the times you've heard that word used as a weapon, and you'll be pretty close.

"Well, see," I said, "it's the Zueck business, you know? I think—"

"*I* think," she said, and when Bridget doesn't let you finish your sentences you know you're playing showdown five-card, nothing wild. "*I* think you should come in today. We have a new client coming in at eleven o'clock, and I would like you there with me to talk with him."

"Yeah? Who?"

"Father Steven Lee, Harry."

"Oh. Right. See you around ten." And hung up.

And speaking of hung, the old familiar headache kicked in just about the time the receiver hit the cradle, a four-Excedrin special, I figured, which is also very bad for cramps in the gut but that can be headed off with a couple of tall glasses of milk and honey. So, chemically prepared to rejoice in the day, I sat with Bandit and watched a half hour of Joan Rivers making dumb with a couple of retired housewife-hookers. I tell you: We made better jokes about that stuff in junior high.

Steven Lee was already there when I got to the office, waiting in the broom closet and a half we call our lounge and reading a month-old *People*. It was a shock to see him in uniform: black suit, Roman collar, the whole Bing Crosby. And it was a relief to see that even in his priest suit his eyes were still dancing to their own private tune, like he was enjoying one hell of a funny joke on everybody but at nobody's expense.

"Excuse me, but haven't we met before?" he asked, jumping to his feet and grinning his ass off when he saw me. And I grinned back, couldn't help it, even though I kept reminding myself that this blackrobe, for all I knew and for reasons I didn't know, might have set me up with Andrea Browder and, in doing that, screwed me up with Janie. Okay, that's what they call association of ideas, but that's the way my head was working.

Maybe some of it showed in my face. "Harry," said Steven Lee as we shook hands, "is everything okay?"

"Hey, man," I said, "you're in my office this time, yeah? You tell *me* if everything's okay." I thought I said it with a smile. I guess I said it mean.

"Yeah, you're right," he said, and I saw a little twinge of hurt in the eyes, and shit, I thought, I do that a lot, don't I.

"Well," I rushed on. "Meat loaf life. You ready to see the boss?"

"Uh—sure," he said. So I had Brenda buzz Bridget and we entered the rainforest.

"Got a Dunhill, Father?" I said as we sat down. He smiled, knowing that I was apologizing and also telling him it was okay to smoke, and fished out one for him and one for me.

"Father Lee," said Bridget, "I know that you've already met Mr. Garnish, and all three of us know that the meeting was under—let's say, sensitive conditions. Now. What exactly do you believe we can do for you?"

He stared at the end of his cigarette. " 'Exactly' is the hard part of your question, Ms. O'Toole," he said. "You see, I know that the reason Harry—Mr. Garnish—came to our house in the first place was because you were checking up on Nancy Browder."

"Father—" began Bridget.

"No, no," he smiled. "You can't confirm that and I don't have any intention of pressing you on it. I'm here to ask for your help, not to make accusations. But since this—oh, golly, this *terrible* thing happened to Nancy—well, you see, we've—I've been getting these phone calls and letters from Professor Browder."

"Oh, dear," said Bridget, almost at the same time I, under my breath, said something else.

"You're both right," Steven said, winking at me. "Phone calls and letters accusing the Sethian movement, and me, of being involved in some—well." And he puffed his second Dunhill into life. It was strange, I thought, seeing him nervous.

"What does 'well' mean?" asked Bridget.

" 'Well' means," said Steven, his smile getting weaker with every word, "some pretty terrible stuff."

"And you're bothered because you think these accusations may damage your work?" asked Bridget again, and I swear I couldn't figure out what her face was saying.

Steven's face, though, was saying the same thing—and it was costing him—that hers said.

"I'm bothered," he said, "because I think Professor Browder might be right."

16

AT MOMENTS LIKE THIS I usually stare at Phil. His big doggy leaf faces always stare back with perfect, goofball-sublime composure. Plants have it knocked. Like, I figure, the Buddha.

"Indeed," said Bridget. I'll bet she's never seen "Star Trek," but every damn time she says "indeed" like that I get the impression of Mr. Spock as played by Roseanne Arnold.

"Look," Steven Lee went on. "I don't know how much you really know about the Sethians."

"The Sethians," Bridget interrupted, "were a Gnostic sect that flourished around the third century A.D. Like all varieties of Gnosticism, they claimed a special, insider's knowledge of the true meaning of the Scriptures and promised a special illumination and freedom to their followers. This particular sect claimed to possess the secret wisdom of Seth, Adam's third son after the murdered Abel and the accursed Cain, and therefore to be the only truly *pure* children of the first man. Is that a fair description?"

Steven's cigarette had been halfway to his mouth for the whole speech. "Wow," he said, with a little smile.

"I know how to do homework," Bridget said, with no smile. "Now, just how does that ancient and obscure heresy relate to the death of young Mr. Donner, the probable death of Mrs. Browder, and your presence here, Father?"

That "Father," Phil and I agreed, was neat; sort of like calling a guy "sir" after you tell him his fly is open, dig?

Steven Lee got it, too. " 'Heresy' is a pretty strong word,

Ms. O'Toole," he said and lit his third Dunhill. "Our, well, you might as well call it our order, was founded in 1968, by the Spanish Dominican Pedro Pardo. He was—"

"I know who he was," said Bridget. "And I've read *The Path of the Chosen*. Twice."

What the hell. She'd been doing homework, she called it, all this time I'd been trying to see how far I could swim toward the bottom of a half pint? Which meant that she'd been taking this shit as seriously as I had? Where had I been? (But if you've never asked yourself that in the mirror on a bad Saturday after a strange Friday, then you can't know what I'm talking about.)

"*The Path*," said Steven Lee. "Then you know that we're—how do you want to put it?—activist."

Phil and I communed some more: Huh?

"Yes," Bridget said. "Believe me, Father, I know about Liberation Theology, and I know how hard it's been for the last decade or so to be Catholic and committed. It's one of the reasons—*one* of the reasons—I'm no longer cloistered. Where did all the promise of 'renewal' go?"

And, swear to God, she was looking bothered, and how the hell had I missed that?

"That's it!" said Steven. "That's why—"

"That's *not* why," Bridget said, "a compilation of fuzzy and clumsily articulated mysticism like *The Path of the Chosen* should become the manifesto of a worldwide insurgency against Rome. I'm sorry, Father Lee, but as far as I can see, what you call your 'order' was badly conceived, and maybe even deeply flawed, from its inception."

Heineken. A tall draft of Heineken with a couple hard-boiled eggs on the side and, of course, the everlasting salt shaker. That's what I figured I could do for this conversation, and I knew I wouldn't be missed.

"I don't know how you can say that," said Steven, getting that true believer gleam back in his face and, boy, that gleam always scares the hell out of me. "You can call it 'flawed,' what we tried to stand for, but don't you think the church is flawed, the way things are now? Do you really think pomp and arrogance and stupidly rigorous doctrine are a way of ministering to people who are dying hungry every day?"

"Father," Bridget said, and goddamn if she wasn't getting the gleam, too, "I care as much about the church's real mission as you do, but—"

"Well I don't," I broke in, and even Phil looked shocked. "Excuse me, gang, but I don't care at all about the church's mission or about the third century A.D. or the path of whoever it's supposed to be the path of, and if the two of you want to spend the morning playing debate society that's no skin off any special part of my anatomy, but I am not in the best damn mood today and I thought this was a business call, okay?"

"Harry—" Bridget began, and I swear I knew she was going to ask me what the matter was, and I was also sure that if one more person asked me that I was going to do something irrational. I don't know, stick my tie up my nose and go "*Ya*-hah! *Ya*-hah!" or something.

"No, you're right, Harry," Steven said. "It's just that you know how sometimes you commit yourself to something because it's so, I don't know, right? And it makes your life seem right, too. And then you find out—or you think you may have found out—that there's a . . . a problem with everything you trusted so much. You know that feeling."

I didn't know that feeling. He could have been trying to explain Picasso to Ray Charles. I did know that he sounded a lot like Denise, talking about all that poetry and such she'd wanted to do before Middlebrook tried to crawl up her sweatshirt. And I knew all of a sudden (the hangover was pacified, so devil number two was coming up to the plate) that what I really wanted was just Janie back.

Everybody was quiet. "Yeah," I said. "I know the feeling. So, you got more?"

He sighed. "This is very hard for me," he said. "Okay. Professor Browder has been accusing us—accusing me—of corrupting his wife, turning her into a fanatic. You know how people get."

"Right," I said, and I must have been feeling shittier than I thought I felt, "in this case, some of the people get dead. Or the next best."

He couldn't have looked more hurt if I'd kicked him in the jewels. And he didn't even fight back.

"But one thing he kept saying stuck in my mind," he went on as if I hadn't spoken. "He kept talking about our Haitian Project."

"Your what?" I said.

"It's called," said Bridget, "the Sethian Relief Fund for Haiti. And what is it really, Father?"

Homework.

"You probably guessed what it is, Ms. O'Toole. Can I assume everything we say here is confidential?"

"You cannot," said Bridget. "In the first place, private investigators do not—whatever you may have seen on television—enjoy the same client-privacy privileges as lawyers. And in the second place, we haven't yet even accepted a retainer from you. So if you're about to tell us something that may compromise you or your order, as you say, then you had better think twice before you speak."

He took out Dunhill four, lit it with one long drag, and spoke to the smoke he exhaled. Know that variation of the thousand-yard stare?

"The Haitian Relief Fund is supposed to be a fund to send food and medical supplies to the people of Haiti. My God, do you know what life is like for the poor people on that island? For the last twelve years, now"—and he saw the looks on both our faces—"all right, sorry. You know. Everybody knows. But what we're doing is making arrangements to get people out of that place."

"Jesus," I said. "You're telling me you're doing illegal aliens?"

He looked at me for a minute. Then, "Yes," he said. "It all

depends on what you think 'illegal' means, though, Harry. We're trying to save people's lives—just one by one, that's okay—but we're trying to save them by any means necessary."

"Malcolm X," said Bridget.

"Wha," said I.

"By any means necessary," she said again. "It's how Malcolm X in the sixties characterized the struggle for freedom. You're probably too young to remember Malcolm, Father." And the irony in that last word was at least sharp enough to make Steven Lee jerk his head back.

"Well—" he began.

"It's not a problem," Bridget went on. "He was, in many ways, a very great man." And now she was staring into some kind of past that I didn't share with her and that maybe I'd never really gone through; except from the look on her face, it looked like one hell of a time to have been alive. Who knew?

This seemed to be my day to break the profound silences and keep the ball in play.

"So?" I said.

"So," said Steven, "we've been bringing Haitians into the country for four or five years now. I can't tell you how we do it. Not because I'm trying to keep anything from you, but just because the whole entry network is hidden in about three or four computer programs that I can't penetrate, even though I've got a modem and I have access to a lot of Sethian data."

"So where's the 'But'?" I said.

"Huh?" he said.

"You get this far blowing the whistle on something, there's always the moment you say 'but,' tell us how it wasn't about what you thought it was about. Am I right? Cut to the chase, man." My head was starting to hurt again.

And it happens sometimes when you talk to a guy who's got something really heavy or vile to lay on you, sooner or later he breaks from his own script and gives you the ugly package. I liked Steven Lee and I didn't enjoy watching him do it, but that's what he did.

"Right," he said, and you could almost hear him gulp as he said it. "Browder kept talking about the Haitian Project in his letters to me. He seemed to think that had something to do with the way we'd 'corrupted' his wife. And Nancy had been really concerned with the problem. She'd given quite a lot of money to us just for the Haitians, you know?"

"So," said Bridget, "you had some checks from Mrs. Browder with the memo line saying 'Haitian Relief Fund' or something like that?"

"Yes, we did," he said. "Quite a few. I suppose that's how Browder got his idea. Anyhow, after . . . after what happened to Nancy and after the calls and the letters started, I decided to try and check into the H.P. file on my modem, just to have some protection against the accusations." His smile when he said that was the kind of smile you don't want to see, if you like the guy wearing it.

"And you found?" said Bridget. She had that look on her face (it must have scared the hell out of kids in her fifth grade class) that said, "And what is the sum?" when you knew that she knew bloody well what the sum was.

"Okay, as I say," said Steven Lee, reaching into the inside pocket of his jacket and bringing out a sheaf of folded papers, "I can't get full access to the Sethian mainframe, but I do have entry into a few programs. Here's the last half-year's accounting for the Haitian Project."

And he handed us both a sheet of paper and even I, who have never balanced a checkbook in my life, could see after a few minutes what the message was.

"Christ," I said. "Two hundred percent profit?"

"Close enough," said Steven Lee. "And here," he said, handing us another sheet, "is a partial list of some of the refugees we've . . . introduced into the U.S. over the past few months. This list cost me a lot of effort to retrieve."

I looked at it. The first few names were

MACQUOT, ABADESSA
DuJOUNIS, ARLENE
SMITH-MARCUS, MARIANNE
DELACROIX, STEPHANIE

And like that. We all looked at the list in silence until Bridget nailed it down.

"So, Father," she said. "You think you might be running a brothel?"

$\triangledown$

17

"I DON'T KNOW," he said after a pause. "I haven't been able to track down any of these girls. Since what we're doing is . . ."

"Try, illegal," said Bridget.

"All right." He sighed. "It's hard to find out how they're placed after we get them into the States, and I'm no computer expert. I just know that I was shaken by what happened to Nancy—she was such a loving, good person. And, I don't know, maybe some of Professor Browder's pain is some of my pain, too. I had to check on the Haitian Project, and now I . . ."

It was odd, and not a lot of fun, seeing Steven as hurt and as screwed up as the fuck-ups (read: humans) he'd tried to help in his little gathering back in South Bend.

"And now you don't know what the hell to do," I said. He looked at me and nodded.

"I think what you should do, Father," said Bridget, staring at the list of girls. "I think you should write a check to O'Toole Agency—fifty dollars will be sufficient, predated last Friday—and then go home and decide whether you want to call the police or the Department of Immigration about all this."

"Huh?" I said.

"Fifty dollars?" said Steven.

"You can make it a hundred if you're more comfortable with that," said Bridget. "The point is that what you've told us is potentially—I'd say probably—evidence of criminal activity. I think your organization may well be involved in the oldest and the vilest form of trade, and I do not mean prostitution, I mean slavery. I think—and so do you, Father, let's drop the pretense that you're confused—I think that your Sethian order is, under the cover of alleviating Third World despair, in fact bringing women into this country to make their lives, if possible, worse than the lives they left behind. It disgusts me."

"Now, wait—" Steven began.

"No, now *you* wait," said Bridget, and damn if in all the time I'd know her I'd ever known her this close to hyperventilating, and Bridget hyperventilating is not something you want to think about.

"I'm not going to argue this with you, Father, because this is not a court of law, and that means that we can talk about the truth we both know without playing silly games over the laws of evidence. I'm asking you for a check, however small or large you choose to make it, precisely because this agency is going to do nothing about what you've told us, hateful as what you've told us may be."

"But—" he said.

"And we're going to do nothing because I honestly believe you didn't know about any of this, and because . . . because Harry likes and trusts you."

Steven and I glanced at one another. Shit. The last thing I needed in all this mess was one more umbilical cord to trip over. So leave it to Bridget to provide one, right?

"So you write that check and you have retained our services. Or our lack of same, and also our confidentiality, so that if you decide to contact the authorities about this business, which I hope you shall, you and we are both exonerated from any blame or charges of obstructing justice. Surely, Father, that's fair?"

He reached into his pocket, took out his Dunhills, put them back, reached into his jacket pocket and took out his checkbook. I handed him my pen. He looked at Bridget and said, "Fifty?"

"Fine," she said.

"Thank you, Father," she said as he handed her the check.

"Ms. O'Toole," he said, "I don't know if we'll see each other again, but if we do, I'd appreciate it if you didn't call me that."

"Please?" she said, and I flashed back to grade school in the fifties, when all good Catholic kids were taught to say "please?" instead of *"what?"* if they didn't know what the hell you were talking about. Ask any veteran.

" 'Father,' " he said. "I'm not sure . . . I'm not sure I want to continue in the priesthood."

I didn't say anything. But what grabbed me was the way he said it. He didn't know if he wanted to stay a blackrobe. Not that he didn't think he could, not he didn't think he should, yeah? *Wanted,* that was what he said. So, okay, by now you know I'm not Sherlock fuckin' Holmes. Like, I hope, most of us, I try to get through the day on intuition and vibes and whatever you call whatever it is that tells you, hey, I can trust this guy. And I'm about fifty-fifty wrong but that's what I have to go on; and the science of deduction, bag it, that's for the movies. Okay? So when Steven said *wanted,* that's when it hit me that he really was straight and that, whatever Andrea Browder had been doing at the Sethian meeting and whyever she had gone out of her way to hang my pelt on her wall, he hadn't been part of the scam.

And that whole thing jumped at me instantaneously (or in the space of three seconds). Isn't that what they call the "neural arc"?

So I didn't say anything. Bridget stared at him for a minute. And then she said, "All right. Good luck."

We shook hands as he left, but he didn't meet my eyes. I wish he had. I wanted to signal the poor bastard to wait for me; I'd buy him a beer, lunch, whatever. But he just left and I looked at Bridget and she looked at me, and, as usual in our staring contests, I wound up being the first to speak.

"So," I said. "What the hell? Are we in this thing or not?"

"This 'thing'?" she said, and as she spoke the word, "bile"

came into my head. "What 'thing,' Harry?"

"Jesus Christ, Bridget," I said, using the two words that I knew would slap her wrist back as hard as she had slapped mine. "We got a lady dead—okay, as good as dead—here. We got a bona fide corpse. We got Steven Lee telling us he works for a bunch of guys, they're running a mail-order whorehouse. We got—oh, yeah, I haven't even told you about this one—we got a student-molesting professor at Northrop—name's Middlebrook, some kind of poet—"

"*Ernest* Middlebrook?" she said, glancing toward her bookshelf.

"Dig," I said. "The same, who when I went to see him yesterday threw his cigarette at my face and who I later found out has been trying to make everybody who gets within six, make it five feet of his office, including they tell me the late Billy Donner. Was a big noise at the college last year, you know? I mean, it ain't third-century A.D. history, it's just history, Bridget. And for all this bullshit, we got so far Barry Browder's fee for checking up on his wife who's now a potted plant and we got fifty fish from Steven Lee for I'm goddamned if I know what. *That* thing, Bridget."

I took out a cigarette and lit it, my hands shaking, and out of breath. I smoke too much.

She stared at me. Just stared. And it's fine by me if you think this is stupid (who the hell are you, anyhow?), but in all the—what?—three, five years I'd known her as my boss, I think it was the first time we'd *looked* at one another. Okay, the first time I'd looked at her. *Looked,* you know?

"And what else?" she said.

Now. If you're a good Chicago boy (probably if you're raised in any real city and that means east of the Continental Divide) the real first commandment you learn is, Thou Shalt Not Spill Thy Guts. You hurt? You swallow it. Like, when I was in high school, one of the very few Czech kids in an Irish zoo, there was this kid, Jimmy Maher, and I don't know why but he hated my ass. And one day, it was November and pissing cold rain, Jimmy and two of his Erin-Go-Bragh buddies braced me on my way to the el. It was the Howard Street station, I remember.

"Hey, Harry," said Jimmy Maher. "You're a freakin' tough guy, right?" (We all said "freakin' " back then, like somebody was listening, already?) "I guess so," I said, because back then I was skinny and I was scared out of my gourd at facing three of these big Micks at once. "Okay," says Jimmy, and hits me—freakin' *hard*—right under what I later learned to call my solar plexus.

That was the first time I saw those little silver bugs swim in front of my eyes (know those little bastards?) and the first time I understood that breathing was, well, a privilege. In other words I thought for a second I was dead. And I knew just what to do. I smiled at Jimmy M. and his two pals, wondering if it was spit or blood running out the sides of my mouth, and I gasped, "That's it?" And since a few grown-ups (no shit, I used to think there were grown-ups), who were also waiting for the Howard el, had seen me get hit and were murmuring, Jimmy grinned at me and patted me on the shoulder and said, "Okay, Garnish, we just wanted to know if you could take it," and he and his pals turned on their heels and I was left alone, stared at by the grown-ups, tasting the tears that I swear to God I must have rerouted from my eyes into my mouth.

You hurt? You swallow it.

And that's another of those three-second specials, neural arc instant memories that grabbed me (I sure as hell didn't want to grab *it*) when Bridget said, "And what else?"

Or maybe it took longer than three seconds. The cigarette I'd just lit had burned out, anyhow.

"Right," I said, lighting up again. "What else is that weekend I spent visiting the Sethians in South Bend, remember? That weekend I got myself laid by this righteous young lady, and guess who she turns out to be? Andrea Browder, no kidding. And I've been lurching around like a blind pig in a soybean field ever since then, and you know it and I know it, and—well, hell, Janie bailed out last night. You think that's enough of 'what else,' Bridget?"

I was trying real hard to stare at the lit end of my Winston. Problem was, my goddamned hand kept trembling.

She stared. Not at me, but at her teddy bear coffee mug. And when she finally spoke, she was still staring at it.

"God," she said and Bridget *never* says "God." "Why can't we just be friends, Harry?"

"Wha," I said.

"Oh," she went on, "I know you think I shouldn't be here. I know you think I'm a foolish, clownish ex-nun on a spree. And I have heard your jokes about Sister Mary Godzilla."

No shit, I flushed and I don't think I've done that since Jimmy Maher hit me in the gut.

"Hey—" I began.

"No," she said, and held up her hand like she was playing Julius Caesar or something. "It doesn't really bother me because I *am* foolish. But so are you, my dear, and so are all of us. But why can't we be friends? Do you know how many people have been watching you suffer and self-destruct for the last few weeks? Do you know how bothered we've been? How bothered Janie has been?"

"Janie?" I said.

"Janie," she said. "You think she hasn't called me? She loves you, Harry, and she's frightened for you. Why didn't you just tell us what was wrong? Is it because we're all just women?"

"It's because you swallow it," I said before I knew what I was saying.

"*What!*" she said. Not "Please?"

"Nothing," I said. "Blurted out. So okay, where are we now?"

"Well, Harry." And she smiled, an odd kind of smile. "I suppose we're *in* it, as you say. What do you want to do?"

And I thought. Really.

"I've got to talk to Andrea," I said finally. "That's for sure. But before I do that, there's another guy I have to see."

"Who?" she said.

"You don't want to know," I said, and when I saw the frown on her face I added, "no, kid, trust me on this one. You really don't."

So we nodded goodbye and I went back to my office to see if I'd left any warm Heineken in my bottom desk drawer. I had. Two cans, but I decided to let them rest there, they looked so damn happy together. And then I dialed the number of the guy I wanted to talk to. Well, sort of *had* to talk to, if I wanted to find out anything about what was really going on with the famous Haitian Project.

Because, you see, he's the guy you want to talk to if you want to find out anything about what's going on—in Chicago or, as far as I know, anywhere on the good side of the Rocky Mountains. They call this guy the "Priest." He is what you would call heavy. And I was pretty sure he'd talk to me.

Because they used to call this guy Jimmy Maher.

$\triangledown$

18

Now as you'll probably understand, I look forward to talking to Jimmy Maher the way I look forward to getting my teeth cleaned: it's hard to tell, in fact, which activity I try harder to put off. So I was surprised, and a little relieved, to see that Steven Lee was still in the reception area, and obviously waiting to catch me. It was that warm glow you get when your dentist calls in sick: a base on balls.

"Harry," he said as I walked up to him. "Got a few minutes?" He was still puffing away, and (silly, but true) it was the smoking that keyed me, more than anything he'd said in Bridget's office, to how much pain he was really in.

Seriously. People smoke for lots of reasons, the main one being, and don't go all pious fascist on me here, because it tastes good. But you use the drug different ways in different situations. Steven at the Sethian meeting, surrounded by a lot of love and trust and (all right, I'll say it) giving a lot of love and trust back, had used it the way you use it when, say, the lights are down and the Paul Desmond/Jim Hall Quartet is on the stereo and the martini is chilled just right, with a little pearl onion swimming around, yet: a cushion that just makes it all more, a word I guess nobody but me uses seriously anymore, groovy. Not now. He was taking deep and quick drags and I don't think he could have held the thing *still* for more than thirty seconds on a dare. It's the way you see junkies smoke when they're waiting for the man (and you always, always have to *wait* for the man) or the way guys betting on margin and way over their heads smoke when they're watching the game.

It was the way I'd been smoking a few weeks ago in Clyde's Cavern, thinking about going back and facing Janie. Hell, it was the way I'd been smoking ever since then, it hit me. So there we were, just two ordinary guys, a mystical priest and a professional creep, who happened to be watching their worlds turn to shit before their confused stares.

"Sure, man," I said. "Want to come to my office? I know it's early but I've got a couple of beers there."

He grinned, and it shocked me. Just because, for all the obvious hurt he was in, it was a really honest, a really (why are we so scared of this word?) *nice* grin.

"Imagine my surprise," he said, and then I grinned, too. "But if you don't mind, I'd like to get out of here. Is there someplace we could get coffee?"

"Great idea," I said. "After—what?—ten Dunhills or so, a nice pot of coffee ought to get you in just the right frame of mind to face the dragons."

He smiled at himself. "So it shows that much?" he said.

"Oh, boy," I said. "Look. Friedman's deli is just around the corner. I'll drive and I'll even spring for the tab, you promise to have something to eat. You look as bad as I feel, Father."

He hardly spoke until we were seated at one of the back tables at Friedman's. Friedman's is to delicatessen what Wrigley Field is to baseball, meaning, if you want to know what it's really about, this is where you look. About twenty years ago they got rezoned out of their old location just off Michigan Avenue near where Sak's Fifth Avenue is now, so Sophie Friedman—who still runs the place—saying *feh!* to the Cossacks all the way, just moved the whole operation up to Skokie, including the old street sign, which is now planted smugly by the front door and which probably violates some city ordinance, but if you knew Sophie you wouldn't want to mess with her either.

In fact it was Sophie, whose breasts I swear get bigger and
her hair more tangerine every time I go in, who ordered us
to our table, poured us coffee without asking if we wanted
it, and barked at us for our order. When I said just coffee
would be fine, and Steven said just a toasted plain bagel, she
got to do what the regulars call a "full Sophieism."

"*You*, I can understand it," she said to me. "A gut like
yours, Harry, they should shut me down for malpractice, I
ever sell you anything but seltzer. But, *Father*"—and that
smile atop those mammaries was living proof that all mothers ought to be Jewish mothers—"you're a *thin boy!* Listen,
you ever have scrambled eggs with lox—*nova* lox? You'd love
it, trust me. We stir in a little cream cheese. . . ."

Steven, fishing out a cigarette, smiled his no thanks, and
Sophie, satisfied at her performance, sighed a masterpiece
of a sigh that ended in, "*Sei gesund* and, I shouldn't say it,
those damned cigarettes will kill you," and stalked off, grum-
bling at one of the busboys on the way.

"She doesn't know it," I told Steven, "but I'm going to
marry that woman one of these days."

"Harry," he laughed, "she would burn you down before
the honeymoon was half over."

"Hope so," I said, and we both dissolved in laughter. It
was the kind of laughter you hear in foxholes and holding
cells and airliners flying through heavy weather, where the
silliest damn joke in the world suddenly cracks everybody up
and you're all horking till the tears come. And it's not because the joke was funny, it's because the laughter is there,
and you're so by God alone or scared that you want to at
least hug that and the other laughers to yourself. I don't
know much about the Holy Grail, understand. But when I
think about it (not all that often), I think about that kind
of laughing.

"So," I said as we both wiped our eyes, feeling silly and oddly
lighter at the same time, "what's to talk about, Steven?"

His eyes suddenly got very clear.

"This is really funny," he said after a couple of beats. "You know, the priesthood is kind of like a . . . a guild."

"Huh?" I said.

"We take care of our own," he said. "I mean, really take care. Do you know, when I was in seminary at Notre Dame, one of the—no, *the* strongest rule they impressed on us was, no outside friendships. Know what that means?"

I'd never heard the phrase before, but I knew. I remembered, from my almost-year there, those pale kids in their black cassocks, marching together into the freshman classes, marching together out of the classes, and never exchanging a word with us civilians. What pricks, we used to think. What poor isolated bastards, I thought now, watching Steven Lee light up again.

"So," he went on, "any problem that comes up within the community, it can be—is supposed to be—handled within the community. Father X has a little problem with the brandy. Father Y seems to spend a lot of time chatting up the younger boys. Father Z has been gone for a couple of days. As I said, we take care of our own, and everybody in the community has a spiritual adviser—they call them 'counselors' now—he can go to when, well, when—"

"When the shit hits the fan," I said, and he nodded. "Pretty fuckin' claustrophobic, or am I getting this wrong?"

"You're getting it just fine," he smiled, and it was a relieved and not a very happy smile. "Pretty fuckin' claustrophobic." And he said that, just as Sophie placed his toasted bagel in front of him, and that gave Sophie the opportunity to call down God's pity for all the foul-mouthed *goyim* with nothing more than a ripple of her ample shoulders and a roll of her cocoa eyes. An eloquent lady.

"So why are you telling me this, man?" I asked. "I mean, I'd think maybe Bridget—"

"She couldn't help," he said. "For one thing, good as she is, I think she's in the same bad place I'm in. She really doesn't know where home is, what world she belongs in.

Look. Ever since I took my final vows, I've been trying to find
some way to—oh, hell— to stay faithful to God and to the
world, too. Does that make any sense?"

It made about as much sense as if he'd started explaining
to me about five-dimensional geometry. And why, in God's
name, was he assuming that I—of all the people he knew,
and he knew me hardly at all, anyway—that I was the guy
he could spill all this to? Sorry, but I'm generally one of those
people, a guy sidles up to me in a late-night bar and talks
about the meaning of life, I start edging toward the door and
thinking about a 911 call.

And yet. I'd seen the guy (I know billy-be-damned about
theology but I know *okay* when I see it), I'd seen him talk
to some pretty wounded people and help them, maybe just
for a while but who cares? feel a little less wounded. And I
saw him feeling like shit right now, and I knew that the
reason he felt like shit wasn't because of anything that could
happen to him, but because he'd—wait a second!

Yes! Because he'd tried, and tried real hard, to be good.
Just, you know, good. Don't we all want that, sooner or later,
and don't we all, most of us, manage to fuck it up? For
instance, the way I'd told myself that I was going to be really
good with, and for, Janie.

But he was staring at me, his question unanswered, and
I realized I'd been drifting.

"It makes sense," I said, "that you're not only a very
strange cat"—he smiled—"but a damned nice guy."

"Harry," he said, waving his hand.

"I'm buying your fuckin' breakfast," I said, "so just shut
up, okay? You *are* a damned nice guy, and you're just going
to have to learn to live with that. And somehow, being a nice
guy, you find yourself anyway half out of your church and
maybe fronting for an international whorehouse. Come on,
don't wince, that's how bad it could be, and, like Bridget
said, we're going to try and find out if it's that bad and if it
is that bad, Father Lee, you're still going to be a damned nice

guy who just happened to have a bad night in the barrel. I really want you to believe that."

And he looked at me very odd. "This doesn't sound like you," he said. "Why are you saying this?"

Well, dammit, why was I? I give advice about as often as I buy Girl Scout cookies and that's never. And then, before I knew it was happening—well, that's a lie, you *always* know it's happening—it all came up.

"Why?" I said. "Because I don't know jack shit about serving God and serving the world and I don't want to, but I do know I've been living with this *fine* lady and I've been treating her like garbage because . . . well, because I have, and I knew I was doing it and couldn't stop anyhow, and last night she split and it's my fault—*my* fuckin' fault, man, not like your scene at all, and God damn it to hell, I just want her back, okay?" I noticed I'd lit two cigarettes while I was talking.

And don't ask me why I didn't, then and there, ask him about Lisa/Andrea. I kept flip-flopping back and forth, half the time sure that he couldn't have a thing to do with it, half the time sure he couldn't not have a thing to do with it. But whatever place we'd come to—in a crowded delicatessen, for crying out loud, over one now-cold bagel—the question just didn't seem all that important.

And Steven Lee did something that, almost any other time, would have freaked me out. He reached across the table and closed his hand around my wrist.

"It'll be all right, man," he said. "Thanks for what you said and thanks for being the friend I needed. Now don't get pissed off at me for saying this, but I'd like to pray for you and your lady. Would you tell me her name?"

And I said, "Look, man, I've got to make some phone calls. You want that bagel?" I still haven't stopped kicking myself for that.

So I drove him back to our parking lot, neither of us saying much, and we shook hands and he walked to his car. "Hey!"

I hollered as he was unlocking the door. He turned.

"We'll take care of business, okay?" I said. He smiled. "And—look, be good to yourself, man." He smiled broader. I've always been glad I said that.

And I walked back to the office, wondering whether I'd just made or missed a friend. Oh, well. Now it was coming on ten-thirty and time to rustle up some old friends, if that was the word.

Time to call the Priest. Time to call Jimmy Maher.

$\triangledown$

19

OR JAMES VINCENT MAHER, you want the pedigree name. The Priest because, after high school, he put in a couple of years in a Jesuit seminary in Maryland. Dropped or got kicked out—nobody was ever sure about that and nobody ever asked, at least more than once—and came back to take over his old man's business, which is selling industrial felt. That's right, industrial felt. The stuff you put on pool tables, the stuff you use in cars and boats and a hundred other things that, you look at them, you never think, Hey! There's goddamn industrial *felt* here! I mean, who grows up thinking to himself, Man, I wanna be the industrial felt king of the Midwest?

But Jimmy's father had done just that—had a stone lock on the felt market in Illinois, Indiana, Kentucky, Wisconsin. And you inherit a business like that, a couple million-plus per year, all you have to do is you have to really keep the supply lines open, the jobbers decently paid, and the clients in line and annually, happily drunk at the big Christmas party you throw at the Ganesha, the best not-Indian-run Indian restaurant in near-south Chicago and therefore convenient to lots of other, interesting, and maybe even fascinating after-dinner places of amusement.

What I mean is that, compared to being, say, a plumber, inheriting Maher Distributors, Inc. is one good gig.

I hadn't talked to the Priest in a few years, I thought as I listened to the phone ring at the other end. I'd done him a favor or two; he'd done me a favor or two. Nothing major:

the little adjustments, tiny lies you do for guys who you used to hate their ass when you were kids together but now you had decades of remembered mistrust between you and that's almost like friendship, right?

I gave the receptionist my Czech name—the name Jimmy used to mainly call me when he was getting set to make my day crappy, and I figured he'd get a kick out of it. He got on the line faster than I'd thought.

"Hey, Haroldski!" he boomed. "You still scrubbing toilet bowls, what?"

Good old Jimmy: never forgets.

"Hey, Priest," I said. "What the hell, man, everybody shits; it's good steady work."

"Mwaaah!" he said. The Priest never laughs. He raises his head forty-five degrees and goes "Mwaaah!" Must drive all the lady sea lions in the neighborhood crazy with desire.

"So," he said, "to what do I owe the extreme pleasure?"

"Jimmy," I said. "I wonder, you got a little time, I could ask you a couple, three questions. A little problem, is all. Nothing righteous."

He was quiet for a few beats.

"Questions on the phone?" he said.

"Questions off the phone," I said.

Four more beats.

"Meet me at the Berghoff, twenty minutes?" he said.

"I'm taking the el, parking'll be a bastard. Forty?"

"Whatever. I buy, like always. Ciao, weasel," and he hung up. Just another endearment from high school, you know?

And, I thought as I drove to the Skokie C.T.A. stop and caught the train into the city, *that* was how heavy the Priest was: I'll be waiting—at the Berghoff, for Christ's sake.

Because *nobody* waits at the Berghoff. Since it opened in—what?—1898, something, on Adams and Michigan, in the heart of the heart of everything, it's been the place every player in town goes for home brew and a you'll-remember-it-at-midnight German lunch, and where every out-of-towner ("Gawd, Martha, ain't them skyscrapers something?") gets told to go for "a real taste of old Chicago," so every day around noon it's a line outside the place and a Bavarian fire drill inside. And the waiters—only *waiters*, dig, this is the Berghoff—serve and clear your plates with all the tender loving care of Vegas blackjack dealers. You dawdle over lunch at the Berghoff, they take you for a rube and count the tip out loud.

Unless you're the Priest. The Priest can sit there all day, he wants to.

Because he eats lunch there five times a week. And, more important, because when he took over Daddy's business, he didn't just sit on his ass, clip coupons, and make football bets at the country club. He became—okay, the only word for this is in Yiddish—he became a *macher*. And what a *macher* does, is, he *does*.

Look. Except a couple of bar fights, Jimmy's never been arrested. Not even called in for questioning, as far as I know. He still lives with his mother in an old, big house in Wilmette. You won't see him in the *Tribune* at the Civic Opera or the Symphony or the Mayor's Saint Patrick's Day Dinner.

But a lot and a lot of people, or people speaking for other people, manage to drop by the Berghoff when the Priest is having his daily long lunch there. And the weekly long-distance calls to and from Maher Distributors would, I figure, pay my bar bills for a good six months. You've got a pesky second drunk driving rap, a little zoning problem for your new store, like that? It can be dealt with, it will go away. You're maybe getting a little too close to the belly button? I mean, the point where whatever your scam is could and probably will land you and the guys you know in some very deep yogurt? You can be dealt with. You will go away. Nothing dramatic, no face-down in Lake Michigan or exploding cars. Just, you know: away.

As I said. What a *macher* does is, he does.

So when I elbowed past the line outside the Berghoff and told the guy behind the desk that somebody was waiting for me, I figured his table would be crowded. And it was.

Winter is when you've got to go there, by the way. You walk in from the cold and you're hit—I mean hit—with this warm mix of sauerbraten, pot roast, noodles, and the best beer in America that, I don't care if your life is melting down the outside of the sugar cone, you feel better about things.

So there was the Priest, in the corner, looking like Ted Kennedy if Ted could just loosen up (in public, I mean) in a maroon turtleneck and a double-breasted camel-hair jacket that said, all by themselves, best not putz with me. With him were two guys sitting over half-eaten plates of schnitzel. The one, in a blue pin-stripe and layered hair, had "incorporated" written all over him and looked like he was wondering why he had to come to lunch in a place like this. The other, a mouse in crumpled corduroy, kept playing with his fork and was obviously wondering if they were going to toss him out of a place like this. Different worlds, colliding over schnitzel and beer: That's why the Priest is the Priest.

"Hey, weasel! Mwaaah!" said Jimmy as I walked toward the table. I smiled and sat down. Just like when he hit me in the gut all those years ago under the Howard Street el.

"Hey, Harry," he said, "meet my friends, Mr. Merkin and Mr. Widget. Guys, this is Harry Garnish I told you about, my old cellmate in Brother Omer's Latin class." They both nodded—no eye contact—and I dug that while it was okay for them to know my real name, I didn't know theirs or that they'd been here, even if I *had* seen pin-stripe on the news a few days before, talking about a bond issue.

"So, hey," Jimmy went on. "These guys have to leave. Sorry we can't all sit and schmooze, but it's a fuckin' jungle out there, yeah?" On cue, Merkin and Widget got up, nodded and mumbled, and left.

Oh, yeah. Jimmy *always* picks up the tab. For everybody.

When they were out of earshot, which in the Berghoff is about two body lengths away from your table, Jimmy turned to me with the old, Irish I-wonder-if-I'll-hug-you-or-just-kick-your-ass smile.

"So, Garnishevitz," he grinned. "Schnitzel or pot roast?"

"Hey, I'll just have a beer, man," I said. "You ate already."
"Fuck that," he brayed, turning—even in the Berghoff at
lunch hour—a few heads. "You gotta eat, weasel. Look. I had
the schnitzel; it's great today. You want the schnitzel? I'll get
the pot roast. I love the pot roast here. Hey, Fritz"—and he
snapped his finger at a passing waiter and you don't snap
your finger at a passing waiter there—"get me a plate, pot
roast, and bring my little brother here some schnitzel, and
two big fuckin' drafts, *Jawohl!* And hey, bring the beer first,
follow me?"

It's why I don't look Jimmy up that often.

"So why'd you look me up, Harry?" he said as the beers
arrived. And his voice was surprisingly soft now. Now we
were doing business.

I took a sip of beer. "Jimmy," I said. "I wanted to find me
a hooker, like, a hooker just off the boat from, well, say, Haiti,
someplace like that. Got any idea where I might look these
days?"

It was a stupid goddamn way of opening, and I knew it
while I was saying it. Can't be helped: All these years, around
Jimmy Maher I still get twitchy.

He looked at me, downed half his glass, and looked again.
Didn't go "Mwaaah!" Didn't turn on the killer grin. Just
looked, and that's when I knew I'd been right to call him.

"Pretty sticky patch, right, Harry?" he said.

"Dig it," I said.

"Now you know I'm not a pimp. And I know you didn't
haul ass all the way down here for a free lunch and to ask
me where you could find some strange tail. Hell, aren't you
still shacked up with that Eye-tie twist, what's the name,
Rugulo, something?"

I got a cold sweat, just like in a gin hangover. How and
why the hell did the Priest know about that?

"Regalbuto," I said. "Janie Regalbuto. And she's Sicilian."

"Hey, no offense, little brother," he grinned, wadding up
the insult in his hands and tossing it over his shoulder.
"What I want to know"—and he paused to glare at the

waiter who was glaring at him as he put our plates before us—"what I want to know," he went on as the guy left, "is just what you're really asking me for, and let's not dick around with any goofball hypotheticals, okay?"

"Okay," I said. "I think there may be some kind of market running here, brings in illegal aliens, and these kids would be from Haiti—that's what I'm interested in, dig, Haiti—and being sold into The Life. More I can't tell you right now, Jimmy. But if you could, like, send out some feelers."

"Nigger whores," Jimmy said. "Man, you know, nigger whores are about as thick as the fuckin' pigeons. About as clean, too. Mwaaah!" That one with a mouthful of pot roast.

And that was it. I pushed my plate aside and stood up. "Okay, Priest," I said. "I came with a question, I figure we go back, I can ask a question, hey? You want to make fuckin' bad jokes? Cool. You don't know where to look? Cool. I gotta go."

"Hey, baby," he said, draining his beer and snapping for another. "Don't get pregnant. For you, little Harry, I'll ask around. Might be something, might not. You can't give me anything else? Hey, sit. Eat your schnitzel."

"Gotta go, Priest," I said. "Here." And I handed him the list of names Steven Lee had given me. "All I got."

He looked over the list of names and looked at me, leering and smacking his lips. "Ooh baby, dats'a what I like," he said, quoting the Big Bopper's one hit, *Chantilly Lace*. "Right, Harry, I'll look. And I'll call you. Like you say, we go back. Hey, you really gotta go? Mind if I take your schnitzel?" he said, already reaching for the plate.

"Enjoy, Jimmy," I said. "And thanks, man. I owe you, you find something."

"Oh, yeah," he said, forking my cutlet onto his plate. "I find something, you owe me, Harry. Ciao, weasel." And concentrated on his food.

On the way out I stopped in the john, put my mouth under the faucet and let the cold water run for about two minutes.

$\bigtriangledown$

20

THE PRIEST WOULD DELIVER, if there was anything to deliver, and, of course, if the information didn't conflict with
any of his own business, which was as tangled as a bowl of
spaghettini al burro. So it was probably worth wasting my
day, and even worth the tinny taste conversations with him
always left in my mouth.

And I realized that I hadn't really eaten anything worth
calling food since my squid—when was it?—around noon
yesterday. And that last night's brandy was still trying to pull
off a palace revolution against my nervous system. And that
it was Christmas season in Chicago, and I hadn't spent any
real time downtown in a while. It was a good, bright and cold
day and the hawk, the downtown Chicago wind, was out: a
dry martini day, a pal of mine used to call it.

So I walked the five or six blocks from the Berghoff to
Marshal Field's, just to look at the Christmas display in their
store windows.

Right: about as square as you can get. But I had had it up
the butt with North Shore *machers* making jokes about nigger whores, with visionary priests running stables of working
girls they didn't even know about, and with nice ladies who
got mixed up with intellectual peacocks and wound up in
hospital beds being fed through the arm. Not to mention, of
course, with lovers who walked out on you just because all
you'd been doing was acting like a two-headed geek. I could
use a little square and dwortzy. Like all my junkie friends

say about what you'll do to get away from the withdrawal
uglies: wouldn't you?

Not that it worked. The Field's windows told the story
this year about how Santa and his elves rescued a little mermaid from the clutches of a grumpy, Grinch-like lobster and
gave all the undersea folk the merriest of Christmases. The
Field's windows usually told you how Santa and his elves
rescue somebody from a grumpy something and give everybody the merriest of you-know-whats, even the now-con-
verted grump.

It was a fuckin' bring-down. Not because it was corny,
mind you. Just because it wasn't corny, because, dammit,
we all do want Santa to rescue the little mermaid and make
the grump an okay guy and for everybody to be—shit—nice
to everybody else. Maybe there's Christmas so at least once
a year we're forced to remind ourselves that it doesn't work
that way: no, that much as we want it, we don't work that
way. And where's the lie here, the fairy tale we know we could
live, or maybe the mess we make trying to live it? It was
about as corny and sentimental as a slap in the face.

And I remembered I'd been planning to get Janie an ankle
bracelet for Christmas. Yeah, I know, very early sixties, but
she'd said that she always thought ankle bracelets were cute,
so what the hell. So I walked into Field's, found the jewelry
counter (or one of the jewelry counters, since Field's main
store is like a ten-acre mall stacked vertically instead of hor-
izontally), and bought, since I'm such a helluva guy, two
ankle bracelets.

And that, natch, made me feel even shittier. Know that
story, "The Gift of the Magi"? The wife sells her beautiful
hair to buy the husband a chain for his supergroovy watch
and the husband sells his goddamn watch to buy the wife a
silver comb for her beautiful hair? Dumb story, if you ask
me. Except if you figure that they were both, at least, trying
to, like, rescue the little mermaid and get the grumpy lobster
to join the band. And in a weird way they did.

And there I was with my gift, but nobody now to give it

to. *Two* ankle bracelets? I thought as the lady behind the counter gave me my package and told me how to get to gift wrapping. So what do I do Christmas morning, clip the bastards together and give them to Bandit to chase around the apartment? With my luck, the dumb little asshole would probably try to eat them and choke to death. Ho ho the fuck ho.

So you can always, you know, have a meal. I escalated up to the eighth floor and went into the Oak Room. This time of day, they wouldn't be all that busy. Got a seat in smoking, lit up, and told the waitress to bring me two Heinekens, both at once, and the Marshal Field Special.

And if anything will set you up on a turn-down day it's two Heinekens and the Marshal Field Special. We're talking, here, and you don't know Chicago you won't believe this, a slice of rye bread; slices of Swiss cheese; a half head of lettuce; slices of turkey breast and strips of bacon and cherry tomatoes, pickles and olives, all dolloped with Thousand Island dressing. What it is, is a BLT with a bad attitude, and it's so damned excessive and hopelessly self-confident, like the city that invented it, that you can almost hear it telling you, "Hey, man, lighten up! It's all going to turn out okay, dig?"

Except, of course (isn't there always an "of course"?) the last time I'd had a Special in the Oak Room had been with Janie last August when we'd been talking about whether we could afford to do a weekend in New York, take in some shows and such, and who to get to watch the cat.

Hell with it. I told the waitress I wanted another Heineken.

And you know that point, you're not really snockered but you've had enough, you're feeling good *enough* you figure you can talk to the people you usually avoid talking to, but now—if you do it right now—you can bring it off? I ate the last strip of bacon and guzzled half the third Heineken and set off for the pay phones.

The first number I called was Wanda. That's Wanda Carnahan, Janie's former roommate and former co-worker before Janie came, I guess, down in the world and moved in with me. Midafternoon is usually a hooker's nap time, of course, but as I say, I was feeling just insulated enough, I didn't care.

"Yeah?" said a husky, sleepy voice at the other end of the line.

"Hey, Wanda," I said. "It's Harry. Harry Garnish. Can you talk?"

She gave a mean little chuckle. "Sure I can talk, Harry," she said. "Can you talk?"

Which meant, of course, that Janie had been to see her.

"Yeah, listen," I said. "I'm kind of worried about Janie. You got any idea where she might be, Wanda?"

Feeble, Garnish: feeble. I was sounding like one of the poor zhlubs who wound up being my clients.

"I got an idea," she said with that mean little chuckle again, "but you got an idea why I should tell you? You got any idea how much she really cared about you? You're a fink, Harry."

"Now, wait," I said, "things haven't been going too good with us lately, but—"

"But my ass," she said. "You guys all think you're so goddamned deep and cagey. Jesus. She knows you been getting some on the side, wiseguy."

"What?" I said. "What makes her think—"

"Oh, *please*," she said, and I swear I felt the ghost of Brother Benedict looking over my shoulder again. "She really loved you, asshole. And if you'd had the balls to be honest with her . . . Oh, shit." And hung up.

And I called right back, and on the eighth ring she picked it up.

"Look, just one minute, okay?" I said before she could talk. "You hate my ass, okay. Maybe I earned it. But just tell me, she's okay?"

"Christ," she said, "what's this, the caring hurt lover number? Okay," she sighed. "She's okay and she's not staying with me. In other words, she's not going back into trade, if that's what you're worried about."

"I didn't—"

"You didn't ask that," she said. "You guys never do, do you? And don't expect me to tell you anything else. You push me on this, man, I know some of the guys you know, and me, they owe some special favors to. Got it?"

What the hell? "Got it," I said. "Thanks, I guess."

"And one more thing," she said before I could hang up. "A little insider information from The Life, I figure you should learn it. You know what makes a john a john? It's because he thinks he's a john. You copy, John?" And hung up again.

Which left me with the other call to make: *the* call, but not before I went back to my table, finished my beer, got a cup of coffee, and smoked two cigarettes. Alcohol, caffeine, nicotine: like the way wrestlers drink honey for the instant rush before they hit the mat.

I know, I know. The private eyes on the tube always have some superior, smartass plan about what they're going to do, how they're going to manage stuff. But I don't live on the tube any more than you do, and, excuse the pun, I didn't have a clue.

All I figured was that if the wrong person answered the phone I'd just hang up, try again later. Pretty damn cagey, huh?

But the ball, for a change, took a home-team bounce.

"Hello?" said a voice, I'd call it in the alto flute register. I remember it, saying some pretty strange things, from the Morris Inn two months ago.

"Hi," I said, feeling a sudden hollowness in my chest. "You remember me, from the Morris Inn, couple months ago? Your name was Lisa back then."

"Oh, *hi!*" she said in a voice that was just casual and loud enough to say that she wasn't alone in the house. "How've you been?"

"So you can't talk, right?" I said.

"That's right," she lilted, and you could almost see her diddling with the phone cord, like some keen teen from "The Donna Reed Show." "So, listen, what's going on?"

"What's going on, kid," I said in a whispered rush—

thanks, Heineken, Maxwell House, and Winston—"is I
want to know what the hell was going on the night you . . .
you what the hell, *got* me and what the hell this is all about,
and if you can't make an arrangement to talk to me, by God
I'm coming up to your fuckin' house and I'm letting Pops
know what his little girl likes to do when she's not going to
the library, or is this not clear?"

"Oh, I wouldn't say *that*," she lilted again and I swear to
God she could have been talking about going to the drive-in
for *Nightmare on Elm Street* number twenty and burgers
afterward. "Look, it's nice of you to call, and . . . well, you
know how worried we all are about Mom"—she said that
knowing she was acting and knowing I knew she was acting
and not really caring and that gave me one helluva chill—
"but I've got a couple of hours between classes tomorrow.
You know where Woodstock's is, right across from campus?
Maybe we could meet there. Oh, *sure*," she added, as if I'd
said something, which I hadn't, "say around one? It would
be good to talk to you again, Helen."

"Be there," I said. "And be ready to talk."

Damned if I knew who'd won that hand. I wasn't even
sure what was wild. Ever have that feeling, usually late in
the game, you're so tired or so drunk or so whatever you
forget which of the cards is supposed to stand for what it
stands for and which is supposed to stand for whatever you
want it to stand for?

Well, hell. I hopped the el back to the Skokie stop and
drove home, stopping on the way to get a six of Löwenbräu
Dark and rent a video of *The Producers*. Know that movie?
I mean, anybody who can invent a musical comedy called
Springtime for Hitler, make a joke that blows you away but
that finally isn't a joke at all about the biggest and ugliest
thing you can think of—well, the guy that can do that at
least has a handle on the way I think things really are.

Anyway, a nice treat for Bandit and me to watch with our
Hormel chili. Yup, things were getting back to just the way
they dammit used to be.

$\triangledown$

21

I WOKE UP AT SEVEN-THIRTY A.M. My head didn't hurt, I didn't feel like I had to go looking for Ernie, and I actually felt *awake* when I was awake. That was all a welcome change from the last couple months.

("Looking for Ernie," by the way, is something I learned from a stewardess I used to see. A passenger gets airsick, he sticks his head in the convenience bag, and goes "Ern? Ern?")

And, oh yeah, there was a knock-knock-knocking on my chamber door.

I threw on a robe and opened the door on a large guy in a fur-collar overcoat and eyebrows like it looked like he'd taken the biggest black caterpillar he could find and taped it as close as he could to his nose.

"So," he said, "you survived another night?"

"You know me, Ray," I said. "Every morning's a comeback. You want some coffee?"

"Naah," he said. "Glass of water, is all. Crummy fuckin' apartment, Harry."

Ray Kelley was one of the guys, used to prowl with Jimmy Maher looking for Bohunks to beat up in high school, and he was still working for Jimmy. Word was, he was a *shtarker*. Not a *macher*, a *shtarker*. Dig: The *shtarker* is the guy, he breaks the bones that the *macher* thinks it might be a nice idea, they got their bones broken. It's not really a complicated system.

"I know," I said, handing him his glass of water. Bandit was trying to hide on top of the fridge, which, don't ask me why, he thinks is the safest place on the planet. "Everybody comes in here, first thing they say is 'Crummy fuckin' apartment, Harry.' It's almost a tradition by now, you know?"

"Yeah. Funny, Harry," he said, draining his glass. "That's what we always liked about you, you were a funny guy. Always with the comebacks, you know?"

Yeah. You make them laugh, they don't punch your gut out at lunch hour. Most of the time.

"And you guys always laughed," I said, lighting a cigarette. "More water, Ray? No? Okay. So what, the Priest send you here or what?"

That "send you" he didn't like, and that's why I said it. He and Jimmy Maher, see, were supposed to be womb-to-tomb pals from the old place, the old neighborhood, the old community, whatever the hell it is you hold on to, makes you feel it's all the way it used to be and it's supposed to be. But then things had happened—years had happened—and here was Ray running errands for the Priest and just coming out of his (you hear about this shit) second divorce with about five kids in the hopper, and basically you break it all down, being *sent* places, at seven A.M. yet, by his old best buddy.

Did I mean what I said to hurt but not hurt enough he would break my balls? Goddamn right I did.

"Busy day, Garnish," he said, not answering my question and getting to his feet. "I can't fuck around here, I got things to do. So here"—and he reached into his inside jacket pocket and took out an envelope—"Jimmy said I should give you this, on my way to work. He also said he may be calling you sometime, but you don't call *him* till you hear from him."

"What?" I said. I was almost enjoying this. "Jimmy tell you he's pissed?" I knew Ray didn't know what the hell was in the envelope: Jimmy had signed it across the seal.

"Fuck it, man," he said. "That's just what the fuckin' Priest says, you got a problem?"

"Not one in the world," I said. "Don't be a stranger, Ray."

"Mph," he said. We didn't shake hands.

After he left I put a tape into my player—Sonny Rollins live at the Village Vanguard, which I swear will insulate against *any* bad karma—and as Sonny began meditating on the changes to "Softly, As in a Morning Sunrise," I opened Jimmy Maher's letter.

It wasn't long. One sheet of typing paper with Jimmy's felt-tip maniac-small printing. So he hadn't dictated this, so that already was a clear bit of information that we were into serious stuff. What it said was:

"Macquot, Abadessa. Call"—and a phone number you don't need to know—"and set up a meeting. Cost you, maybe, two hundred. That's what you get from me, except WATCH YOUR ASS on this one. P.S. Now you owe me." No signature. "P.P.S. Ask for Summer, ain't that called a nom de guerre?"

Well, so the Priest had asked just enough questions, off my little list of names, to find out where the first of our lost waifs was hanging out these days, and also to find out that he didn't need to get any further involved in whatever it was he had *really* found out. Steven Lee's worries about the righteous quotient of the Sethian Haitian Project looked a lot less like moral fidgets in the cool glare of Jimmy Maher's single sheet of paper.

And, of course, that business about "WATCH YOUR ASS" wasn't just old school chum solicitude. Jimmy was telling me that he *had* called in a marker or two to get this shit for me, and that one day I was going to pay him back for it, and he didn't want me to get, like, dead before he could collect his debt.

It works that way.

"That Sonny, he never makes a mistake, does he?" I asked Bandit as I opened a can of something called Salmon Kitty Treat (Janie had bought it) and tried not to gag. Bandit had come down from his fortress of solitude and was sitting next to his food dish, accusing.

"Goddamn right," I said, spooning the mess into his dish. "Every note, soon as he plays it, it sounds like the only fuckin' note you could put there. Like fuckin' Mozart, dig? Hey, you mind if you eat alone this morning?" He seemed not to.

"Groovy," I said, getting dressed (the way I felt, a shower wouldn't have done much good, anyway). "But really, just listen to Sonny. It's like Bird. Everything he does, you just know it's absolutely spontaneous, he just thought of it, and you know it's just the right thing to do. How do you get to be that way, make it all work out that way, like you're just sailing over all the jagged edges of the world?"

His nose buried in Salmon Kitty Treat, Bandit didn't give a shit. That *I* could tell.

"Well, what's a fuckin' cat know, anyhow?" I said, all dressed up now with I didn't know where to go. So I cut Sonny off in midphrase and turned on MTV. Bandit likes MTV and that shit's not complicated, so I usually leave it on for him when I'm out of the house. They were showing a really good live concert by Queen, and I thought about Billy Donner and . . . well, I thought about Billy Donner, you know?

"Enjoy, asshole," I said as I left. "And hey—Janie calls, just tell her I'm doing fine, all right?"

I was going to call the number for Abadessa Macquot. Don't ask me why, I just didn't feel like calling it from my apartment.

$\triangledown$

22

So I got to the office, for once, earlier than anybody else, and it felt kind of nice. The apartment now was echoing with bad vibes like a haunted house from a low-budget drive-in movie, and the street—anything outside your door is always, break it all down, the street—was lately getting all tangled with complications and half-kept secrets that, personally, I'd rather have chopped liver on rye. But the office, with no Bridget, no Brenda, no phones ringing yet, felt . . . well, safe: a nice sterilized womb to crawl into. I even, for the hell of it, locked my door, which I never do, leaned back and lit a cigarette, and promised myself to start getting up early and doing this more often, a promise I knew I wouldn't keep but it felt good, anyway.

And then I looked at yesterday afternoon's mail on my desk.

There, on top of some letters and bills I didn't bother to open, was a little box wrapped in brown paper. I recognized the handwriting, addressed to me at the office, God damn it. Knowing what it was, I opened it anyhow.

When Janie had first moved in, I'd bought her (okay, this is soap-opera sticky, so sue my ass) this little ceramic brooch, two cats leaning against each other on a wood fence. It seemed like the thing to do, and back then it looked like everything was coming up seashells and balloons (you mean *you* never felt that way?).

And there it was, all nicely nicely cushioned in tissue paper. With a note: "I'm really sorry. Janie."

Damn if it wasn't my morning for interesting correspondence. I threw the brooch in the wastebasket. Then I fished it out, made sure it wasn't chipped, and put it in my bottom drawer, right next to the two cans of Heineken who were still, like puppies in a pet-store window, trying to get my attention.

Screw them. Screw everything.

And then, just like it was a bad movie (ever think that life maybe *is* a bad movie?), I heard voices in the hallway. Bridget and Brenda, naturally, who I guess always arrive close enough to the same time they could qualify for one of those dopey coordinated-doing-something events they have in the Olympics now. They were nattering happily about something when I stuck my head into the hallway, and when they both saw me there, at that hour, I think it may be the first time you could have at least tried (we're talking serious total tonnage here) to knock at least one of them down with the famous feather.

"Harry," said Bridget, "is everything all right?"

"Bridget," I said, "know what a moratorium is? Of course you do, you're so educated and everything. Well, that's what I'm declaring on the question, 'Harry, are you all right,' okay? From now until such time as I decide to lift the damn thing. Brenda, you're in on this too, right?"

Brenda just stared. Bridget, however, did something that upset me almost as much as getting Janie's package had.

She looked at me, made the smallest of smiles, and—I swear—winked.

Say what? I thought. I'd seen the O'Toole do a lot of shit, but winking? Forget it.

"My office, fifteen minutes?" she said.

"Unh, yeah," I said. "Sure." And went back into my office, where Janie's note was still lying on top of my desk. I crumpled it to throw into the wastebasket and stuffed it into my jacket pocket.

"So what was that wink about?" I asked as I sat down in Bridget's office. She had her hands folded on the desk before

her: one of those mother-superior effects—you get it with
reformed junkies, too—that I'd learned meant, "Let's have
a little chat, shall we?" Very self-assured; a very different
Bridget than the one I'd left yesterday afternoon. Dammit,
she'd been up to something.

"Harry," she smiled. "Are you—oops, I forgot about your
moratorium on that question. Well, anyway. I think it's all
going to work out."

"It?" I said. "*It* is all going to work out? Bridget, I'm a very
tired guy at this point, so I'm probably thinking even slower
than usual. So in all this mess, you want to give me a clue
what the 'it' is that you say is going to work out?"

"Well," she said, "to begin with, I spoke with Janie last
night."

"Where is she?" I said before I knew I said it.

"She doesn't want you to know, Harry, and I promised her
that I wouldn't tell you. I'm sorry. But she's all right. She's
with . . . friends."

"So you told her about—" I began.

"About Andrea?" she said. "No. Of course not. But she
knew that something like that had happened. Don't you
realize, the way you've been behaving, you were trying to tell
her something had happened? Men!" she sighed, and for just
a moment there I couldn't tell if I was listening to Bridget or
to my old pal Wanda.

"Okay, fine," I said. "Janie's all right and that's just great.
But—hey, excuse me, I may be getting a little stupid here—I
thought we were trying to find out what happened to Nancy
Browder and Billy Donner and whether or not Steven Lee is
involved in running a tax-sheltered slave trade. Or did I miss
one of the changes? And now you're telling me that it's all
going to work out because you talked to Janie? What the hell
does Janie have to do with anything?"

"In one sense, nothing," she said, "and in another sense
quite a lot. You see, your . . . well, your problems with Janie
have really been parallel to the other developments in this
matter."

I didn't believe it. Or I didn't want to. I lit a cigarette.

"Aces," I said. "You're going to get all mystical on me, aren't you, Bridget? I was stupid, I got tired, and I told you what went down when I was in South Bend, and now you're going to orchestrate some big drama of guilt and repentance. That's your scene, right?"

"Harry—" she began.

"Harry, my ass!" I said. "Look, Bridget, I'm a little—okay, okay, a lot—screwed up right now. And that's all right, too. I bought the grief, I can work with the grief. Just don't tell me—please—that you're seeing mystical connections between my problems and whatever killed this kid."

"That's the second time you've used the word 'mystical,' Harry," she said. "I don't know what you think it means, but I can assure you I'm not playing around with fuzzy, occult connections and paranoid fantasies of connectedness. I leave that to Dom Pedro Pardo and the Sethians."

"So?"

"So I merely meant to say that, after I talked with Janie I realized that you're a lucky man. She still cares about you, Harry, as much as you have hurt her."

"Look—" I began.

"No," she said. "You look. I don't know if she's going to come back to you. I don't think she will, myself, and I can't say that I blame her."

"Well, hey," I said, "don't sugar coat it for me, Bridget, just let me have it straight."

"The point," she added, "is that after I left Janie I began thinking about why you've been so swinish for the last few weeks."

Jesus, I thought. This was the kind of crap people usually paid to hear about themselves, and I was getting it all for free. Sure must be Christmas.

"And I realized," she continued in her lecturer's tone, "that you'd been so vile to Janie—and to me, Harry, in case you hadn't noticed—just because you felt you had already hurt her, and probably also somehow betrayed me or, per-

haps, the agency, and so you did what people naturally tend
to do. You kept on hurting."

"Look, Bridget," I said, "I've got some phone calls to make,
so—"

"No deep psychology here, Harry, just observations about
the way people act," she said, and Christ, even Phil looked
uncomfortable. "You see, all this nonsense about the unfaithful husband bringing his wife flowers and candy is a lot
of . . . a lot of stuff. Usually—consciously or not—he causes
his wife more pain. And do you know why?"

Do you know why? Do you want, like, your own videotape
of your last root canal?

"Because he wants to earn the pain that he's already in-
flicted," she said, "but can't admit to inflicting." And she
looked at me with the same placid expression you see on
your teacher when she's just solved a quadratic equation on
the board.

And then I got it. Old Martin O'Toole wouldn't have gone
such a long way round the barn to get there, but I got it, and
it wasn't sloppy mysticism and it didn't even have a hell of
a lot to do with my problems. My problems were just a way
into the situation, like a flip-top on a can of worms. It was
O'Toole thinking and I recognized its sense.

"Damn!" I said. "You mean, you think we're dealing with
some kind of—Jesus, what—some kind of pecking order here?"

She smiled. " 'Pecking order' will do," she said, "although
I'd rather call it a trail of pain. You know, the way people talk
about a 'paper trail' when they're investigating embezzle-
ment or fraud? Before Professor Browder came to see us the
first time, someone was hurt. I don't have any idea who it
was, but I'd bet my life that someone was. And somehow
that hurt got multiplied and passed on and passed around,
until it ended with young Mr. Donner dead and Mrs. Browder . . . well, let's say it, dead, too."

"So you think it was a murder?" I said.

"I don't know," she said. Loud enough that even Phil
jumped a little. "Harry, I don't know if we're dealing with a

crime here or just with a—what did you call it—a grief. All I know is that now we have to find its nest. Where it started."

"And why's that?" I said.

She looked me in the eye, maybe straighter than she'd looked at me since I'd known her.

"Because that's the only thing that will help you, dear," she said.

Well, shit. I ground out my cigarette in the Harry Garnish Memorial Ashtray on her desk, and without another word I went back to my office.

The hell with psychology and guilt and every other damned thing. It was time to check out the only bit in this whole business looked like it had something to do with the real world, at least the real world the way you and I see it.

It was time to call for Abadessa Macquot.

23

"PYRAMID TALENT AGENCY," said a voice somewhere between a coo and a purr. "May we be of service to you?"

You know that voice. You've heard it on TV, you've heard it selling you booze or cars or shaving lotion or, for crying out loud, mineral water. You may even have heard it if you've ever dialed one of those 900 numbers from the back pages of certain magazines. It's a comfy, welcoming, reassuring voice that hints at everything, except itself.

"Uh, yeah," I said. "A friend of mine gave me this number, told me I might want to call it, I was interested in . . . well . . . a good time." Pretty lame, I know. But if this was the sort of place I thought it was—and the Priest had confirmed that without saying a thing—lame was what you wanted to sound: made you for a mark.

"Sir," she said, "we're an escort service. If you'd like an evening in the company of one of our girls, and if you have a credit card, we can arrange for her to meet you at your home or some place you designate. The escort fee is two hundred dollars, plus of course you pay for dinner, or a show, or whatever you'd like to do."

"Sounds fine," I said. "Now, this friend of mine, he said that he really liked this one girl. Her name was—gosh, I think it was the name of one of the seasons. Somebody there named, I think, Spring?"

She sighed. Johns are such dorks. "We have a young lady named Summer," she said. "Now Summer is a black girl. Is that who you're looking for?"

"Yeah, yeah," I said, trying to sound like Herkimer Jerkimer Jones right off the farm. "That's just right. You want my credit card number?"

And down it went, just like when you order your L.L. Bean hiking boots on the toll-free line. Summer would be on my doorstep at seven that evening, and the lady told me she hoped I would have a real good evening. I thanked her, and resisted the temptation to ask if Summer would be delivered UPS or Federal Express. Then I sighed, lit up, opened my bottom drawer, stared at that damn cat brooch, and told my two cans of Heineken that I didn't feel like playing just now.

It was only—Christ!—nine-thirty, and I didn't have jack pissant to do until my meeting with Andrea at one.

And then I noticed the book on my desk.

It must have been there this morning when I came in, but I just hadn't noticed it. Aligned square with the upper left-hand corner of my desk, a skinny paperback with a blue cover and in white one of those big triangles with an eye in the middle of it and underneath it a drawing of the Earth. *The Path of the Chosen*, by Dom Pedro Pardo. Translated by J. S. Nienow. Tenth printing, 1989. And a folded note inside the cover: "Harry, FYI. Bridget."

What the hell. I opened to page one.

Two hours, one can of Heineken, and a half pack of Winstons later, I'd found out this: that the Gospels really aren't at all about what you think they're about. As a matter of fact, the whole Bible isn't what you think it's about. Abraham and Moses and David and those guys and then Jesus and Paul and Peter? Forget it. The whole book—get this—is a secret message—"absolutely open and absolutely secret," is the way brother Pardo says it—and what it's about is (okay, I'm not going to get this right but this is as close as I can come) the "infinite self-revelation of the NAME" (that's, natch, brother Pardo again). And the NAME is, well, it's basically the fact that if you can dig the NAME, then you're, like—God.

Right. I was pretty surprised to find that out, too. And the beauty part, as Jimmy Maher would say when he was laying you down a deal, for a small opening stake, you couldn't lose your ass if you tried, was that only *you* could tell if you really dug the NAME. Here, let me quote Pedro Pardo himself:

> *The meaning of the Book has been suppressed and deformed for so many centuries just because its revelation, if allowed to flower, would spell the end of all the large codes of fraud and woe and domination that are the mortar of the Judeo-Christian prison house. And when the chosen come to know that they are the chosen, they will change the world by re-imagining the world, casting off the age-old lies of sin, privilege, and rank and glorying in the NAME because they are all the free children of the NAME and they* are *the NAME.*

No shit, the guy could write. Except, I couldn't help thinking, it all sounded like you got to grade your own final exam. Or you got to decide whether or not to write yourself a ticket for going through three red lights. "To the elect, all things are permitted." Pedro kept quoting that line, and I thought, that's pretty goddamn nice for the elect, but what's it got to do with the skinny ass of Abadessa Macquot, aka Summer?"

Anyhow that's how I spent my morning until it was time for me to head north again and meet Andrea Browder. Pedro Pardo, the back cover of the book said, was a Dominican who had founded the New Sethian movement in 1968, been reprimanded by his order and finally removed from his teaching position in Barcelona by the Roman Curia, and had mysteriously disappeared in 1979, on a visit to a Sethian community in Chile.

Fine by me. Maybe right now he was getting a cherry Slurpee in a 7-Eleven with Elvis and I hoped they were both happy as clams.

And Andrea Browder was sitting, good as gold and pretty as an MTV video, in Woodstock's when I got there at 1:10. Black turtleneck, jeans, and a leather jacket thrown over her shoulders, if you're interested. And a smile like the girl in the Tanqueray ads.

"Hi!" she said, Gidget-cute as I sat down across from her. "Aren't you going to have something?" She was drinking a Coke and swirling the crushed ice around with her straw. I hate it when people drink Coke and swirl the crushed ice around with their straws.

"Thanks," I said, "but I think I've had enough already. You really want to have this conversation *here?*"

"Why not?" she beamed. "We're not going to divulge any deep dark secrets, are we?"

And I'll tell you. I've talked to I don't know how many people, and some of them have been telling the truth and a lot more (them's the odds, son) have been liars, and a few have been flat-out loony, and when she said that I didn't know which the hell I was dealing with.

"Uh, look," I said. "I don't know if you're scamming or if you're really from Oz, here. But you do remember the Morris Inn, don't you? I mean, don't tell me you weren't the girl or some crap like that. Now this is—"

"Are you about to tell me this is serious business, Harry?" she smiled, and when she said my name, exactly as she had that night, I felt like I'd just stepped into a bear trap. I just stared.

"Oh, Harry," she said, still smiling. "I can see you're all confused, poor thing. So you want to talk in private? Look, my dad's gone for the day. Why don't you come to our house?"

Now go ahead and tell me all the reasons why going with her to Barry Browder's house was exactly the last thing I wanted to be doing: like, I couldn't trust her in the first place; like, she might be round-the-bend crazy; like, if Barry Browder came home and found us talking it would put an already screwed-up situation way over the rainbow; and, yes, like, as crappy as I was feeling about Janie and as angry as I was at Andrea, I knew myself well enough to know that if Andrea decided to turn back into Lisa and suggest an afternoon round of meat marbles, odds were—not good, but bettable—that I'd wind up taking a hand.

So I climbed back into my car and followed her home, thinking to myself, as I fiddled with the heater, to the elect, all things are permitted.

The Browder house was in Kenilworth, a few miles and a few more tax brackets north of Wilmette. You walked through a big, double door that desperately wanted you to believe it was oak into a sunken living room that was about the size of my whole apartment, with white carpeting and pneumatic-looking sofas that Bandit, I figured, could have happily spent a month or two turning into yarn. This immediately helped solve the problem of the unpredictable Garnish gonads. It's not that I hate the rich. It's that I hate it when they remind you that they're the rich, and they've got a thousand ways of doing that—ways, I wonder if they even know they're doing some of them.

Andrea—there wasn't much Lisa in her now—flung herself, and that's the word, flung herself on a big pearl gray sofa, kicked off her shoes, and asked me if I'd like a drink now.

"I'll pass," I said, although there was, dammit, a full bottle of Glenfiddich on the booze caddy in the corner. "Now, you agreed to see me. And I don't know what the hell you think you're doing, but your mother—"

"You leave my mother out of this!" she snapped, and I guess it was the first human reaction I'd gotten from her. "My mother has nothing to do with . . . with whatever you want to talk about."

"Bullshit!" I said, and without knowing I was doing it, walked over to the caddy and poured myself one hell of a Glenfiddich.

"Listen, sister," I said and I hate it when I sound like an RKO Coming Attractions, "two months ago you pick me up, you screw my brains out, and then you go off the map. Now don't tell me you hit on me in South Bend because it was an enchanted evening and I was the stranger across a crowded room. You knew who I was, and you knew why I was at the

Sethian meeting, so your mother's got every goddamned
thing to do with this, and, by the way, I don't notice you
exactly draped in mourning over her—"

"*Shut up!*" she shouted, and damn if she didn't pick up—
you know those little crystal, ceramic eggs people, I don't
know why, put on little stands and put on their whatnot
shelves, cocktail tables—anyway, pick up one of those things
and throw it at me. These college people liked to throw stuff,
I figured.

It missed me but scored a direct hit on the neck of the
Scotch bottle which, unbroken, tumbled off the caddy and
proceeded to spill on that nice white carpet. I got it after the
first healthy gurgle (some things are too important to waste,
even in the middle of high melodrama) but by that time
Andrea was already at me, her hands bunched into fists and
shouting in my face from less than two inches away.

"You sono*fabitch!*" she shouted, near tears. "Now look what
you've done! All over Daddy's carpet! Now he's bound to find
out! Now everything's wasted, all the—oh, you bastard!"

So since we'd dropped into a B-movie scene, I thought,
why not go all the way, and did something I had, honest to
God, never done before to anybody. I grabbed her wrists and
wrestled her back to the sofa. She was still calling me variations of sonofabitch, but there's something about forcing
somebody to sit down: You just can't be as angry with your
butt settled on a nice cushion.

"Now," I said, when she ran out of breath. "If you'll get
me some ammonia, some baking soda, and a nice big damp
rag, I'll make the big bad stain go away and Daddy won't
have to know anything, okay? Or don't you know where they
keep the household shit around here?"

She stared at me for a moment and then got up and walked
toward, I supposed, the kitchen. I lit a cigarette and for the
first time in a long time laughed at myself.

It was, you have to admit, funny. I mean, the keen-teen
sex goddess turns out to be the sinister, daughter-of-the-
wealthy-guy lady of mystery, and then what does *she* turn

out to be? Well, I wasn't sure quite yet, and I still didn't have a clue why the hell she had jumped my bones under the shadow of the old Golden Dome, but now I did know that one thing she was was a probably spoiled and surely scared girl who'd probably screwed around too much, who loved and feared her daddy, and who didn't know, for crying out loud, how to get a whiskey stain off the carpet.

"Be on your guard against romance at all times, boyo," Martin O'Toole once told me. "It's appealing, it's simple, it's lovely, and it will always, sure as God made the rabbit for prey for the wolf, blind you to the true and glorious sloppiness of life. *Nobody* ever wore a glass slipper."

When she came back with the stuff I got to work on the stain. "No biggie, see?" I told her as I scrubbed. "You get to be as old as I am, go around the track often enough, booze stains on the floor get as simple as hangnails."

I thought that might get a smile. I was wrong.

"So," I said after I finished (a good job, if I say so myself), "what were we talking about? Oh, yeah. You were going to tell me why you came all the way to South Bend to fuck my brains out. Weren't you?"

She was silent for a minute and I waited. "Look," she said finally. "You've got to know that my m—that I love my mother. I mean, she'd been acting a little weird lately, things haven't been . . . too good around here, but I love her, okay?"

I didn't say anything.

"All right," she went on after a while. "I knew that Daddy was worried about my mother and those . . . people. We've never had secrets, he and I, and he's got this important job that he might be on the verge of getting, and he's been worried that—"

"Yeah, yeah," I said. "So cut to the chase."

"So he told me that he'd hired . . . you people to check up on the . . . the . . ."

"Sethians," I said.

"Right. And he told me about Miss O'Toole, and about you, and so I just thought that I'd, well, *you* know."

"That you'd track me to the meeting, try to get me between the sheets—which you did very nicely, by the way—so
that you could what? Compromise me? Maybe blackmail me
to give your dad the kind of information he wanted to hear
to keep Mommy away from the Sethians? *What*, for Chrissake?"

Now there's a gesture people make—you've seen it a hundred times—when they try to tell you that they don't know
what they're trying to say, or why they did what they did. It
isn't even a gesture, really. It's a lot of different waves of the
hand, shrugs of the shoulder, or just tosses of the head, but
they all mean the same thing, and one of those is what
Andrea did then.

"Got it," I said. "You just wanted to be in on the action
and help Daddy any way you could, and you guessed the best
way to do it would be to use your body to rope in the ol'
private eye, right?"

She nodded and shrugged at the same time.

"And Daddy still doesn't know, does he?" I said.

The alarm on her face was her answer.

"Do that a lot, do you?" I said. "I mean, screw guys to
help out ol' Dad's career? You could get a disease, you know."

And she was about to start another B-movie scene but I
stopped her. "Don't bother," I said. "That dog won't hunt,
anyway."

"Huh?"

"Your dad," I said, "may have told you about Bridget and
me being in on the case, but he had no way of knowing that
I was going to go to the Sethian meeting that Saturday night,
and I'm sure as hell that Bridget didn't leak the information.
So either you'd been going to the meetings on a regular basis
yourself, or you tipped the Sethians that I was coming and
they tipped you when I was coming so that you could set the
whole damn thing up and that means this whole business
about your dad being worried about your mother's activities
is a bunch of bullshit. Dig? What story you want to tell
now?"

Funny. I should have been angry about how this whole thing had fouled up what it was I had with Janie. I should have been concerned about Nancy Browder, lying somewhere in a hospital bed with her mind halfway between brain-dead and everlasting nightmare, for all I knew. And I was. But what was really on my mind when I asked her that (don't ask me why) was Steven Lee. I really wanted to know whether he'd been involved in scamming me from the beginning, or whether he was the . . . well, dammit, just *likable* guy I'd come to think he was. I don't know. Maybe I just wanted to hear that there was one person in this whole business who was just what he said he was.

Not that I got my answer right then. Andrea stared at me, ran her fingers through her hair a couple of times, pursed her lips and was just about, I thought, to speak when the front door opened and Barry Browder walked in.

24

"M<small>R.</small> G<small>ARNISH</small>," <small>HE SAID</small>, no expression on his face, and walked to the liquor caddy and poured himself a drink. "May I ask why you're here?"

"Dad—" Andrea began, and I could see she was just this side of hyperventilating.

"Sorry, sir," I jumped in. "I should have called, but I was up this way on some other business, and I just thought I would stop by on the chance you were in. Your daughter told me you probably wouldn't be back for a while, so I had a drink of your Glenfiddich—hope you don't mind—and was just about to leave."

He stared from one to the other of us, and obviously didn't buy it. "But you told me that there was nothing else you could do for my . . . situation," he said finally.

"Well, yeah," I said. "But I kind of wanted to see how you were doing, to be honest. I mean, are you—well, hell—all right?"

His face softened. "That's kind of you, Mr. Garnish. Thank you. Nancy is just the same, and we're, as you see, coping. Would you like another Scotch?"

I would have loved another Scotch, but if you don't know when to walk away from the table, you shouldn't sit down for the deal.

"Thanks, no," I said, "gotta go. But you wouldn't mind if I checked in with you once in a while? I mean, I'm so damned sorry things—"

"Yes, of course, and Andrea and I both appreciate it. And give my regards to Ms. O'Toole."

He was as glad to see me out of there as I was to be out of there. I shook his hand, nodded at Andrea (we both knew we'd be talking again), and left, thinking about the way the critters used to exit stage left in Warner Brothers Cartoons, wishing I could do that.

So. How to portion out the rest of my busy afternoon? I could go back to the office and fiddle around with my files (which is mainly what I do with my files) and try to keep out of Bridget's way. I could call Wanda again and try to wheedle, beg, or piss and moan her into getting a message from me to Janie. I could call Steven Lee, who at this point was looming larger and larger as the big question mark in the whole business—I mean, *had* he set me up with Andrea, or what, and if so, why was he now asking us to check on his own damned people?—and just brace him. Or, it hit me as I swung through the S curve where Sheridan Road starts to parallel Lake Michigan, I could call the Priest back, and ask *him* to brace Steven Lee. And when the Priest asks you a question, you always tell him the truth. Sooner or later.

Now that was an appealing idea. Jimmy Maher had told me, of course, that he didn't want to be any more involved with the Sethians or whatever livestock trade they might be engaged in. But that didn't mean—that never meant—that I couldn't press him for a little more information. It just meant (this was never, you know, said or printed on a contract or anything) that when payback time came around, the interest rate would have gone up. Maybe a little, maybe a lot, but payback time always came.

So no to that idea, too. At least for now. So I had three, four hours till Summer. The hell with it. I drove home, had a half pot of coffee, shared a jar of schmaltz herring with Bandit, put my tape of Chet Baker's last great concert into the machine, and went to sleep.

Maybe it was the Glenfiddich—that stuff could probably

stop a nuclear meltdown—or maybe it was just the last two months crashing in all together, but I fell into one of those sleeps that, even when you're in it, you somehow know you're as deep down as you're going to get, and you're not all that sure you ever want to come up out of it again. The kind of state junkies are really talking about when they talk about being "on the nod": not just a doze or a nap, but an escape inside yourself so insulated and so heavy that nothing, like, for example, walking out of a burning room, seems worth the trouble in comparison to the nod.

Which is why, when at seven P.M. my doorbell rang, all four of my limbs jumped out in opposite directions, like trying to find a handhold or toehold in free fall, and I shouted something like "MrrARGH!" sending Bandit clear to the top of the fridge, and didn't for a few *long* seconds have the slightest goddamned idea where I was.

Like Martin O'Toole always said, "Always get ready to interview a body, laddie, like you were getting ready for a concert performance."

"Harry?" she said when I opened the door.

Pyramid Talent Agency, whatever else it was, was a professional outfit. She was dressed in what you come to think of as A-drawer hooker style. A big blond overstuffed fake-fur coat, and underneath it a modest and damn form-fitting black dress that underlined the Nestlé-Quik, warm hue of her skin. No cherry red miniskirts and half-moon earrings for Pyramid, man. And (no kidding) high heels that brought her almost up to my height, and I'm a short guy, as I think I told you.

And no smile. That's what got to me, because, of course, a seasoned pro always wears that hey-let's-be-best-buddies smile, just like airline attendants and used-car salesmen and other people 90 percent of whose trade depends on their being able to convince you that you are the most important person in the world to them. Presidents, too, I guess.

She hadn't gotten to that phase yet, no matter how much she'd been coached by her handlers. She was a kid, for crying out loud, sent to meet a man she knew jack shit about, especially about what his idea of a good time might be, and she was scared. I checked her pupils: small enough that she'd taken, or been given, something before they sent her out for her night's work, but she still wasn't enough of a user that it could completely cancel out the deep-shit fear she had about whatever was going to come down this time around the track.

I wondered what had been done to her on earlier dates— that's what they're called, "dates." And I wanted, Christ, I don't know, to buy her a Chicago Cubs sweatshirt and some tennis shoes and take her to an amusement park. And I wanted to go back into the righteous nod she'd woken me out of.

"Summer?" I said. "Come on in."

$\triangledown$

25

THE NEXT DAY—WASN'T Thanksgiving coming up soon? I wondered as I drove to the office, or maybe I had missed it already—I found out that Steven Lee was dead.

I walked into the office at eight in the morning, and there, waiting for me, were Bridget and a guy I'd never seen before, but who had "cop" written all over his face. Maybe (no kidding) six and a half feet, with a face like five miles of bad road and a nose like a Polish sausage, in a corduroy jacket and a checkered shirt with a black tie that came halfway to his belt and that kind of stare (you see it in cops sometimes) where you figure, if a toad pokes its head around the corner twenty feet away from them, they'll notice it.

"Harry, this is Lieutenant Wingate of the South Bend Police Department," Bridget said as I walked into the reception room. Lieutenant Wingate smothered my hand in his and in a voice like a thick steak suggested that we go to Bridget's office to talk.

I'll spare you the dialog, which (Wingate was one of those cops who took quite a long time to get round the barn) went on much longer than it needed to. The evening before, the little old bird-lady, Clara—remember Clara? turns out she wasn't only Steven's receptionist but also his housekeeper and, as a matter of fact, his mother—anyway, Clara had come up to Steven's room in the Sethian Center at about nine o'clock, as she always did, to see if he would like his brandy toddy nightcap and a little chat before she turned in and he started out on his nightly reading and writing. But, just like in the movies, this night there was no answer when she knocked on the door. And, just like in the movies, she knew that he hadn't gone out that night, so she tried the door, found it locked, and when she let herself in found Steven on his bed, in his Roman collar, with an empty bottle of codeine tablets on the nightstand and a plastic bag over his head, neatly and firmly tied just around the Roman collar. The paramedics got there right in time to watch him flatline.

"Was there a note?" asked Bridget, very softly.

"No, ma'am," said Wingate, flexing his hands. He was one of those guys with hands the size of New York strip cuts, who seem constantly flexing or bending or cracking their knuckles. "But the reason I called you so late last night, we were trying to find out from his mom" (that's what he said, "mom") "if he'd been depressed lately or anything—you know, the usual stuff you ask—and she mentioned that Father Lee had been talking about seeing you folks on some business. Wouldn't tell his mom what it was, but she sort of sensed—you know how moms are—he had some kind of burr up his—some kind of bee in his bonnet, and it appears he set great store by you people. So, I'm just wondering, well . . ."

"Yes," said Bridget, "Father Lee was a client of ours. But, Lieutenant, as sorry, as terribly sorry, as I am to hear this news, I'm sure you'll understand that we can't really, ethically, tell you the nature of his business with us."

He locked his fingers together in something that looked like one of those knots you could never get quite right in Cub Scouts. "Well, yes, ma'am," he said. "I sort of expected you to say that. It's just that"—and he took out a notebook, paged through it, and made a clicking sound when he found the page he wanted—"it's just that we noticed, checking over Father Lee's record book, that Mister Garnish here visited the Father's, unh, center last September. See, Father Lee made this little note next to the name, 'Garnish,' that said 'O'Toole Agency, Chicago.' " He looked at us. "Now, accord-

ing to what we've heard, that was considerably before he
came in to you folks as a client." He was quiet.

"I'm sorry, Lieutenant," said Bridget after two or three
beats. "I'm really not sure what we're talking about here.
You're not suggesting, surely, that Mister Garnish's visit to
the Sethian Center was somehow the cause of Father Lee's
later retention of our services, are you?"

"Well, ma'am—" he began.

"Because if you are," she went on, "then I have to tell you
that it sounds very like you're accusing us of either coercing
or even blackmailing Father Lee. And if that is the case, then
I think you had better make your inquiry a formal one, because as I'm sure you know, we have certain legal recourse
to take in the event of allegations like that."

"Now, just a minute—" he began again.

"No, look," I said, and Bridget tried to glare me into silence but for once it didn't work. "Let's not all get pregnant
here, okay? Lieutenant, I went to Steven Lee's shindig because I was on a case, and it had nothing to do with Steven's
people, just the person I was supposed to be checking on."

Yeah, it was a lie. Sue me.

"And," I went on, "Steven's people or Steven was smart
enough to twig that I was a P.I., and Steven braced me with
that before I got to his meeting. Now you gotta trust me on
this, but we thrashed it out between the two of us, and he
agreed to let me come to the meeting anyhow. Hell, I really
liked that guy. And when he came to us, just a few days ago,
it was I guess because he liked me, too, and figured he could
trust us on his business, which, don't worry, I'm not going
to tell you. All street legal, if you get my drift. Like, you got
car trouble and one of your friends happens to be a mechanic,
who you going to call?"

He gave me a cop stare. If you've ever gotten one of those,
I don't have to describe it to you. If you've never gotten one,
I can't.

"Does that listen?" I said.

And he tried not to smile. Using the cop's favorite phrase

for how you tell bullshit from nonbullshit—it either listens or it doesn't—I'd let him know that I knew the rules of the game we were playing and also, I hoped, that I was playing it straight.

"We'll see," he said finally, and fished a pipe the size of a small fishbowl out of his jacket and lit it. Meerschaum. I was getting to like him.

"That'll do for now," he said. "I hope you folks won't mind if I maybe get in touch with you again. Nothing formal, ma'am"—with a smile at Bridget—"just in case we need any other help." And he rose to leave.

"If I could have one more moment, Lieutenant?" said Bridget, and I knew she was going to ask him what I wanted to ask him.

"You say that Father Lee's death is being treated as a suicide," she said. "And you've driven ninety miles this morning to speak with us, and you've obviously checked Father Lee's records fairly exhaustively since the body was discovered. Now we've been candid with you"—that with a short and, I think the word is, *telling* glance at me—"so, as far as your official duties will allow, could we ask for some candor, too?"

"Ma'am?" Wingate said in an aw-shucks voice that meant he knew exactly where this was going.

"Lieutenant," Bridget sighed. "Do you think it was a suicide? Or is there something else about all this that's—forgive me, sir—obsessing you?"

He made that suck-pop-suck noise on his pipe that experienced pipe smokers seem to find so comforting.

"All right," he said. "I'll tell you this, because you've got a good report, Miss O'Toole, and because you, Mister Garnish, have a reputation for being smart enough to keep on the right side of things. Most of the time."

Damned if I'd known we had reputations at all, especially in, for crying out loud, South Bend. Old farmer Wingate, it appeared, might not be old farmer Wingate at all.

"Sure, it was suicide," he went on, staring into the bowl

of his pipe the way Martin O'Toole used to do right before
he trumped your ace. "Don't see how it could've been anything else. Heck, there's even this book out now, tells people
how to kill themselves if they want to, and Father Lee followed that guy's instructions right down the path. Naah, he
killed himself, all right."

And he stopped a minute. Stared into his pipe like there
was some message down there, tamped it, and relit it.

"But, you see," he went on, "a lot of people really liked—
well, tell you the truth, loved—Father Lee. Oh, I don't know
anything about this, what do they call it, this Sethian stuff.
I'm a Methodist, anyway, so—no offense, ma'am, I know
you're a Catholic—all the high church business looks pretty
much the same to me, kind of like do you want mint jelly or
parsley on your lamb chop. But Father Lee. He was a really
good man, don't you know? My own daughter, my
Wendy . . ."

And sonofabitch if it didn't hit me then where I'd seen his
face before. Well, okay, not his face, but those eyes and that
peculiar cast of the lips, whatever the hell it is that marks a
personality, makes a shape you recognize as a person, or tells
you that one person is related to or is damned close to another person. I know it's not scientific, but if you've ever met
the father or the mother of your best friend and instantly
seen the resemblance between the two in just the way they
dance with their faces, you know what I'm talking about.

It was the girl. The girl back at the Sethian meeting, back
in September, back before I wound up spending the night
playing four-handed grabass with Lisa (check that, Andrea)
and before all the shit, whatever shit we were in, came
down. The girl who was skinny as dental floss and was still
blind-shit scared that she was going to be fat and whom
Steven Lee had hugged and whispered to and finally made
her give a teary smile to the rest of us and let us know she
felt a little better than when she'd walked into the room.
Looking at Wingate's bulk and seeing those same tricks with

the eyes and the mouth and all those other little muscles in the face that you can't name but that're clearer than telegrams, I understood why this wasn't really a cop thing for him and why he cared about what had caused Steven Lee to buy the farm for himself. And (you might think this is funny) I realized that I cared the same way.

"My Wendy," Wingate went on, "she had some . . . some trouble a little while ago. Nothing real serious, you understand."

Right, I figured: living on bottled water and Ritz crackers and purging, probably, with Ipecac is just one of life's little annoyances.

"But," he continued, "she saw some people about her problem, and she started seeing Father Lee, too. And to this day she's convinced that Father Lee really saved her life."

I don't think I've ever seen a man that big look that uncomfortable.

"I understand," said Bridget after a while. "Lieutenant, if there's anything we can reasonably do to be of any help to you, we'll certainly try. Does your daughter know that Father Lee is dead yet?"

Good old Bridget. She can find a vein even when she's not looking for one. I saw Wingate wince.

"Well," he said, "I guess it'll be in the morning papers."

"Then," she said, "maybe it would be a good idea to go home to her and comfort her. Would you like to call her from our office?"

He said thank you, ma'am, no, stuffed his pipe (I hoped it wasn't still lit) back in his jacket, told us he'd keep in touch, and left.

And Bridget and I stared at one another.

" 'May you live in interesting times,' " I said finally.

She smiled sadly. "I know, Harry. Father's 'ancient Chinese curse.' Poor Father Lee."

"Poor Nancy Browder," I said. "Poor Billy Donner. Great weather for suicides these days, ain't it?"

She looked at me oddly.

"You've found out something, haven't you?" she said.

"Maybe," I said, lighting a cigarette—my first of the day, I noticed. "Maybe not. So Wingate called you last night? Why didn't you call me?"

"You're avoiding my question," she said. "But if you must know, I didn't call you because it was very late."

"Not good enough," I said.

"And because," she went on as if I hadn't spoken, "I was hoping, quite frankly, that I'd be able to talk to the lieutenant by myself this morning."

"Well, dammit, that's nice," I said, stubbing out one cigarette and lighting another. "Maybe you'd like to tell me if I still work here, while you're being so fucking candid?"

"You know how I hate that word," she said.

"Okay," I said, "so fucking *frank*. That better?"

Heavy sigh. "Harry," she said. "When do you ever come in to the office this early? In the last year or so, only twice. The first time was yesterday, and I don't know what you really did yesterday, but it was pretty obvious that it was, as you say, 'heavy.' The second was today, after you found out whatever it was you were going to find out yesterday. Now, be honest with me, Harry, how am I supposed not to think that you're doing something, planning something, that you really don't want me to know about? Have you found something about the Sethians? It's too late to help Father Lee, but if you know something, I think we owe it to him, don't you?"

I took a last drag, lit another, and stared at Phil for a moment. Three cigarettes in the morning on an empty stomach will, I don't know if you know this, get you damn near stoned. I looked at Phil and he looked at me and, with his good old vegetable telepathy, told me to go for the goal. I did.

"Okay," I said. "I'll tell you what I found out about the Sethians and about the Haitian Project and every other damn thing you want to know."

"Well, thank you," she said.

"*Sei gesund*," I said. "But first you tell me where Janie is."

She picked up her coffee mug—nobody had had any coffee yet that morning—and communed for a minute with the teddy bears around its rim.

"All right," she said. "It may be the right time, anyway. Janie is staying with me, Harry."

$\triangledown$

26

I WASN'T SURPRISED, REALLY, but I *was* surprised. Kind of like when you're pretty sure you're overdrawn but then the afternoon mail comes with your overdraft notice anyhow, yes?

"Do tell," I said. "No shit," I added.

"No kidding," she said, and coming from Bridget, that was almost like a nudge in the ribs on a bar stool. "Nobody wanted to deceive you, Harry, but Janie had nowhere to go. I mean, she didn't want to go back to . . . unh . . ."

"Wanda," I said.

"Well, yes, if that's what you want to call it," she said. Bridget knew the phrase The Life, but she was damned if she was going to say it.

"So, now the cat's out of the bag, you think maybe I could talk to her?" I said.

"Harry," she sighed. "Do you know what Father used to say? 'In every marriage,' he used to say—"

" 'One grows stronger and one grows weaker,' " I finished for her, " 'and the one who grows weaker is the one who loves more.' Yeah, Bridget, that was Martin's basic training lecture for handling divorce cases. I've heard it. I'm a little surprised he told that to you, you being a nun and all, but—"

Something in her expression stopped me. I don't know, a little crookedness I hadn't seen before in her smile as she looked at her teddy bears, maybe—it could have been—a slight, a very slight shaking of her head, like she was remembering something that I'd never really get to know about. What the hell: I'd never thought about Bridget that way. So this was my season for revelations.

"What I mean . . . ," I said, trying to shift gears.

"I know what you mean, Harry," she said, in her softest voice. "Let's let it go, all right? The point is I don't think you should talk to Janie, at least not yet. And I know that you're a good man. So I know that, even now that you know where she's staying, you won't disturb her."

I hate it, no seriously, I hate it when people tell you what a good person you are. It's like—what? Well, once I was going out with this waitress. Nice lady. Face and a smile like a harvest moon on a balmy night, right? So the night of the big score I take her to the Jazz Showcase—it was in the old, now defunct Holiday Inn on Lake Shore back then—to hear Phil Woods, who is to the alto sax what Colonel Sanders is to fried chicken, the guy can't miss, and between the jazz and the Rob Roys and my dazzling repartee I figure I can't miss, so I drive her back to her apartment and at the door she, just a tiny bit more snockered than me, which was my plan, heh heh, smiles at me and says, "Oh, thanks, Harry. You're such a *nice* guy." So I goddammit give her a big hug and a big kiss and shuffle back to my car, which is in a no parking zone and I've already been ticketed and drive back home planning to kick Bandit, which I didn't have the heart to do either. And that's what it's like, being told what a good person you are.

"You see," Bridget went on, "I don't really know which one of you is the weaker in this situation, because I can't really tell which of you loves more. All right, you may think me silly. In fact, I know you often do think me silly. But really, Harry, you and Janie are so good together. Why can't you stop hating—I mean, hurting—yourself just because you were, let's say foolish, for one stupid evening? When you hurt yourself that way, you hurt Janie, too, you know."

I lit my fourth cigarette and broke through to that early-morning, empty-belly clarity that hits you sometimes like a fire alarm in a movie house.

"Right," I said. "You know as well as I do that you meant 'hating,' not 'hurting,' and I'll even—what do the lawyers call it?—I'll even stipulate that. And I'm not going to bother you or Janie till one of you tells me it's okay, okay? Hell, you wanted to, you could fire my ass and Janie could get a court order, something. And, like the man said, what's this got to do with the price of eggs on the moon?"

"I beg your pardon?" she said.

"I think maybe you ought to," I said. "You're right about my coming in early, Sherlock. And the reason is that I found out something last night that, I know you hate the word, scares the shit out of me. Steven Lee wasn't just right about the Sethians running an elaborate stable of illegal-alien hookers, he was righter than he thought."

"Meaning?" she said.

"Meaning that these guys are not only running the stable, but they're keeping as close tabs on the girls as the baddest pimp on Blackstone Avenue. These kids are scared, Bridget. I had a date with one of them last night."

"What?" she said.

"Oh, come on," I said, "I dropped three hundred dollars for two hours of conversation, which, by the way, I expect to take out of our slush fund, if we still have one, and when I asked her about Haiti and mentioned the Sethians, she freaked more than if I'd trotted out the handcuffs and the riding crop."

"Harry—" she began.

"Sorry about that. Anyway, I promised her an extra yard— the going rate is only two hundred—and let her believe that I was working with the cops on this—remember that Precinct Pass I wheedled out of downtown a few years ago?—so I had her almost, that's *almost*, as spooked by me as by her runners. She doesn't, natch, know a damned thing about the way the thing is organized or about *The Path of the Chosen* or any of the metaphysical fruit salad. What she does know is that around Port-au-Prince, that's her hometown, it's pretty general skinny that if you want to get out of the shit down there, maybe make some bread to send back to the family from stateside, and if you're a young girl—or a young boy, Bridge—with all four limbs and decent teeth,

there's an address you can go to, and, when your name gets
to the top of the list, you close your eyes and wake up in
Chicago or, for all I know, San Francisco or London, making
a pretty good buck by lying down on the job."

"And do you mean to tell me," she said, "that you sent
the girl back to that—"

"It's called a talent agency," I said. "No choice. She was
terrified when I told her she could stay with me, and when
I realized that her runners had my name and address I sort
of had to agree with her. But you're missing what they call
in Washington the big picture, Bridget."

"I don't think I am," she said. "Just short hours after
Steven Lee comes to see us, agonized over what he thinks is
a betrayal of everything he's been working for, he's found
dead. You're thinking that you'd like to see a record of his
phone calls for the last forty-eight hours, aren't you, Harry?"

When she does a slap-shot like that, even I feel like standing up and cheering.

"Yes," I said. "You know more about this vocation stuff
than I do, but when he was in here talking about maybe
giving up the priesthood, it hit me that—"

"That for a man like Steven Lee to give up the priesthood"—when she said it you could hear the capital "P"—
"would be very like giving up his life. Yes. I know how that
must feel. "

"Yeah," I said. "I don't know how the hell you go about
proving something like this. Damn, it sounds like one of
those JFK assassination conspiracy theories, doesn't it? But
you had to see how really scared Abadessa—that's the kid's
name—was last night. She figures these cats, like, even know
when she goes to the john. And I've got reasons to think she
wasn't just panicking here. The guy who put me on to her—
never mind his name—is a guy who knows a *lot* of guys, and
he doesn't want me to ask him any more about this scene.
You want to know what I think, I think Steven stirred up
the stew enough, somebody from way high in the Sethians
gave him a call, told him a thing or two—what the hell,

maybe mentioned some bad stuff, it could happen to his
gray-haired old momma, and Steven pulls the plug because
he figures his life is a waste anyhow. We are dealing with
some very heavy hitters here, if I'm not just round the bend."

"Thank you for not mentioning any of this to Lieutenant
Wingate," she said. "An interview with an illegal-alien pros-
titute, a conversation with an anonymous friend whom you
claim to be highly informed about the underworld, and the
suicide of a priest. Do you realize how wild all of this sounds,
Harry? Do you realize that you're accusing a religious organization—an organization that has ties, however tenuous,
with the Catholic Church—of trafficking in human flesh?"

I smiled. "Yeah," I said, "and I know that tone of voice,
boss. You just about more than half believe me already, and
you're waiting for me to take you the rest of the way around
the track."

"Well," she harumphed at her empty coffee mug. Really:
she can harumph.

"Just ask your house guest," I said, maybe a little more
bitterly than I wanted. "It's a gold mine, if you run it right.
And the payoffs—if you have payoffs, and a classy enough
organization can even get around those—are tiny compared
to the taxes you *aren't* paying. And assume that the Sethians
really *are* doing all kinds of good work all around the world:
I mean, I can't believe Steven was that much of a patsy. This
is one sure-fire way to pay for a lot of good works, especially
since, as Dom Pardo likes saying—"

"I know," she said. " 'To the elect, all things are permitted.'
It's one of the things I could wish Saint Paul had never written. The Manichaeans, the Cathars, the Brethren of the Free
Spirit—do you know, Harry, how many radical sects have
used that as a basis for the most outrageous self-deceit?"

"Not really." I yawned. "But I know you can't play bridge
if you get to change trump every trick. Is that what you call
theological?"

"Very," she smiled. "So, assuming that you're right, what
do you think we should do?"

"Bail," I said. "I know you don't like it when I tell you this, but Batman and Robin we ain't. We're a business and much as you dig being the masked avenger and such, if—*if*—these guys are the *pezzi novanti* I think, then a mom-and-pop grocery like ours is just not going to jerk their chain."

I saw that look—*that* look—come into her eyes. "Steven Lee is dead," she said, "and you want to walk away."

"Hey," I said. "Life in the big city. It works that way sometimes, Bridget. If Martin was here, he'd tell you the same thing: it's how you keep your kneecaps, minor stuff like that."

"So Barry Browder was right all along," she said.

"Barry Browder was right all along," I said, "and look where being right got him. The poor bastard. I don't like him, but Jesus, finding out his wife's been fidutzing around with one of his students. I'll tell you, kid, this whole business has been bad karma from the get-go, and my take is, we crawl under a bush, lick the scars clean, and wait for the rain to let up."

She stared at me. For a long time. Long enough that I got the antsies, reached into my pocket for another cigarette, and realized I was fresh out. Bad omen.

"I'm afraid we can't, Harry," she said at last.

"Oh, come on," I said, "you want to mount your big white horse and charge into the fray, is that it? I'm telling you, this is just too damn complicated a situation, Bridget. Listen to me for once, okay?"

"You don't understand," she said. "If I could take your advice, this time I would."

"Well?"

"Harry," she said, "I know how . . . difficult your life has been lately, and I didn't want to disturb you any more than you've already been disturbed. But I have another reason for believing you're right about the Sethians. Here." And she reached into her top drawer and handed me two letters.

They were both dated three days ago. And together they meant that O'Toole Agency was about to be, like they say in the animal shelters, put down.

$\triangledown$

27

THE TOP LETTER WAS from the good folks who owned the building where our office was, and it said that starting in January our monthly rent was going up. As a matter of fact, it was going up to about two and a half times what we were currently paying. The second, on classy paper and a letterhead that said Nova Security Network and a New York address (Fifth Avenue, yet), was an offer to Bridget to buy out the business, the license, the whole gefilte fish, at a price that was about two and a half times what you would figure the agency could possibly be worth, if you were a little drunk when you were doing the figuring.

I wished I had a cigarette. "Ever get the feeling," I said finally, "that you're caught in something's teeth and it's picking at you?"

"Exactly," she said. "Look at the envelopes," and handed them to me.

I looked. "So?" I said.

She sighed. "The letter from the landlord is postmarked from Chicago the day before it was delivered," she said. "The one from New York is postmarked three days before it was delivered. And both letters arrived on the same day, *dated* on the same day."

"Beautiful," I said. "They want us to know. Draw one card, then double your bet, scare everybody else the hell off the table. And it usually works, too. What are you going to do?"

"What am *I* going to do?" she laughed. "Are you dissolving the partnership, Harry? Or have you forgotten that this is

Father's agency, and have you forgotten how much trust and love Father invested in you? What am *I* going to do?" And— shocked the hell out of me—she slammed her mug on the desk and turned to look at her plants, shaking her head.

And damn. I'd never seen Bridget O'Toole frightened before. It struck me that I'd never *thought* of Bridget being frightened before, and at the same time it struck me that maybe, because of that, I'd never really thought of Bridget being all the way human before. I don't know if that makes any sense to you, but it did to me, and before I knew what I was doing I had reached across the desk and taken one of her pudgy hands in both of mine. I could feel the jolt go through her.

"Okay," I said. "You want to tough it out, I'll try to keep up with you. Can we make the rent on the plant for January?"

"For January and February," she said in a voice that was strained and oddly soft at the same time. "I have just about that much in savings. After that . . ."

"Don't worry," I said, "after that if we haven't beaten these bastards, you'll be back in the convent and I'll probably be hitting you up for a gig as janitor there." That got a smile, and I'll tell you, it felt really *nice.*

"And you think we can beat them?" she said.

"Honestly? No," I said. "Bridget, I've never fought any of the really big guys in my life. And a half hour ago I was ready to cut bait, let the last three months wear off like a bad hangover. Now, if you want to try to save the homestead, I'm with you. I love old Martin, too, you know? But I have to tell you. The only way I know to bring it round is going to be to talk to some guys I know; these guys are into some stuff, you would not like to know what it is. Understand?"

"Harry—" she began.

"Nope, not yet," I said. "And besides the stuff they're into, these guys are also not the ASPCA. I mean, they do you a favor, they find out things you want to know, and, Bridget, *they will get the favor back.* I want that clear, right at the top of the deal."

She gave one of those smiles that you know it's not a happy smile. "You make it all sound very . . . Faustian."

"Screw Faustian," I said. "I'm not even sure I can get my friends to come along here, but if they do, I'm giving out some very large markers, and that means you are, too. And once I ask—that's just ask—we're already in. Look, you're Martin's daughter. You know exactly what I'm talking about. So do I make some calls?"

She looked at the teddy bears, but they weren't being much help. And, tell you the truth, I was half hoping they'd advise her to drop the deal. I don't know. Did you ever make a commitment—I mean, a commitment you knew you were going to pay some dues for—almost before you knew you'd made the damn thing? And then hope that somebody in the recording booth would call for a retake?

No such luck. "All right," she said. "Make your calls."

"Dig," I said. "Cheer up, Bridget. They can kill us, but they can't eat us. That's against the law."

Which is how come, two hours later, I was sitting in the cocktail lounge of the Ritz-Carlton at Water Tower Place, sucking alternately on a Beck's and a Lucky Strike (emergency therapy for nicotine withdrawal), staring out the big window at the wet snow shlumping all over Michigan Avenue and waiting (you got it) for the Priest.

$\triangledown$

28

AT THE VERY TOP OF Michigan Avenue, Water Tower Place, which they only finished around the midseventies, is to Chicago what his last quartets are to Beethoven: a summary of what the whole thing's been about, you know? Like Marshal Field's, it's one big shopping mall, but stood on its end, vertical, not horizontal, and it's right across from the old Water Tower, one of the few buildings that survived the Great Fire of 1871. And what it does, after the Great Fire and the Capone days and depressions and wars and even after Reagan and Bush turned the idea of America into damn near a joke, what it does is it rears up on its hind legs and stares around the horizon and says, at least to me, "I'm still Chicago. Fuck you."

I like going to Water Tower Place.

Even today, even to meet the Priest.

The Ritz-Carlton is one of the latest ornaments on the Christmas tree that's Water Tower Place, and the cocktail lounge on the twelfth floor is like the set of an Astaire-Rogers big number, all chrome and glass and plush, and that's okay with me, too. At that hour (eleven) nobody was playing the piano in the center of the lounge, but they were piping in some pretty classy Muzak, sounded like "Mister Tamborine Man" played by the hundred and one flutes or something, and I was just about set to order a second Beck's at the bar when a big hand clasped around the back of my neck, sort of friendly-like, sort of not, and a voice just behind and above my right ear rasped to the bartender, "Two Johnnie Walker

Black rocks, Mustapha. Water side." The bartender, of
course, was an Indian or Pakistani guy.

"Priest," I said, half turning round.

"Weasel," he said, taking a Lucky out of my pack on the
bar and lighting it. "I told you on the phone, I tell you now.
Kelley's supposed to tell you I didn't want to mess with this
anymore. He told you that?"

"He told me that," I said. Certain dealings with certain
guys, they take on this ritual feeling.

"Good," he said. "I'd hate to think Ray was slipping, you
know? So he told you."

"Priest," I said, "he for Christ's sake told me."

"So," he said, laughing, not what they call an "infectious"
laugh, "what the fuck am I doing here? I mean, I *tell* you I
don't want to see you, you get the message, then you call me,
for Chrissake, so here we are, sitting here having our nice
morning jolt, and what the fuck is going on here, Harry?"

Time to trump the ace. "That's what I want to find out,
Jimmy," I said. "Why *are* you here? You're the *Priest*, Chrissake. You need guys like me the way Godzilla needs lice,
right? So I call you, I tell you we got to talk, you piss and
moan over the phone and then you show up here, just like
a goddamn Boy Scout. So am I missing something here,
Jimmy, or did I maybe push one of your buttons, there?"

The Johnnie Walkers had arrived. He drank his—one
toss—and then he drank mine—one toss—and sucked down
a tall glass of ice water. Jimmy Maher never had much sense
of mine or thine; that's part of why he is the Priest. And
stared at me.

"Okay, Harry," he said after the last neural kick of the
booze tapered out, and don't tell me you don't know what
that feels like. "Are we doing *Geschaeft*, or what?"

That's a very serious word, that *Geschaeft*. In German,
or in Yiddish, whatever, it just means "business," right?
Wrong. With the guys who know what the hell is going on—
the guys with hair, at least that's what we call them this
year—the guys who finally and really decide which precinct

gets new street lights or which building contractor gets left alone and which one gets sent South, or who gets to be mayor next time around, with these guys *Geschaeft* means something like "the business of business," the kind of dealing, I mean, they don't let you, after you won your thirty or fifty or a hundred bucks at a simple-dick game of seven-card stud, walk away from the table with an out-of-towner grin on your face and catch your cab back to the Holiday Inn, got it?

Geschaeft is, like, *later*. And in all my years in Chicago, that was the first time a real player used the word with me. It scared me, because among the guys who counted, this was as good as a contract. What had Bridget called it? Right: Faustian.

"Yeah," I said to the Priest. "This is, you want to deal with it, *Geschaeft.*"

Maybe it was the two Scotches or maybe it was my acquiescence (like that word?), but Jimmy Maher's face softened and he gestured for us to move to one of the tables away from the bar, and away from the good overdressed folks who were parading, variously, into the lounge at the prelunch hour.

We sat down at a little table far away from the piano. "So," he said. "Tell."

So I told. Not the partial bullshit version of things I'd told Bridget, or Janie or maybe even (it hit me while I was telling the tale) myself: I told him the whole story the way I've just told it to you. Full confession to the Priest, yeah? Well, not exactly. More like, you want the man to get you out of the shit you're in, you'd best tell where all the shit *is*.

When I had finished, he was quiet for a minute or two. Signaled the bartender for another shot. And when he spoke, his voice was very soft.

"Good story, Harry," he said. "How do you want to write the ending?"

The waiter put down his Scotch, and before he picked it up I tossed it off. It was okay: I was in the loop now.

"How I want it to end," I said, "is these schmutzes trying to foreclose on the agency somehow get their tits caught in

the wringer, back off, and leave us the hell alone. This can
be done?"

"You know what you're worth, Harry?" he said.

"Come again?"

"What you're worth," he said, holding up two fingers for
two more Johnnie Walkers. "What O'Toole Agency is worth.
You want to see your net assets from the last fiscal year?"
And he reached into his jacket pocket and, swear to God,
took out three folded sheets of copy paper.

"What the hell—" I began.

"Harry, don't go doofus on me," the Priest said. "You
know how I make my nut. I make it by *knowing* stuff. And
the more stuff you know, little brother, the more stuff you
can find out. Information, Harry. Jesus. No offense, but you
cock around with adulteries, drugs, whores, insurance
scams, that shit, and you think it's the fuckin' real world,
right? Wrong, my man. These are the fuckin' nineties.
What's real is what you know, and what you can pass on to
the folks who want to know what you know, and you do that
so they'll tell you what they know. It's—what did Brother
Brian call it, back in algebra?—yeah, it's exponential. It's
Trivial Pursuit, baby—you move around the board by knowing shit. Shit like"—and he unfolded the stats—"that as of
your last tax return you and old O'Toole are worth, you factor
in the property, the equipment, everything, aah"—and he
ran his finger to the bottom of page three—"about seventy,
eighty K." He looked at me. "Harry," he said, "that wouldn't
pay my entertainment expenses for the year."

"So," I said, "it can't be done."

"I didn't say that. You want to do *Geschaeft*, we're doing
Geschaeft. I'm explaining to you, pumpkin, why I'm going
to help you out here."

"Don't tell me," I said. "Information."

"Bingo," he said. "You're that fuckin' smart, what you
doing working for the fat old lady? Matter of fact, I help you
turn this thing around, Harry, you won't be working for her—
not altogether, anyway. You understand that, don't you?"

I'd understood it when I made the call. I told you, the Priest isn't really into anything on the messy side of the sheets. But, like he'd said, it's his business to know stuff. So, when I'd sat down in the Ritz-Carlton bar, I'd know that, if the agency kept afloat, the agency would never be the same. Because, if it kept afloat, then one day, and probably sooner than later, Jimmy would get in touch with me, that's not Bridget but me, and there'd be this little thing, maybe about an alderman, maybe about a lawyer, maybe just delivering a message to a certain guy, that he'd like me to take care of. And I'd do it, because things work that way. And Bridget, for everything I'd told her before I called the Priest, would never know what was going down, because for her it would mean the agency had been—what's the word she would use? yeah, "compromised."

That was the deal. "Got it," I said, and the deal was closed.

And goddammit if it didn't hit me: The debt I'd incurred by asking the Priest for the first favor—getting Abadessa Macquot's number—was just this, I mean, asking him for the second favor. I don't know. It was like, when I'd screwed Lisa/Andrea in South Bend, I was already, in some way, kicking Janie out of the apartment. Or like, when Barry Browder came in to ask us to check up on his wife, somehow—I'm just saying *somehow*, dig—Nancy Browder was already on her way to irreversible coma in that damn motel room, and Steven Lee was on his way to the big eighty-six.

There was this thing in the *Tribune,* one of those Sunday-magazine-science-for-idiots pieces they run every month or so, on something called "Chaos Theory." As far as I could tell, the geniuses who put this thing together had decided that—surprise, surprise—the real world was actually as screwed up as most of us had already thought it was. The example I remember from the piece was that a butterfly fluttering its wings in China could, eventually, cause a hurricane off the coast of California. Like I said: Everything is as screwed up as we thought it was all along. The idea, especially as it applied to me and my recent adventures in the flesh wars, made me a little dizzy, but it seemed a helluva lot closer to the facts than Pedro Pardo's jive "to the elect all things are permitted."

But what do I know? I'm not a philosopher. At the moment I was a P.I. selling out his boss and his agency to save the agency and to save his boss's pretty big, psychological ass. Bridget wouldn't have to know: The world I live in, that's already a good cut of the cards.

So Jimmy slapped me on the back and told me not to worry, this shit would all get itself worked out, this kind of shit always did, and that I could go back to whatever I'd been doing, he'd call when he had something. And left. We could have just been laying down a bet on the next Bulls game.

The problem is, I *did* worry. I looked at the empty Scotch glasses and I worried, maybe too much. Maybe that's why everything turned out as bad as it did.

$\triangledown$

29

BRIDGET WOULDN'T HAVE TO KNOW. But I'd know, and now that I'd dumped all my problems in the Priest's lap, I got, not relief, but that nagging feeling that maybe there was something I could have done that I hadn't, because I was either too dumb or too lazy to do it. What the hell. Guilt is more like a cold sore than anything else, am I right? You just can't leave it alone.

So I went back to the office, sat and smoked and finished off the last Heineken in my desk and stared at the walls. I've got one picture in my office, the famous photo of John Coltrane sitting in a wicker chair, his head bent over, staring at his soprano saxophone. Now that's the kind of meditation I can believe in. I asked Trane what I should do (yeah, I do that sometimes), and, as usual, he didn't have anything to tell me.

But (and this happens sometimes, too) as I was asking Trane what to do, I got a little clearer in my own mind about how to start, at least, doing it.

I called the Northrop College switchboard, and after some hassling and to-and-froing with the lady on the other end of the line, got the home phone number of a Denise who roomed with a Heather. Heather answered.

"Hey," I said, "I don't know if you remember me, but I'm the guy—"

"I remember," she said. "You're the guy got Dennie drunk and sloppy. What do you want?"

"Well, this may sound pretty strange, but I'd like to talk to you guys again."

"Jesus! You've got to be kidding," she said.

"No," I said, "but I wish I was."

"Do you—"

"Believe me, I do. I'm a pain in the ass, right? And you and Denise would be real happy never to see my granite profile again, right? What do you kids call guys like me these days? Am I still a bummer?"

She didn't laugh, but she was forcing herself not to. My business, you learn to hear things like that.

"Look—" she began.

"Wait," I said. "All I want—Scout's honor—is about an hour's worth of your time. No more. And if you'll give it to me, I'll blow you guys to the best Greek lunch you can get on the North Shore. I'm in kind of a sticky patch here."

"Yeah," she said, "that's what you said last time we talked to you, and Dennie was screwed up for two days afterward."

"So talk to her when she gets home and call me, okay? She's not screwed up anymore and I still am, if that means anything. Just let me know, anytime after seven tonight, if you'll do it. I don't hear from you, that means no, and that's cool."

"So why?" she said.

"What can I tell you?" I said. "If I told you I was still bothered about Thor's death would you believe me?"

She was quiet for a minute. "You're a bastard, aren't you?" she said at last. "No, I don't believe you. But one of us will probably call tonight. Is that all?"

That was enough. I gave her my apartment number, hung up, and called Pyramid. The same, infinitely promising voice, answered. I wasn't sure it was the same person, but it's always the same voice.

"Hi," I said. "Listen. I know this is short notice, but could I maybe get a date with one of your escorts later this afternoon? Her name is Summer."

Pause. "Have you used our service before?"

"Yeah, just yesterday," I said. "Garnish, Harry." And I waited while the Muzak kicked in—it was an electronic-piano version of that great song, "Love for Sale," I kid you not—and the receptionist punched up my name and current credit status on the computer.

"Hi, Harry," she breathed when she came back on. "Sorry to keep you waiting. Summer would love to get together with you again, but she's going to be busy for most of the afternoon. Would you like to meet one of our other girls?"

And *that* was a problem. If Abadessa, aka Summer, had wound up being more scared by Pyramid, aka the Sethians, than she had by me, she would have told one of them what had happened on our "date," and my ass was already fried. On the other hand, if she hadn't blown the whistle on me, and was really busy for the afternoon, then everything was still manageable.

I looked at Trane again. And hey, he told me, they're taking over the ranch anyway, right? So how much more fried could your ass get?

"That's okay," I said. "Any chance of seeing her like, later?"

"One minute, Harry," she said, and the Muzak came back on right where it had left off.

Either they were deciding to send a collector to rearrange my posture, I figured, or, if they were really checking Summer's evening schedule, they had their girls working pretty damned hard.

"Harry?" she said. "Would six o'clock be okay for you?"

All right. I told her that would be just peachy, and we agreed on the price and on my place again as the launch pad.

I walked down the hall to Bridget's office.

"Harry," she said when I sat down. "How is . . . everything?"

I laughed and lit a cigarette. "Bridget," I said, "if I could give you a straight answer to that I'd die a happy man. I talked to my guy, he told me he'd cut us a little slack, so unless my guy, like, has a safe drop on his head in the next few days, I'd assume we're going to keep in business."

She stared at me. "Then why am I not relieved?" she said.

"Maybe it's because you're smart," I said. "Look. I've been

screwed up since the minute I walked in here and said hello to Barry Browder, okay? No contest. I don't know. Maybe, in some weird way—you ever hear about something called chaos theory? Oh, hell, of course *you* would have. Maybe, somehow, this is all my fault."

"All?" she said.

I shrugged. "Whatever 'all' breaks down to," I said. "Dammit, Bridget, I'm asking you if you want to *do* something, is all."

"Very articulate, Harry," she said, and then when she saw my face she said, "I'm sorry, dear. What is your plan?"

I had to laugh again. "Plan," I said, "is about as far from what I've got as—oh, hell, as luck is from fate. But I want you to come by my place tonight around five, five-thirty and talk to somebody with me. The girl I told you about. Abadessa Macquot."

"Why?" she said.

I couldn't think of a better question.

"Because I'm asking," I said.

"Good answer," she said. "I'll be there with you, Harry. In every way."

That was good. That left me with only one more phone call to make. I told Bridget I'd have the coffee on for her and went back to my office.

▽

30

AFTER THE PHONE CALL, the rest of the afternoon went by in that hazy state of expectation you slip into when you're waiting for something important to happen that you're not sure *will* happen: you know, Sunday afternoon in Wrigley Field at the bottom of the fourth inning and working on your second beer and waiting for the Cubs, for Chrissake, to *do* something: like that. Not pleasant and not un-.

So I got home around four, four-thirty and fed Bandit, who was as always miffed that I thought anything in the world was more crucial than his Tuna Bits, spooned out the coffee for Bridget but didn't start heating the water, got myself a beer, and flipped on the Gerry Mulligan Concert Band, from all those years ago, playing "More Than You Know." If there's something, besides sex, better than the way Gerry Mulligan wrote for a big band when he was at the top of his form, I'd like to know what it is because I think it ought to be outlawed. And that association, naturally, started me thinking about Janie— goddamn, I'd gone almost a whole day without thinking about Janie—so I turned Gerry off and put on the young Sarah Vaughan. Well, *that* was no help. And rummaged around my tapes till I found Glenn Gould doing the Goldberg Variations. Okay, like the Franciscans used to say, take a cold shower.

Variation number thirteen or fourteen was probably the one that put me away. Anyhow, when the buzzer buzzed at five-thirty on the dot, so I might have known it was Bridget, it took me a minute to remember where the hell I was and what the hell I was planning to do.

I made the coffee and we made small talk, really small talk, the kind you don't even want to hear, for about fifteen minutes that felt like a working day.

"So why am I really here, Harry?" Bridget asked on her second cup of coffee and my second beer. And I had my answer all prepared.

"As a witness. As somebody to sit here and hear what's going to go down and know that I'm finally off the hook for all this shit, okay? Somebody to say, even if I did wind up running to Jimmy Maher after things got hairy, I was still able to do something worth doing. Hell, I don't know. Look. There's something Abadessa said when she was here last night. It didn't register—maybe I was goofy, who knows? Didn't register till after I talked to the Priest and sold our butt down the river, and maybe it doesn't mean a goddamn thing anyway, but I want to take just one more roll of the dice before we cash out here. That's why."

And that's what I was going to say. I didn't get a chance to say it, though, because just as I stubbed out my cigarette and took a pull on my Beck's (this was going to be a special night) the buzzer buzzed again.

Abadessa. Summer.

She looked smaller—hell, I don't know, more scared—than she had last night. And she was dressed in the same outfit; I guess her handlers had to economize somewhere, and when she walked into the place it hit me—okay, it just hit me then, I'm dumb—that she'd come here, knowing who I was or who I said I was, like, the heat, and that she'd come anyway because she was too frightened to rat on me to her runners or now not to come back to me for another grilling.

And then she came all the way in and saw Bridget. You've got to realize. This kid was from Haiti. I mean, one of the Olympic class capitals of very ugly stuff that the grand old U.S. of A. always manages, somehow, to ignore, maybe because they've got no oil there. So figure. She's raised on the set of a horror film and now she's laying it down for nickels and dimes in the land of the free and the home of the brave and she thinks I'm a cop and she's got no choice but to come back here and she sees that now there's two of us. Third degree or threesome?

As I watched her eyes widen, all the energy I hoped I'd mustered for this thing went out of me. My chest felt hollow, you know?

"Hey," I said, and I didn't even have the guts to take her hand to reassure her. "It's okay. Nothing bad is going to happen here. This is my friend Bridget. Bridget, this is, uh, Summer."

And the kid nodded to Bridget and looked at me, and said, "That's okay, Harry. What would you like to do?"

And—okay, okay, I know I'm one foul-mouth sonofabitch and I know this is a corny thing to say anyhow, but when she said that, it damn near broke my fucking heart.

Bridget saved the moment. She got out of her chair and took Abadessa by both hands and sat her down on the sofa. "Summer," she said. "What a nice name. We only want to talk, dear, just as you and Harry did last night. Isn't that right, Harry? Gosh! Your hands are cold. Would you like some coffee? Is Summer actually your name?"

You (or, okay, I) have to hand it to Bridget. Her tone of voice, her choice of words, whatever it was, seemed to relax the kid more than anything I'd been able to do the night before. Abadessa even managed half a smile—that's half a real smile, not half a hooker's smile, if you know the difference—as she sat down and told Bridget, yes, she could use some coffee.

By the time I came back from the kitchen with her coffee, Abadessa was schmoozing with Bridget like they'd been to convent school together. Well, sort of.

"The Life—that's what we call it."

"I know, dear," Bridget said.

"Well, you know, really, it's not so bad. I mean, I'm a Catholic girl, and I know it's a sin and everything. But compared to the stables some of the girls talk about, they treat us pretty good. And, you know, in another two or three years, when I get enough money together . . ." and her voice trailed off.

Bridget looked at me and I looked at Bridget. Bullshit, we said to one another silently. Dig, it's *always* "another two or three years" for a lot of the kids who wind up in The Life. Problem is, by the time those two or three years go by, you're either in hock up to your navel to the company store—and the company store deals in the kind of shit, they don't sell it to you, they sell you to it—or you're burned out enough, and "burned" isn't exactly the right word, you really don't give a damn no more, no how.

"Well, Summer—" Bridget began.

"Call me Abadessa," Abadessa said.

"Even prettier than Summer." Bridget smiled. "And someday soon, perhaps we can have a long talk about all of this. But now I think Harry has something specific he wanted us to cover. Isn't that right, Harry?"

I could see Abadessa go tense. Bridget had sounded just enough like a cop—good cop veering toward bad cop, in fact—that the kid was reminded where she really was, and also how vulnerable she really was just by showing up here.

Well played, Bridget, I thought. The kid's blind scared and we both hate it that she's blind scared, but you use that anyway. A few more years on the job, I thought, with a little regret, and you'll be just like the rest of us.

"Well, yeah," I said, wondering if I'd arranged everything just right or if this was going to be another, patented H. Garnish screw-up. "See, Abadessa, when I was asking you yesterday about your . . . uh . . ."

"We call them johns," she said. There wasn't a trace of irony in her voice and her eyes were as wide and uncomplicated as if she'd been reciting her catechism.

"Right," I said. "Now, you were telling me that some of your johns wanted . . . uh, well, this is sort of hard."

"Why?" Abadessa said. "Because Bridget's here tonight? It's okay, Harry. This is my business, I'm not ashamed. You wanted to ask about the name thing, didn't you?"

Empowerment. That's what they call it in the magazines

and such: you know, who's in control of the conversation, who's defining the terms you talk under, all that stuff. It's basically who's got the stick, which is the way we used to talk about it, and I still think that's as good a way as any. But any way you want to splice it, Abadessa was *empowered*—big goddamn deal, right? She could talk about the shit I was shy to talk about, and that meant that she was a lot more in control of the situation than I was. Bridget just watched the two of us, wondering what was going on.

And then what I'd hoped was going on went on. Before I could speak, the buzzer buzzed again and in walked Barry Browder and his daughter.

$\triangledown$

31

EVERYTHING I NEEDED TO find out I found out before anybody spoke.

Barry Browder froze as he came into the room. Just for an
instant, but he froze. You know the kind of freeze: Your worst
nightmare just came true and it's staring you in the face and
there's, for Chrissake, other people around? So your body
kicks in and floods your system with—what?—adrenaline
and endorphins, which is like a speedball: cocaine and her-
oin. It feels like your head's been chilled with Novocaine,
but at the same time like you're in absolute, almost mechan-
ical control of every muscle in your body. And it only takes
a second, so that you can say, coolly, as Browder did after
he'd seen Abadessa on the couch, "Mr. Garnish. Miss
O'Toole. And . . . ah . . . I'm afraid I haven't met the young
lady."

Abadessa was pretty good, too. After she and Browder
locked eyes, she just stared at her wrists, lying one over the
other. For all the kid knew, you see, this could just be an
added touch of kinkiness.

But I'd caught the instant of freeze-up, and though I
wasn't sure about everything it meant, I knew damn well
one thing it meant.

Andrea just looked stone-faced. And that I couldn't read.

"Yes, sir," I said. "Will you have a seat? Something to
drink? Okay. Thanks for coming. This lady is Abadessa
Macquot, and the reason I asked you over here is because
she's had . . . uh . . . connections with the Sethian people

and I thought you might want to know about this thing they call their Haitian Project. Abadessa's from Haiti."

Barry Browder was one smart guy. Probably a lot smarter than me, if you want to know the truth, and the kind of smart that in the right circumstances and under the right conditions you can *see* the intelligence dancing around behind the eyes, looking for a way out.

"And what exactly do you have for us?" he said. Andrea hadn't taken a seat. She was standing by the door staring at Abadessa, who was still discovering all kinds of interesting things about her wrists.

"Well," I said, and this was the hard part, because to tell you the truth all I'd been looking for was the look on Browder's face when he came into the room. "Well," I said, "I just thought it might interest you that Abadessa, here— Miss Macquot—was actually brought into this country illegally, and by the Sethians. She's . . . uh . . . gainfully employed here, and I'm sure you'll understand that everything she's told me is in confidence. But I wanted you to know that we're, you know, on the case. And I thought you might like to ask Miss Macquot a question or two."

He looked at me and I looked at him and we may as well have had an hour's worth of conversation.

"I have to say, Miss O'Toole," he said, turning to Bridget, "that this is a very strange way for a professional investigator to behave, and I thought you were a professional. Was it really necessary to drag me and my daughter all the way down here just to deliver this piece of noninformation? I'm surprised. Not to say disappointed."

"Professor Browder," said Bridget. "I can assure you that I have no more idea of the reason for this meeting than you do. But Mr. Garnish is my trusted associate, and I have full confidence in his professionalism."

Good for Bridget! She was going to back me up, even if she didn't know what the hell I was trying to do. I tried to catch her eye as she finished, but she wouldn't even give Barry Browder the satisfaction of letting him see her looking at me.

Goddammit, she *was* my friend: This whole thing was getting pretty trippy.

"Nevertheless," he said after a minute (was he weighing how much he thought *Bridget* knew? I wondered), "I think Andrea and I will be going. I hope you aren't planning to charge me for this visit."

That was a nice touch of bravado, I thought: "grace under pressure." Who said that? One of the writers Browder wrote about?

And then the phone rang.

"Just a minute, folks," I said, and picked it up. In the kitchen.

When I'd hung up and came back into the living room, with a fresh glass of Beck's, they were all sitting quietly, just like I'd left them—another "Twilight Zone" scene, right?

"Sorry," I said, sitting down and lighting a cigarette. "That was one of your former students, Professor Browder. Kid named Denise. You probably wouldn't remember her, you teach a lot of kids, I know." I was checking Andrea out of the corner of my eye, but she didn't stir. Was I enjoying this? Goddamn right I was enjoying this.

"I was hoping to talk with her," I went on, "but she says she's just not up to it. She was a friend of Thor—Billy Donner, you know?" Still not a twitch from Andrea or from the good professor.

"Anyway, she's got this friend, Heather, and I talked with them a little while ago about this . . . uh . . . problem with one of your colleagues, a guy named Middlebrook."

"Ernest," said Browder, sort of the way you'd spit.

"Right," I said. "Point is, this guy Middlebrook, he's got kind of a problem, aah, keeping his hands where they belong, right? I know you know all about that, being from the same college and all—"

"I'm not here to discuss college politics with you, Mr. Garnish, and I'm certainly not here to bandy gossip. As I said, we're leaving." And he rose to go.

"Okay, sorry," I said, rising with him. "The only thing is,

this Denise. Well, see, Middlebrook hit on her, too—bet you didn't know that. She told me that the first time we talked, and—"

"And I don't think we need hear any more of this, thank you," said Browder, heading for the door.

"But, Pyramid," I said. And he stopped and turned. And, that's right, Andrea still hadn't said a word.

"What?"

"Pyramid," I said again. "Dig it, I just wanted to ask Denise if she'd ever heard of an outfit called Pyramid Entertainment, Pyramid Escort, anything like that. That's where Abadessa here works, you see, she's a kind of a, well, paid companion for folks."

Abadessa stayed as still as Andrea.

"And since the Pyramid people are connected—how, you got me—with the Sethians, I just thought the association might be worth a shot. And dammit if she didn't tell me just now that when she was in his office, uh, you know, sort of fighting him off—if she didn't notice, on his desk, this like big folder—I don't know, brochure, advertising, catalog, whatever, with the word 'Pyramid' in big red letters across the top of it. I'm sorry, sir. I know you've got to go, and I apologize for dragging you down here for what you think is nothing important. I just wanted to let you know that there seems to be some kind of connection here. Promise: Next time I'll send you all the stuff I find out in a letter. Thanks for coming."

And they left. Without another word.

And nobody spoke after they left, either.

Until I said, "Anyone for tennis?" I am such a witty son-ofabitch.

"I think we've had enough obfuscation, Harry," Bridget said, "unless there's some reason you think playing more will make you feel better."

"Obfuscation," I said. "Nice word. Means lying, doesn't it? Okay. Sorry for all the melodrama, but I really didn't know any other way to find out what the hell it was I wanted to

find out. I hate to tell you this, Bridget, but you know that
phone call I told you I was going to make this morning? The
one that I told you would solve all our problems? Well, here's
the scene. I made the phone call. I put us in hock to this guy
I told you about. No, don't frown, I didn't sign anything or
promise anything. But I asked him for a favor and he agreed
to do me the favor, and, Bridget, I don't really have to tell
you, do I? The kind of guy I'm talking about, you ask him
for something, you're in hock, you want to keep working in
Chicago."

"Yes, Harry," she sighed. "We've been over this before."

"Well, yeah, we have," I said, and I lit a cigarette, because
this was the bad part. "Dig. The thing is, I don't think we
had to."

"*What?*" And, yeah, you could hear the italics in her voice.

"I screwed up," I said. "After I talked to the Pr—to this
guy I told you about, I remembered something Abadessa here
told me when we were talking last night. Don't ask me why
I didn't get it at the time. Maybe I was—what do they call
it?—maybe I was repressing or something. I don't know.
Abadessa, it's okay. You know what I'm talking about, don't
you?"

And Abadessa, for the first time in a long time, raised her
eyes from the carpet in front of her feet. I had to give it to
Pyramid; they were professionals. First thing you want to do,
you want to run a hooker, you make sure they feel beat. Saves
a lot of arguments about what is and what isn't allowed on
a date.

And Abadessa was about to speak when Bridget said,
"Not yet."

Come again?

"Dear," Bridget said to Abadessa. "I know that Harry has
told you that he's with the police. And I know that you think
you're here under official constraint. You're very frightened,
aren't you?"

"Well . . .," she began.

"All right," Bridget said. "Before you say anything else—

anything, dear—I think you should know that we're both just private detectives, and that you don't have to tell us anything if you don't want to."

And, aah, shit! I thought. I thought this was going to be one goddamn big discovery scene, and here comes Bridget, just like always, I should have known, fouling things up.

"Harry, I'm sorry," she said to me, "but I just can't continue anymore with all this . . . this tacky secrecy. And whatever Miss Macquot has to say, I think she should say of her own free will and not because she's being deceived by you or me or anyone else. Do you understand what I am telling you, dear? If you just want to go back home, we will make sure you're paid for your time and we will not bother you anymore. That's a very serious promise."

Bandit, just then, strolled through the living room. He looked about as pissed off as I was, but I realized it was because he hadn't gotten his eight o'clock dried herring. (It's a thing I do: alas.)

"I understand," Abadessa said. "You're a good lady. And I thank you for being a good lady." Her eyes—funny, but when I'd been talking to her the night before I hadn't noticed how, what the hell is the word, how *warm* her eyes were—her eyes, anyhow, were shining. Moisture? Trust? Beats me.

"And I think I ought to go," she went on. "I don't . . . I don't want to get in any trouble with my people, you know? They're . . . strict."

"That's fine, dear," Bridget said.

I didn't say anything.

"But," Abadessa went on, "I guess I'll stay anyhow. At least until you ask me to go. There's nothing I can tell you that Harry can't tell you if I leave, anyway. So maybe, if I stay while you hear it, you'll take care of me?"

And she looked at both of us. It wasn't a hooker's bargain. It was a scared and very smart kid's bargain. It was honest and it was a good deal.

"Dig," I said. "You got it. Now tell the nice lady what all this is about."

"Could I have a drink of water?" she said.

Killed me, right? I got her one.

"Thank you," she said when I gave her the glass. Just like I'd handed her a glass of, I don't know, lemonade, something, at a damn lawn party. You ever get that shiver? Like, I mean, when it hits you that damn near everybody, you cut close enough to the bone, is damn near everybody else?

Okay, forget it. I'm getting what Bridget calls metaphysical.

"Let's see," said Abadessa to Bridget after she'd had some water. "The thing I think Harry wants you to know is that guy that was just here—what was his name?—well, anyway, that he was one of my . . ."

"Johns?" said Bridget.

"Johns," said Abadessa.

32

"Harry?" said Bridget.

"Yeah," said I. "I'm one of those guys, always gets the right answer on *Jeopardy!* right after the bastard on the screen gets it, I guess. Anyway, after I make the deal with this guy, I remember. Abadessa—"

"Call me Dessa," she interrupted.

"Yeah. Dessa, when I was asking her last night about her business, she told me about this one guy who was kind of a regular client, you know, once, twice a month. Always met her—isn't this right, Dessa?—somewhere downtown, the Palmer House, whatever, for dinner, then wound up in one of the Loop hotels. So, it hits me, the description Dessa gave me of this guy sounds a little like our Professor Browder."

"And that's it?" Bridget said.

"Not all of it," I said. "Thing is, this dude, Dessa told me, while they were . . . uh . . ."

"Making love, Harry," said Bridget. "I'm familiar with the concept."

Dessa laughed. "Men!" she said to Bridget, and Bridget smiled back at her. "What Harry's trying to say, *en toute la longue de la route, c'est que ce gars-la, pendant que nous faisons le zoumba—tu comprends zoumba?*"

"*Bien sûr,*" said Bridget. What the hell?

"*Bon. A la longue du zoumba, ce gars-la, il a insisté de m'appeler 'Lisa' et c'est toute l'histoire que je lui ai racontée.*"

"Excuse me?" I said.

"The man Dessa told you about insisted on calling her 'Lisa' while they were making love," Bridget said. "And what did this tell you?"

"It told me that Barry Browder's got some kind of trouble with his family life," I said. "Okay. 'Lisa' is what Andrea called herself when she seduced my ass at the Morris Inn, dig? Now I know that's not exactly probable cause, and I know it doesn't exactly solve all our problems, but damn, Bridget, ain't it fascinating?"

I thought I'd been a very clever bear. I mean, I'd discovered that ol' Barry Browder III had a—what do they call it?—an unnatural attachment to his daughter, maybe. At least, he was going around town turning tricks and calling them what his daughter called herself to me when she reamed my brains out. I'd been a real goddamn detective, right?

Bridget looked like I'd just disemboweled a chicken and then asked for her approval.

"And you let them leave?" she said. I don't think I can tell you how her face looked. Ever stare down the lights of an oncoming semi on a rainy night?

"Well," I said.

"Well be *damned!*" she said and, swear to God, that's the first time I ever heard her swear to God. "Those people are wounded, Harry. Can't you do anything without hurting someone? Do you know what you've just done to them? Harry! Do you have Browder's phone number?"

And what happened after that, if you'll excuse it, gets kind of confused. I tried to find Browder's phone number but somehow I couldn't get my eyes focused on my damn address book. Dessa said she had better be going, and Bridget took her aside in the kitchen for a couple of minutes before she split. I finally found the number, punched it up, and Bridget took the phone out of my hand.

"Professor Browder," she said, "this is Bridget O'Toole. When you get home—and I pray you're going home right now—*please* call me at Harry Garnish's number. We have to talk, and I *promise* you that talk is all we'll do. I'm so sorry for this"—with a glare at me—"this terrible thing, and I just want you to know that—"

She hung up. "The tape ran out," she said.

So we sat. And didn't speak. For about forty-five minutes. Finally, I said, "Call the cops?"

"And tell them what?" Bridget said. "That we think— think, mind you—that Browder and his daughter may be involved in incest and we're worried what they might do, now they've been discovered? *Harry*." And I hope I never hear anybody say my name that way again.

After another half hour we called again. This time the phone just rang: no answer machine. "Switched off," I said.

"We'd better go," said Bridget.

And midway up Sheridan Road toward the Browder house I got to hear my name pronounced again the way Bridget had done it back in the apartment.

"How did that girl—Denise?" she said.

"Yeah," I said.

"How did she remember the material from Pyramid on Professor Middlebrook's desk? If he was trying to seduce her, I'd think she would have been fairly distracted."

"Well, see, she didn't, really. She called to tell me she didn't want to talk with me anymore. But I thought I ought to let Browder know that I knew about Pyramid, and that maybe some other people around campus did, too."

"*Harry*," she said: Just That Way.

There were lights on downstairs at the house. I rang the bell four, five times with no answer.

"Can you spring the lock?" Bridget asked.

"Are you kidding?" I said, resting my hand on the knob. And the door swung open.

And there, sitting on the sofa just where she'd been last time I was in the house, was Andrea. She hadn't even taken her coat off. The room was fully lit, something that sounded like Vivaldi was coming over the speakers, and she had half a tall glass of Glenfiddich in her hand.

She smiled.

"Professor Browder's having a nap just now," she said. "I'm afraid he can't be disturbed, he's been working so hard lately. But if you'd like to wait for a while, perhaps I can show you some of his books."

"Andrea—" I began.

"I'm Lisa," she said. "Andrea's upstairs, asleep in her room. I'm afraid she can't be disturbed, either. Would you like to look at her father's books?"

"*Go!*" whispered Bridget, sitting down beside her and taking her hand. I took the stairs two at a time and after opening two wrong doors found Browder in his study.

No blood on the walls, no plastic bag over his head, no pill bottle beside his typewriter. He was breathing normally and staring straight ahead. The light from his desk lamp, the only light in the room, formed a halo on the center of his desk, where there was a bundle of envelopes that had once been blue and now were a kind of tainted white (ever notice how old stationery gets puffy, kind of like toaster waffles?) and this photograph.

It was an old photograph, like from, remember when Polaroids always came out with the colors all looking like a bad print of a Warner cartoon? And it showed a gangly young guy in a polo shirt grinning with more teeth than possible at the camera, with his arm around a skinny blond girl with hair that looked like it went all the way to her waist—you couldn't tell—in a halter top: somebody's living room.

I called Browder's name a couple of times but he didn't answer. He'd gone away, damn if I knew for how long. And I stared back at the photo and finally made the young guy grinning so confidently at the camera. The girl had a wisp of her long blond hair caught in her teeth (I've always thought that was sexy). And I turned the photo over. The writing on the back said, "Barry, honey. Love you forever. Lisa."

When I went back downstairs, leaving Browder staring at whatever he saw past the desk lamp, Andrea was curled up asleep on the sofa with her head in Bridget's lap.

I called 911.

$\triangledown$

33

NEXT MORNING—JESUS, WAS it the next morning? Damned if I can remember. Anyway, a day or so after I got a phone call from the Priest. I was in my office.

"Harry!" he boomed. "Jimmy! Listen, so your guy Browder went round the fuckin' bend, hey? Some fuckin' teacher, right? Hell, they're all assholes, am I right?"

"The doctors call it catatonia, Jimmy," I said. "Near as I can figure it means you just don't give a shit anymore." And I was beginning to know what that must feel like. Was Bridget going to walk in someday and find me staring at Janie's goddamned ceramic cats? "So, you got something?"

"What I got you're gonna love, and you're gonna be eternally grateful to your uncle Jimmy," he said. "It's all a matter of following the right paper in the right direction, sonny. Know that gig, that high-paying gig Browder said he was in for? Turns out it was some kind of what they all it, lectureship in—let's see here—yeah, in religion and literature at some big university, which I can't tell you its name but you can guess away. Very big bucks."

"And that's what you got?" I said.

He sighed. "Harry, let me finish. You want to guess who was bankrolling this damn lectureship? No. Don't guess. Fuckin' Sethians."

"Say *what?*" I said.

"No shit," he said. "These guys, they're running whores, they're foreclosing on real estate all the hell over the place, and they're setting up this lecturing crap, colleges all the hell over the place. Want to guess why I'm telling you this?"

Now that was a joke. You know the Priest as long as I know the Priest, or maybe you know Chicago as long as I know Chicago, and, a question like that, you don't have to guess.

It was because Jimmy Maher had asked some questions. But, being Jimmy Maher, which is to say a guy with serious hair, he'd made sure that when the questions got asked, people knew who was asking the questions. And people knew who was asking the questions, and how—let's say accommodating—the asker could be, you could just naturally answer the questions, but answer them so that the asker wound up being one of the friendlies. He learns what he wants, he owes you, he makes a little *Geschaeft*, you make a little more, and like that.

It's how things are.

"Juice," I said.

"Dig," he said. "So anyway, your professor, he knew all about this shit from the starting gate."

"Then why—" I began.

"Why'd the dumb shit come to you guys in the first place, ask you to check out the folks, they're going to give him all this bread? Goddamn if I know. Like it turns out, asshole's crazy, yeah? Self-destructive."

Yeah, I thought. Like, the guy's self-destructive. Like, he's obsessed with his daughter—no, with Lisa, whoever the hell Lisa was or whatever lost chance Lisa was, and he's screwed up his kid and he's screwed up his marriage because of that. And he finds out—*when* did he find out?—that the sophisticated whorehouse he's patronizing is tied in with the people who are going to make him rich and famous for teaching the moral truth. Or his wife finds out, and she starts going to Sethian meetings because, what? Because she can't stand seeing him look at his—their daughter like *that!* Because she thinks maybe it's a way of making everything okay again? Why do people do the desperate things they do to make love stay? Is that how Thor figured in? Was Nancy

Browder really screwing him out of some need to be, for Chrissake, real, and not just a shadow in Barry Browder's own search for Lisa?

Browder was still staring straight ahead of him. Nancy was still in a coma, waiting—I'd guess—for somebody to pull the plug. Andrea? She was in County, for all I knew talking about her good friend the professor and calling herself Lisa. "Yeah," I said. "Self-destructive."

"So anyway," the Priest went on, "you'll be happy to know that everything's been smoothed out, by your old uncle, and that you and Sister Godzilla can keep the ranch. Matter of fact, the Sethians—well, actually they're a pretty big conglomerate with a fancier name—are kind of grateful to you for putting Professor Stupid out of commission, not to mention for bringing them and me together. This is all, of course, if you don't do anything stupid about the . . . uh . . . the socializing side of the business, yeah? I told them you'd be cool. I was right, wasn't I?"

What do they call it? A black box problem. You've got this machine, see, and it does something: waves a flag, plays "Dixie," makes no difference. But the machine's in a black box that you can't open, really *can't*, because if you try to open it, the machine inside will self-destruct, right? So how do you reproduce the machinery that produces that same effect?

The answer? Simple. You build your own machine to produce *just* and *only* that effect, and then you say, whatever the hell is inside the box, you've replicated it. Even, dig, if you don't and never *will* know what's really inside the box.

"You were right," I said. "Except there's this one kid—"

"Abadessa, right?" he said. "Garnish, what the hell kind of organization you think I got here? Fuckin' Little League? We know all about her and you, and I figure you, being the sentimental sonofabitch you are, would like her sprung from the stable. What, you want her to fill in for the Dago twist, old buddy?"

"I just want her cut loose and set up," I said. And yeah,

that's all I said. You want to screw with the Priest? Be my guest.

"Done," he said. And that was that. He hung up.

So Steven Lee was still dead, I assume killed by an ideal that backfired. And Andrea/Lisa would be a long time coming back from wherever the hell she was: She's still there as I tell you this. Oh, yeah: Nancy Browder finally just went away, and Barry Browder hasn't spoken in one damn long time.

Bridget and I started speaking again, very gingerly at first, about a week after the Priest's call. I didn't tell her everything he'd told me, but I'm pretty sure she realizes things are going to be more complicated now than they were before. So business goes on, except Bridget and I look over our shoulders a little more these days.

And then, on Christmas morning (no kidding, life can be corny) I'm sitting in the apartment in my underwear spooning out some tinned salmon for Bandit—it's Christmas, hey?— and the doorbell rings. I put on my robe, go to the door.

It's Janie.

"Try it again?" she says.

"You sure?" I say, after five beats.

"You?" she says.

"Christ," I say. "Nothing wild?"

"House rules." She smiles. "Nothing wild. Redeal. So let's try."

So we did. And we do.